ALSO BY NED WHITE

Place
(createspace)

The Very Bad Thing
(Viking)

Inside Television: A Guide to Critical Viewing
(Science and Behavior Books)

CALLING OUT
YOUR NAME

a novel for young adults

by NED WHITE

ACKNOWLEDGMENTS

Thanks to our Georgia-born friends for
training my ear to the poetry and color of southern voices,
and for their adventuresome spirit
that inspires much of what happens in this book.

DEDICATION

This book is dedicated to
Sam, Amy, Molly, Gillian, Martin, and August

ONE

My zoo-headed younger brother pulled his five-finger discount about fifty-seven times before it finally got him into serious trouble. You'd think his luck wouldn't run that good over the years, but the truth is in the small town of Ogamesh, Georgia, where we lived, most everybody knew him and seemed to have a soft spot in their heart for him, even when he was stumbling out of Crews' Groceries with a handful of Snickers bars that every other decent soul had to pay for. Whenever I lost sight of him in a store, he'd grab something, even if it was totally useless to him, like a box of wing nuts or a jar of silver polish. They'd say – and I'd overhear them say it – "that's the Elmont boy. The slow one. He don't mean no harm." Harmon Crews, the owner of the store, spoke like that more times than I can remember, as I was shoveling out change to pay for the stolen candy bars or else returning the totally useless wing nuts. He also strongly advised me to put him on a leash like a dog whenever we came to the store, but then he'd wink at me.

My brother was born Aubrey Elmont, but everyone called him Tick. Some think it's *Tic* without the "k," because Tick's eyes can be twitchy and he tends to speak in small explosions, but that's not it. The name came from our Mom, who called him *Deertick*, probably because he was a cute chubby baby who might grow into a bloodsucking pest, and it shortened from there. Evidently, something went wrong at his birth, I never learned just what, and Tick popped out as blue as a popsicle and a few pickles short of a barrel. Technically, they tell me, he wasn't mentally retarded, just a bit off his nut and with a temperament more rambunctious than a ferret. I'd seen it hundreds of times, and the truth

1

is it wore me to a frazzle because it was me that was mostly responsible for him getting through the day without causing a major disturbance or accidentally killing himself or somebody else. He could just plain exhaust me. On a good day, Tick was a typical pain-in-the-ass thirteen year old younger brother who happened to be a kleptomaniac. On a bad day, he was a complete mangle of hysterical guffawing and sobbing, shin-kicking and cursing, and stealing some of my favorite clothes, which were all too big for him, or pilfering my arrowheads, which was worse.

Aunt Zee kept reminding me, "you're your brother's keeper," which to me was like a doctor saying "you've got a brain tumor, but isn't life just a long disease anyway?"

Actually, I had to put up with both of them. We'd been living at Aunt Zee's house since our Mom died, which was ten years ago, and I guess Zee had hung on to most of her marbles back then, when she was seventy, because I remember she actually cooked for us and changed Tick's soiled pants and whatnot, but something happened to her brain after that, and one day about a year ago I remember she could not for the life of her know if it was Tick or me who came out of the kitchen with a plate of cookies and muscadine jam for her while she watched some useless soap opera on TV.

"Why, thank you, Tick!"

I thought she'd gone blind. "I'm Woody."

"I believe, for a moment there, you looked like Tick."

"No, ma'am. Woody. Woodrow."

I remember thinking, what all's happened to her head, I look like Tick as much as a possum resembles a snake, she can't be getting soft yet. But she was losing it all right, and we've been putting up with her foggy mind ever since, doing chores and errands for her.

To be accurate, we have some help. Down our street a few houses is Tychander Williams, a black girl who just graduated from high school, and she comes by a couple of times a day to do cleaning and cooking, and to drive into town to Crews' to get groceries or go to the bank to take money out of Zee's account or deposit her pension checks. She's friendly enough and we do have some fun, but it irritates me that she seems to favor Tick because of his shortcomings and starts to play ball with him outside while I'm cleaning up dinner dishes, being ignored. Still, we do need her for driving around since I don't have my license yet, and I make sure she gets paid the right amount everyday. I turned sixteen in August and *should* go get my license, but the lines at the Georgia DMV are pretty long up in Macon and I just haven't gotten around to it yet.

It's good having Tychander come and go. She's the only other one here with a teaspoon of brains, and I enjoy every chance I can get to talk to someone in the house who actually makes *sense*.

So I have to get to the story about where Tick's raw dumb luck with shoplifting stupid useless stuff finally ran out, and what happened afterwards that basically completely messed up my life, which seemed to be going along fairly smoothly till then.

It was October last year and I came back from school on the bus with Tick to find Aunt Zee and Tychander on the front porch in the middle of some brouhaha while Zee was snipping hydrangeas and sticking them in a vase. She'd been talking about having a dinner party for some friends, but you never knew if she really meant it or not, her brain was so squishy.

Well, evidently she meant it, because she was lashing out at Ty.

"No, not *paper* doilies, *lace* doilies!"

"Can't find no lace doilies in Ogamesh," said Ty.

"A dinner party needs lace doilies, and my old ones got moth holes in 'em, and paper won't do and if y'all were raised right you'd know it."

Tick and I were headed inside the house for our usual snack of sweet tea and cookies or leftover hushpuppies or whatever else wasn't nailed down, but Zee whipped out a shout, *Tick Elmont!*, which had the same effect as a hand grabbing him by the collar. He stopped quick.

"Ma'am?"

"Tick, you know who's invited to my party?"

"No, I don't."

"Well, specifically, I'm asking the *governor* and his wife, that's who."

"The governor, wow. *That's* good."

Tick missed the huge wink Zee tossed at him.

"I'm just messin' with you, son," she said.

Tick chewed on this for a second before hooting out a laugh, proving he saw some humor in it. I sure didn't – I was hungry and thirsty – and Zee's kidding about inviting the governor didn't seem to have a point.

"Not likely the governor would come way down here for *nothin'*," she added. "But proper folks are invited all the same, and we gotta have fine lace doilies, so I'm asking Tychander to take forty dollars and go buy a set of six, and you boys can help her. That mall should have them."

"What color you want, Miz Morton?" Ty asked her.

"Only come in white. If they come in something else, avoid 'em. Now off with y'all, all three."

We weren't off just then, because we hadn't raided the fridge yet, and also I needed time to figure out a way to wriggle out of this whole thing, because I'd made other plans. I'd talked to my friend Natalie Starke at school and we'd made a date to go look at some guy's old Honda motorcycle sitting in his yard and priced right, at three hundred dollars. It looked just about my size, though I'd have to repaint the tank and the fenders because he'd spray-painted them a disgusting orange. Well, the problem was that Tick would *kill* to go to any mall, and my guess was it would be the one near Macon that has all the lah-de-dah shops in them, which is perfect if you're looking for lace doilies. When it came to shopping trips, Ty said many times *I can't manage that boy, much as I like him,* and she meant it because of his kleptomania. So, like it or not, I'd have to go.

Zee hollered for Tick to come back out onto the porch again, so I had some time alone to wrack my brains and try to come up with something. Just announcing that I had other plans wouldn't amount to a peehole in Georgia clay, because it was traditional in our house that I *always* had other plans and they were never too important to change. Well, I came up with nothing and ended up being foiled as usual, so I had to call Natalie to change our date for seeing the orange bike up close.

When I got back out to the porch, Zee was having a whispering session with Tick, which I didn't understand, but soon enough it broke up and we all hopped in Zee's car and headed for Macon. Ty and I, up front, discussed the party and theorized whether or not Zee would actually pull it off. She'd talked about having supper parties before, but her thoughts just flew away with the wind and went poof. Still, Ty figured, if she's sending us off for the afternoon to shop for doilies, she might be serious about it.

Zoo-head was in back picking his nose and blowing at my hair, which was usual for him. I thought, the kid's thirteen and he *can't keep acting seven forever,* but I was probably wrong. In point of fact, our doctor and the school psychologist said the same thing, that he was only *mildly disabled,* but the main thing was that his brain was wired differently from most people's and he was *emotionally challenged.* He could actually do much of the schoolwork other kids his age could do, even though it took him quite a bit longer. He also kept getting distracted or losing interest or having one of his weird-out moments where he'd just stare out the window at birds perching in our big live oak tree in the yard. He could sit and stare, like in a trance, for hours on end. Now he was blowing at my hair and picking his nose and I kept swatting at him, *knock it off.*

In time he did, just as we were arriving at the mall.

"Now you stick right with me," I said to him as we got out.

"I'm good at that."

"You get the worst Indian wrist burn *ever* if you don't." Well, he winced at this, because I'd given him those before. The problem was, he was into a growth spurt now and getting pretty strong, and though I had a few inches on him in height I was more on the skinny side and if we ever started fighting or wrestling like we meant it, I'm not sure I could take him. He had thick shoulders and strong arms and more leverage than I did, *plus,* he tended to fight dirty.

"Maybe not the worst Indian wrist burn ever, but a bad one just the same," I warned, easing up a bit.

"Do as Woody says, I ain't watching you," Ty chipped in.

He grunted, and we strolled into the mall's main entrance.

And into our crazy future.

Ty kept kidding about finding the "doily store," like they had such things, but soon we found a big place that sold all kinds of gifts from kitchen stuff to clothes to jewelry, and sure enough they had a stash of formal dining things like placemats and napkins and white doilies that *looked* like lace and maybe were polyester or something, but we figured Zee would settle for them since they had a nice pattern to them and cost only about four bucks each. So Ty and I grabbed six of them, and after a brief discussion I grabbed two more as extras in case her guest list expanded. Now here's where things get a little hazy. I was *certain* Tick was in our aisle, or at worst in the one next to us looking at tablesetting things like glasses and such, but when I called out for him he didn't answer. As it happened, this store had a lot of shoppers in it, and tall shelves to boot, so it was hard to see very far.

Ty told me, *he's sprung loose on you,* and I had to agree.

We popped out of the tableware section and into a more open area and that's when I spotted his scruffy blond head bobbing along past some displays of leather handbags headed for the door, with his hands jammed into his pockets. Ty and I made a beeline for him and as we did we passed a young couple at a jewelry counter who seemed suddenly distressed by something that was missing. Well, we paused long enough to see they had several rings out on the glass display case, rings that were glittering with diamonds and emeralds and other stones, and the clerk was saying *well I know we had six of them out.*

"I'm not goin' after him," Ty told me.

"Okay, *I'll* do it, you can buy the doilies and I'll see you outside."

That's when the distress at the jewelry counter started to pick up steam. I hustled out of there and into the main mall.

One thing about Tick, he truly deeply *hates* being chased, unless he's sure it's a game. Even if you're taking baby steps toward him, he'll start to freak out and make a run for it. But if you're totally casual about approaching him with a normal everyday kind of walk, and saying things like *hey Tick, you should check out the cool doilies we just bought,* then he's clueless that you're going to grab him by the collar of his dirty tee shirt and handle him like a crazed pit bull. So far I was lucky. He caught sight of me as he ducked behind a cart selling stuffed animal toys, then poked his head out again and gave me a goofy grin, the kind of lopsided smile that was all too familiar to me because it was saying *I did it again.*

Now I'd come to realize about Tick's *I did it again* wasn't gloating or pride, it was a mix of astonishment and embarrassment, because he truly seemed to be on another mental planet when he stole. It would be fascinating to get inside his head during those times, but impossible too.

I smiled back to assure him I wasn't going to kill him, and that's when this big burly security guard appeared from nowhere right behind him, a dumb-looking white guy who looked like he just escaped from the Marines.

Tick had never stolen from a mall before, and it's a different experience from a little neighborhood shop in Ogamesh. This guy was not kindly old Harmon Crews at the grocery store or Mrs. Coulter at the gift shop, this guy was the law of the land and Tick was so amazed he didn't even budge.

¤ ¤ ¤ ¤ ¤

Piecing it together later at the police station, when Tick wasn't snuffling or whimpering, it seemed he actually had a *reason* for stealing the ring, unlike almost all the other times. He'd gotten the totally wacko idea that Aunt Zee's party was actually for her *birthday* and he needed to swipe her a present. Well, this was October and Zee's birthday is in May sometime – I forget the exact date until it's a few days before it and she reminds me – and Tick should've known this. In fact, he has an uncanny knack for remembering details like birthdays or the time you almost cut your finger off with the lawn mower, and it bothered me he could pluck such an idea out of nowhere and make such a mess of things because of it. The other hugely irritating part of this escapade is that he snatched a piece of jewelry costing nine hundred and seventy-five dollars for the "birthday present," and because of that the overweight sourfaced policewoman looked at all of us with daggers for eyes.

We were in this back room with not much in it – a table where she sat, and a bench for the three of us. She started in on Tick, but it didn't last long.

"That wasn't a pack of gum you stole, son."

"No ma'am. It's a ring for my aunt."

Her eyes grew wide at him.

"I'm *saying*, this is a serious crime."

He nodded at her. "Ma'am, I sometimes don't know what I'm doing."

"It's true!" I blurted out. "He doesn't. You see –"

"Hold on!" She put her hand up to stop me and looked back to Tick. "Aubrey Elmont, do you have a kind of disability?"

"Yes, ma'am. What they say is, my mind's not right half the time."

Well, I'd never heard him speak it as such, and I was kind of proud of him.

He added, "They don't got a name for it."

"Is it okay if I talk to your brother and Miz Williams?"

"Sure."

Well, Ty and I both jabbered out all the truth that we had at our fingertips, me particularly because I was so anxious, and soon enough the cop knew that Aubrey Elmont was disabled since birth and had a long history of taking things from stores and not being consistent about how wrong it was. They also learned that our legal guardian, our great aunt Zelda Morton of Ogamesh, had her bright spots from time to time but was aging fast and sometimes didn't know lunch from supper, so she was our guardian more in a legal way than actual. Tychander, as much as me, was the responsible adult for us, though not on any piece of paper.

It was a good thing I did most of the talking because any chance she could get, Ty launched in with her disgusted whine voice, as in *that boy ain't never hurt anyone, why you pickin' on him so?* and *I ain't nobody to tell you how to do your business, but you got that boy's life in your hands, just so's you know. You can treat him right, or you can just throw him away.*

The cop might have been impressed by our loyalty, but it didn't show in any way that counted.

"Now son," said the cop, "whether you understand this fully or not, we're gonna have to charge you with a crime, which is called a felony, and arraign you and then have a hearing. And it would be appropriate for all of you to come, along with Miz Morton, if she's able."

Tick hung his head low and shook it. "No jail." The tears had dried on his cheek and left muddy streaks.

"Son, you're not going to jail. But you can't be loose as a tomcat in the world taking anything you want just 'cause it's pretty or someone's got a birthday. If you were a few years older, you *would* go to jail 'cause it's larceny and a serious crime, and it's also unethical. You understand about that word 'unethical?'"

Tick shook his head.

"His mind doesn't work just that way," I suggested to her.

"Well, he's old enough so he should catch up on it. Now let's get to the paperwork."

Two

One of the problems I have with friends is that I don't have very many of them. I'm not much interested in sports, especially football, so after school I tend to get on the bus with Tick and go home, leaving the other kids behind. Some days I send Tick home alone and ask or bribe somebody on the bus to keep an eye on him, so I can walk back to town with some of the guys or hook up with Natalie. But more often than not I'm on the bus with him, with my face pressed to the glass looking at lawns and gardens in front of houses. The other kids *understand* that I have to care for my brother, but they don't do much to compensate for it, like coming over to the house or inviting both of us to go somewhere and do something. They tend to like Tick because he can be funny, but they usually give him plenty of room because they know he can explode at any time, or just act like a pain in the ass.

A couple of my good friends either died or went away. Jake Culpepper hanged himself in his barn when he was twelve, and no one could figure out why, since he was so good-natured and popular. Jupiter Strange is a black kid who lived in a trailer with his Mom and sister next to Jameson's cotton fields, and he was my age and a lot of fun, but he went joyriding in a neighbor's truck when he was thirteen and the sheriff took him for a wise guy and threw the book at him. Meaning, in this area, he got shipped off to juvenile detention for a year or so, and then to St. Anselm's Home for Troubled Youth. Jupiter Strange was his real given name, though you'd have to ask his Mom why she bestowed it on him.

It seemed pretty obvious to me, and just about everyone else in Ogamesh, that the court would do the same thing to Tick – shoot him directly off to St. Anselm's. I'd been there once to visit Jupiter, hitching a ride with Mrs. Strange, and it seemed a decent enough place with lots of lawns spreading out among the buildings, and a big shady grove of pecan trees next to a pond that was loaded with bullfrogs. Jupiter said he liked it there just as much as his trailer, but he missed his friends (like me). It was about twenty miles away, so making a visit took some planning.

After Jake and Jupiter were gone, my collection of friends basically shrank down to Natalie Starke. It could be awkward and challenging getting to like her, for several reasons. First, as people around here would say, she was a "damn Yankee," having recently moved here from Ohio with her mother and new stepfather, a rich professor named Dr. Hawkins who decided to retire. I had nothing in particular against Yankees, but her accent and her manner sometimes made it hard to communicate. Second, she was too educated for her own good, I thought. She could talk circles around me, and always kept me off balance with her philosophical view of things and her endless questions that had no easy answers. She liked to drink after school, which made it worse, since liquor loosened her tongue. Third, she was probably the richest kid in Ogamesh and everyone knew it. The family had bought an old cotton farm a mile or so out of town and they'd added so much on to the original house it started to look like a mansion, as if they were trying to show us all up. Fourth, she wasn't exactly the best looking girl in my grade, and though it didn't matter much to me what she looked like, I got teased now and then just for hanging out with her sometimes. Natalie was built like a fence post, straight and thin, she had bony shoulders and elbows, and the most noticeable part of her face were her thick black eyebrows that were trying to grow together over her nose.

One thing that will never change, from the beginning of civilization to the end: kids will always pick on other kids because of their *looks*. I swear, I never could figure it.

On the plus side of things with Natalie: if you don't count Tick, she was the only friend I ever had who actually seemed interested in me and wanted to know what was on my mind. Another big plus was that she was the fastest girl runner ever on our track team because she had those long scrawny legs that could leap out about half a mile in front of her and never get tired. Lastly and best of all, she had her license and *owned her own car,* an old Buick that her stepfather snapped up for her at some auction.

But she could be tricky, as you'll see.

About a week before Tick's hearing, I finally got a chance to get Natalie to pick me up so we could go over to take a look at the orange Honda. When she pulled up in front of the house, I left Tick swinging on the old tire hanging from the live oak in our back yard and ignored his annoying, singsongy *Woody's got a girlfriend.* Ty was coming over any minute to help with Zee, so Tick would be all right.

I hopped in the car and we were off, down our street three blocks, then left onto Route 12, the main drag through town. Natalie was an exceptionally careful and slow driver, which was too bad since the Buick had a very strong small block engine under the hood, a three-fifty.

"So, you should *know,*" she started in, "that you've got a lot of friends in this town."

News to me. "I do?"

"People tend to like your brother, and don't be surprised that a bunch of them show up at the hearing. But they also know how hard it is for you. They're *behind* you."

It didn't feel quite right that she seemed to know so much about what other people thought of me. Also, I caught a potent whiff of whiskey, so maybe she was stretching the truth.

"They also know you have to deal with your aunt."

"Well, I don't pay much attention."

"They say you're long-suffering, the patience of Job, things like that."

I hadn't thought about it that way, and this surprised me.

"You're very handsome, you know."

Hadn't thought about that either, not in any concentrated way.

"How you talk," I said, rathering she wouldn't. She was getting tricky on me. "Especially since you've had a nip or two."

"Well, Woody, I think it's *healthy* to exchange personal views like that, just so we understand each other better, even if you're shy about it."

"I'm not shy, and I think we understand each other *fine* without talking about looks."

"I think you'll look cool on that motorcycle, even if it's utterly imprac-tical. Have you got the money yet?"

"Look, it's *not* impractical, I'm going to put saddle bags on it so I can help do errands and maybe go to school with it next year, and no, I've only got about two hundred so far."

We rumbled over the railroad tracks headed for the other side of town. I was eager to get to the guy's house, but Nat barely drove the speed limit. A huge log carrier, fully loaded, was passing us with a loud roar.

"Might be the best thing for Tick," she said when the truck pulled in front of us and it quieted down.

"What might be."

"St. Anselm's. They've got people who can give him the right kind of therapies and treatments."

I nodded slightly, but inside of me it was a huge nod. I'd secretly gotten to the point where I could imagine carrying on my life at Zee's without the constant shadow of my crazy brother. In a way, I was glad he got caught, but I didn't want him thrown into juvenile detention, which I'd heard was a snakepit, but rather straight off to St. Anselm's, which was more of a residential treatment place.

"You think?" she prodded.

"I'd miss him. But it would be okay."

"What would you do?"

"What would I do?"

She tsked at me and tried a new approach.

"Woody. If Tick weren't with you, what kinds of things would you do? Perhaps this is like asking, what do you *want* to do? Now, and in your future?"

The odd thing is, I'd been more focused on Tick's ideas about life than my own. I haven't gotten into this yet, but he was nutso about being a champion surfer, and more specifically, a champion surfer in Malibu, California. He'd five-fingered a surfing magazine at the News and Gifts Shop and kept it right under his pillow. There were photos of people surfing at some competition in Malibu, and he kept telling me *that's where I wanna be and that's what I wanna do.* He'd never done it, of course. He was great on his skateboard, I have to admit, until a truck ran over it on our street and squished it, so I guess he had the coordination to be a surfer, and he was a decent swimmer to boot. But I tried to warn him you can't make a living surfing, you can only do it when you're young. Naturally he shot back at me, "Well, I *am* young."

The problem was, we lived four hours from the nearest waves and about two thousand miles or more from California, so it was just a fantasy for him. Even if I had a car, I was not driving him to California.

"Your *future*," she said again. "Do you want one?"

"C'mon."

"Use it or lose it. Plan it or can it."

She was sermonizing, but I was still thinking how zoo-heady it was for Tick to be obsessing about surfing, when there were so many opportunities for fun here in Georgia. Every adult I know, practically, and tons of kids too, go hunting and fishing. Hunting is all about wild boar and deer, and fishing for crappies in the lakes or catfish in a pond can keep your mind unoccupied for hours. In school, football and basketball and baseball are the most popular, and kids also get into their cars and trucks and motorcycles. So why surfing?

"Just a thought," Nat said, and I snapped back to attention.

"I'm not sure yet."

"What gives you pleasure, Woody?"

"Well." And it hung there for a few seconds. "I like going to look at a cool motorcycle with you. In other words, what we're doing right *now*. In fact –"

"Now, my dear boy, is a very short time."

"My soon-to-be future is that motorcycle and you just drove by it."

To hurry things along, we turned around and got back to the guy's house. He came out to meet us and he showed me everything about the bike that was both good and bad. The main problem was that one of the cylinders had below-average compression and might need a ring job, so that's why the bike was going cheap. I didn't care that much, because I figured I could work on it after school at Winkler's Garage, where I was a part-time employee doing simple things like changing oil and rotating tires. The guy lent me his helmet, I went for a spin down the highway and came back *knowing* this was my bike. It fit me great, and with 450 ccs it had plenty of juice in it, in spite of the bad cylinder.

Of course, I didn't have the money yet, and I told him so. Well, being a regular guy trying to sell something, he said he'd have to unload it to the first three hundred dollars that came along.

⋈ ⋈ ⋈ ⋈ ⋈

Nat was right about the hearing. I swear half of Ogamesh showed up at the courthouse in Macon, and most dressed up for it, too, with coats and ties and long dresses. Nat and her family came, along with Harmon Crews, both of the Winkler brothers, and a bunch of teachers and parents from the school. Aunt Zee didn't come; she said she was feeling kind of pokey, and wasn't sure what all kind of a mess Tick had gotten himself into anyway, so the proceedings wouldn't make much sense to her. Since Tychander had to drive us all up, Zee had her friend John Dandridge come to the house to help her out for the day.

The policewoman, the one who'd hauled us into that little room, proceeded to lay out her case about the theft of the ring, and the judge listened carefully and nodded a lot while he looked at Tick, and then at me. He was a juvenile court judge, and therefore a specialist in a case like this, but for all his experience he seemed very sad about what he was hearing. He was also a thin man with a bald head, and reminded me of a Sunday school teacher I had once who was gentle and friendly.

When the policewoman finished her story, which included her understanding that the young boy was developmentally disabled, the judge announced that he wanted to meet with the family "in chambers," and also asked if other qualified witnesses were present, like school-teachers or doctors. I turned around and saw a bunch of people leap to their feet, but eventually the judge sifted through them all and settled on the school psychologist and Tick's teacher, Miss Sproul. They followed Tick, me, Tychander, the policewoman, and the judge into his back office.

Sad as he was in the courtroom, he got downright depressed when we were all together in his office and he started asking about our family. I did most of the talking in this regard, explaining that great aunt Zelda Morton became our legal guardian after my mother's death when I was six and Tick was three, but that she'd probably had a few mild strokes because it was she who now needed attending, not us. The strokes must have been mild, because from one day to the next we didn't see much change in her.

He asked about our Mom, Martha Elmont, and I was forced to tell the truth that she'd taken her own life, with pills, for reasons that she never shared with us, not that I could remember much since I was just six. We were staying with Aunt Zee anyway back then, for a lengthy visit while Mom was "sick."

"And your father?"

I remember Mom saying *he's moved away and I don't know where,* and that was the end of it.

"I don't know, sir. He left about three years before Mom died. Before Tick was born, in fact. So I've been told."

"It's so sad, so sad," he said, shaking his head, and I thought he might burst into tears.

The policewoman reminded him that a felony had been committed and that the matter was before him.

"And no one's contested the facts of the case," she threw in.

The judge turned to Tick to take in a long look, knowing my brother's future was in his hands. Now I have to say, in preparation for his day in court, Ty and I had worked pretty hard on him to trim his hair, clean him up and dress him right since he'd be disinclined to do any of this himself. Ty was the chief barber, trimming his hair at the collar and raising it over his ears, then using the electric clippers to shave the back and sides of his neck. I got out his only white shirt with buttons and ironed it on the kitchen counter, and did the same with a pair of gray wool trousers that I figured might still fit him. It's obvious that if we ever went to church his clothes would be more up to date, but Zee gave up on church a few years ago so we all stopped going. Ty and I helped wash his face and, for the first time ever, I decided to let him use my deodorant.

The pants were too short but still fit around the waist. The white shirt was too snug at the throat, so we left the top button open and I tied his only necktie so it pulled the collars together, more or less. All in all, he looked spanking clean and as innocent as circumstances would allow.

"Is there anyone here," the judge began, "who can say with certainty that this boy had a clear understanding of the consequences of his act?"

All I could hear was my own head pounding. I was actually pretty nervous about all of this and my heart rate was up.

"Son?" said the judge to him. "Just give me the best answer you can. Why on *earth* did you steal that ring?"

Well, Tick's mouth twisted into that impish grin he sometimes makes, and he came out with this:

"Woody says I'm a klepto."

Somebody chuckled – I think it was the school shrink, Dr. Tinkerman.

"But why the ring?" the judge went on. "Why not – a toy?"

"Don't take no toys," Ty chipped in. "He takes *stupid* things, like boxes of screws and such."

"I'd like the boy to respond."

Tick fired up for his answer. "It was a present for Zee. She wanted something nice for her birthday. She just has bracelets, no rings. It just sat there on the glass. She told me, get me something nice. I don't have no money. I have three dollars in my magazine box. Under my bed. Zee's good to me, I wanted to get her something pretty. But after I took it, my mind told me, you didn't really take it, you just dreamed it. That's what happens sometimes. I take things, and I don't believe I actually did it. Until I feel it in my pocket."

The judge was hanging on every word, it seems. He was leaning forward on his desk trying to focus on Tick's face.

"When you feel it in your pocket, what do you tell yourself?"

Tick screwed his face up into a grimace.

"Uh oh."

The judge sat back and put his hands behind his head.

"I'm not sending this child to juvenile detention."

Well, nobody dared react with a hoot or a holler, but you could hear a lot of exhaling. I felt my shoulders relax and drop down about four inches.

"I invite your thoughts and recommendations. St. Anselm's, anyone?"

After brief discussion with Dr. Tinkerman and Miss Sproul, there was no question how this would all end up, because St. Anselm's seemed like the perfect place.

"St. Anselm's it is. Son, you'll be remanded there for a period of between twelve and eighteen months, depending on your progress. You'll start the first of the year, and I will strongly recommend that you receive the best treatment for your disability."

"Okay, judge," said Tick.

"It's a good place where people can visit you, and they say the food's not so bad."

"Okay. I'll go."

THREE

Through the spring, Aunt Zee's physical problems started to catch up with the general slippages of her mind. Mostly it was in her lower back and hip, and I thought maybe she'd cracked one of her hip bones the way elderly people sometimes do, but no, she said it was the mugginess in the air that was tightening her joints and keeping her bent over. In any event, while she used to be able to stagger around on her own with only an occasional helping hand, now she needed one of those walkers to help her up off the couch and get to the kitchen or the bathroom. If mugginess were to blame, then it seemed to tighten up her voice, too; instead of asking for help the way she usually did, now she just barked it out. *Woody! Tick!*

That's right, Tick was gone to St. Anselm's but Zee couldn't wrap her brain around it. In a way, I became both myself and my brother, especially when she needed help, which was more often than I'd like.

Tick!

If she called his name out, it was me showing up in the doorway.

"What can I get you?"

"Where's Tick?"

I'd explain, again, that he was off to St. Anselm's for a visit and wasn't due back just yet, and I was cheered that she seemed to recall it. But then she'd be alarmed that he was gone for so long, just like he'd packed up and moved out.

"Is it the food?" she'd ask. "Tychander cooks a good meal."

Ty and I, and sometimes Natalie, did some house rearranging to try to smooth things out for Zee. The big change was shifting her bedroom from the upstairs into the spare room downstairs, which overlooks the front porch. It happened that she had *tons* of stuff up there in boxes and old knitting bags that she wanted close by in her new room, but I didn't dare go through any of it because so much of it seemed personal, like old letters and such. We just brought it all down and stashed it around the room as neatly as we could. The letters, I assumed, were mostly from Uncle Carl Morton, probably when he was off to war in the Pacific and he and Zee were freshly married. Carl was my mother's mother's brother, but I never met him beyond seeing his pictures in the hallway and on Zee's dresser upstairs, because he died before Tick and I were born. As did our grandparents.

Other changes upstairs had to do with our bedroom, since Tick was no longer in it. I shoveled most of his stuff into the closet, or into a stack in the corner of the room next to his desk. He had tons of magazines about skateboards and motorcycles, guns and ammo and surfing, and just as many comic books, mostly superhero stuff. A bunch of them he piled into his trunk to take with him to St. Anselm's, but most of them he left behind for me to deal with. I didn't touch the posters and magazine covers he'd taped to the wall over his bed; they were generally surfing pictures and the word "Malibu" made with huge cut-out letters in a kind of rainbow over all the photos. It seemed all the guys and the girls in the pictures were blond, like him.

My desk was between the two beds, and I cleared off one end of it where he kept his pocketknife, buffalo head nickel, useless tube of anchovy paste that he stole, and hand-squeezer exercise thingy he used to strengthen his grip. I put all these things in his desk drawer. So I had my desk back all to myself, and also the view out the window to the live oak dripping with Spanish moss and the tire swing hanging still from the lower branch. It was a nice long, easy spring, and most days I left the window open so I could catch a whiff of whatever was growing in our neighbor's garden beyond the tree while I tackled my homework. In the summer, with the wind from the east, you'd practically drown in the aroma of their gardenias.

I *liked* those smells, I liked flowers, and I wondered if maybe my future might have something to do with plants or nurseries. Or maybe forestry, because I liked being in the woods and understanding trees. Natalie had a point; it was time to think about what I wanted to be.

With Tick gone and Zee downstairs, it was amazingly quiet in the room, and I grew to adapt to it. Before the changes, I'd have to deal with Tick's raspy night-breathing and hollering in his sleep, and also the sounds from Zee's bedroom next to us, her snoring and the trumpet-like farts that she fired off when she was stirring in the early hours of the morning. She kept her closet door open, which was right through the wall, and I swear it acted like a loudspeaker.

But now she was safely and quietly downstairs, and spending more and more time in bed. Tychander's hours and duties expanded, so that she was in and out of the house all the time, helping Zee into the bathroom or toting in lunch on a tray. Cream cheese and olive sandwiches and sweet tea were the usual.

A couple of times Ty drove me to St. Anselm's to visit Tick, otherwise it was Natalie in the old Buick, going *ever so slowly* and I swear I was tempted to wrench the steering wheel from her hands and leap over to do my own driving at a sensible pace. I was usually impatient to get there and see how he was being treated, but you could only go during visiting hours on Wednesday evenings and Sunday afternoons. Either way, I didn't think the staff did much to gussy up their behavior during visiting hours, since I heard plenty of loud, stern voices from the staff chastising the kids for one thing or another, just as you'd expect on a normal day. Also, the place looked raggedy here and there, with some of the buildings in need of paint, and they didn't go out of their way to pretty it up just for visitors. In a way, it was comforting, because St. Anselm's wasn't trying to make a big show of being something it wasn't. It was a fairly strict halfway house kind of place, designed to straighten out kids who had some major kink in their lives or their behavior, and it wasn't any summer camp, for sure.

Nat and I would take turns using my baseball glove to play catch with Tick out on the main lawn, and sometimes Jupiter Strange would join us. They both lived in Magnolia House, in a big open dormitory with about twenty beds on the second floor, all with the same Navy blue wool blankets. Each kid got a dresser and a small table, and they stashed their trunks under the bed. It was all neat and clean, with a military feeling to it, but there was a strong odor of mildew and dirty socks which made it homier than you'd expect, and comforting.

I got a kick out of hooking up with Jupiter again. He was the same, big old goofy guy with a huge smile that showed which teeth were missing, but he'd lost some weight in the last year or so and looked much more athletic than before. One time, I think it was late April, he and I scooted off away from Nat and Tick, who were playing ball, and moseyed down to one of the ponds jammed with bullfrogs. I remember he said,

"I'm tryin' to teach the scamp some morals."

Which naturally led to a discussion of how teachable my brother was, but Jupe (as I called him) was sure he was making some progress. Tick had swiped one of Jupe's baseball cards, as it happened.

"Sometimes," I said, "he doesn't know what he's doing."

"Uh *uh*, he knows just fine. He just keeps testing. I told him, do that again I'll rip your arm out of its socket. That got his attention – he straightened right up."

"No, Jupe, he *pretends* to get the message –"

"You shoulda tried that, threatening to rip his arm out."

"I gave him Indian wrist burns –"

"No *no no*, worse, it has to be worse. And you gotta stick your eyes into him like you want to kill him, that's how to educate him. Fact is, he wouldn't be here if your aunt Zee hadn't told him it was her birthday and she wanted something nice."

Well, I still couldn't see Zee lying to him on purpose, just to get a free present – not in her condition. Also, Jupiter was in one of his know-it-all moods, which added a grain of salt.

"She's just as zoo-brained as he is," I said.

We looked around the pond and the pine trees on the other side. At some point when you're visiting St. Anselm's, it dawns on you. There are no fences. If you hated being here, you could scoot off just like walking out your front door. It happened sometimes, they said, but then you'd get caught and be shuffled right off to juvenile detention without so much as a how-do-you-do.

"Tick and I," said Jupe, "we're *tight* now. He's always lookin' to me for the next lesson. 'S like he never got no morals, so I am imparting my wisdom to him."

Well, if I believed him, I would've been ashamed of myself, since it had always been my job to show Tick what was right and what was wrong. I knew well enough, you don't have to spout it off all the time, you just need to behave a certain way and it'll be noticed. I'd behaved more or less the same way all my life, and often as not Tick was right at my side to catch onto it. When he did catch on, it was gratifying, and when he didn't – like with shoplifting – I blamed it on his troubles at birth. So I didn't think Jupe was barking up the right tree, wanting to impart his wisdom to a kid whose brain-wiring was a spaghetti tangle of short circuits. Also, I believed Indian wrist burns were a better teaching tool than dismembering Tick's arm, which on the face of it was a ridiculous threat and easy enough to see through.

I found out Jupiter's time at St. Anselm's would be up in July, if all went well in how he managed himself. He said he liked it there fine enough. The school part of it was as good as any school back in Ogamesh, he thought, and he believed the food tasted about the same as it would from his mother in the trailer, though they tended to serve too much macaroni and cheese and greasy burgers to suit his taste. As a rule, he told me, he and Tick would go through the cafeteria line together and Jupe would command him to stay away from the fatty stuff.

"It's training," he said, as we walked back from the pond. "If he's going surfing, he can't lard up like a farm hog."

"Jupe, he's not going surfing."

"That's his dream. You don't deny a dream."

I let it go at that. If they wanted to have some fantasy about surfing, so be it.

¤ ¤ ¤ ¤ ¤

On a Friday in June, right after we'd gotten out of school for the year, I finally broke down and agreed to go on a "date" with Natalie. It had several conditions which, if I were the girl, I might back away from, but she stuck right to her guns. First, I told her I couldn't spend any money because I was *this* close to piling up three hundred dollars for the Honda, which no one had bought yet and was now stashed inside the guy's garage. Second, it had to be in the afternoon instead of night, and here's where I shoveled it on a bit, explaining to her that Ty didn't normally work past seven at night and someone had to hang around to help Zee, namely yours truly. That's true except for the fact that Ty will come along to the house *any*time day or night, as long as she gets her usual hourly wage, and I know aunt Zee is always good for it because of the terrific pension she has, and an annuity, too. But you have to give Ty a day's notice, as a rule, just to be polite, and I hadn't bothered working on it. In any event, Nat said fine, she'd treat me to a couple of shooters of whiskey and an early supper picnic over on the banks of the river by Jameson's cotton field so I could be back by seven.

Now I need to say, I liked Nat as a *friend* up to this point, and only a friend, and I knew she had ratcheted up her interest in me a little past that, so it was going to be tricky to keep it simple. For the life of me, I can't figure out her problem. I didn't have a tenth her brain or a millionth of her money or a zillionth of her car, and I wasn't a star athlete. All those things mean a lot to most all the girls in this town. She'd said I was handsome, which maybe I was on a good cloudy day around dusk to a half-blind fool, but I'd come to sense that girls didn't care so much for handsomeness as long as the guy had a good car and some cash for a fun evening out. Also, after a couple of hours working at Winkler's Garage changing tires or oil, it was almost impossible to get all the grime off me and I wasn't much to look at, especially the knuckles and under the fingernails. The other problem she raised was the shooters of whiskey. She knew I'd take a small sip and that would be it, leaving the rest for herself, just as she wanted. Basically what she had planned for herself was philosophy and some food by the river and a hell of a buzz.

There's a nice grassy spot between the cotton field and the river, and Nat spread out a big blanket. Next to it she arranged the cooler and a picnic hamper, and then patted the blanket for me to come sit by her, though I was distracted by the river and the antics of some water bugs playing in a little eddy. After I obeyed her, she took out the bottle of whiskey, two short glasses, and some ice. I pinched my thumb and forefinger together, indicating I wanted just a tiny bit, and of course she said *good, all the more for me.*

Well, she slugged the first one down while I accidentally spilled mine behind my back, careful to aim for the grass instead of the blanket. *Freakin' idiot* I muttered to myself, then took a sip of the half-thimbleful that was left. She topped her glass off again while I put my hand up to say, *couldn't touch another drop.* Call me a total country idiot, but I'd much rather have a Dr. Pepper on a hot June afternoon rather than beer or liquor. What she *did* have in the hamper that excited me was crawfish salad, which she'd made from scratch because she knew it was one of my favorite things, along with some bread to make sandwiches. And some cold andouille sausage. I was ready for it any time, but she felt compelled to talk first.

"*Friendship,*" she said like it was important, "requires a certain intimacy. If it's to be a *good* friendship."

"Intimacy?" I knew the word, of course, but I needed more direction with it.

"Trusting the friend," she explained, "with your innermost thoughts and feelings."

"I've done that, haven't I?"

She was slugging her whiskey again and she almost gagged on it she started laughing so hard. But she got it down.

"You *do* entertain me, Woodrow."

"Well, I *listen* to you," I rejoindered, believing that listening was as intimate as talking, in a way.

"I don't want to pry or psychoanalyze, but sometimes I just can't figure you. I mean, at home, do you ever talk about serious things, share things, with Aunt Zee?"

Now it was my turn to laugh.

"I believe she's about as intimate as a wild boar."

She shook her head in dismay.

"And as congenial, too," I added. I started sucking on a whiskey-flavored ice cube.

"Well, I guess your aunt is not your friend."

"Not so much. But I'm intimate with my brother. We talk about all kinds of things."

"Can you talk to me the same way? Or do I sit here staring at your skull wondering what's going on in all that moosh."

Nat could get kind of snippy when she was drinking, but the fact is I didn't really mind because there could be some wit to it and she'd make me laugh.

"Try it," she went on. "Talk to me like Tick. I just transformed, I'm Tick."

"Hi Tick. You smell like booze."

"Gee, Woody, booze makes me feel better, 'specially when I get sad thinking about how we got no parents, only Aunt Zee, and she ain't no real parent."

She did this goofy retarded voice that didn't sound much like Tick, but I got the idea. His voice sounded more jittery and sharp, and actually kind of musical sometimes.

"Well, that's our lot. We make the best of it."

"Don't you miss 'em, Woody? Our daddy ran off, didn't he? Why'd he do that? Didn't he love us or nothin'?"

"Husbands do that, and so do wives. Now drink up, Tick, and quit whining in that phony voice, I'm hungry."

"Y'never give me a good night kiss, Woody."

Oh Lordy, how she got tricky.

"I've *never* kissed a brother and I never will, I just swat you on the bum and that's it, and I'd do the same to Natalie Starke next time I see her."

That more or less killed the game, which didn't satisfy her, I don't think. She finally got into the hamper and assembled some crawfish salad sandwiches as best she could and drank some more whiskey. As things unfolded, I could see I was going to drive us home.

The truth is, Tick never whined about not having parents, but we hadn't skipped over the issue either, because he was interested. Our father was a man named Milton Clayne, according to Aunt Zee, and he was a lumberman who lived and worked in our area for a few years before moving on. He and our mother never got married, so the town had plenty to talk about, particularly if you consider that Tick and I came three years apart, which was plenty of time for him to pop the question or for our mother to go find someone else who would. It's always been the truth to me that our mother loved Milton, in spite of his waffling on the subject of marriage, and it was all but a gunshot to her head when he finally left town, before Tick was born, to seek his fortune elsewhere. Whether he was upright and honest or a total scoundrel is a mystery to me. It doesn't matter, because I don't remember him at all, and there are no pictures.

I'd told all this to Nat before. But she couldn't seem to get it out of her head that I must have *cared* in some way for this guy and therefore had to confront the business of his running off and deal with it. She was digging for anger, but there wasn't any. Most of my teenage years, I was too busy trying to manage my brother and my addle-brained aunt to get angry at some guy I'd never known.

Still, it was irritating that he'd bailed on us when we sure could've used a father around the house.

With some fathers I've run into, you get the impression their kid is only alive because of *him*. That's true in a factual way, of course, but it's the sort of swollen-up pride that has nothing behind it. I swear Tick and I would've popped onto this earth one way or another, in some different shape, no matter who made us. That's how I felt.

When I drove us back along the access road past Jameson's cotton fields, Nat tried to describe for me what all she'd been building up to, but she was so full of whiskey it came out in a series of gurgles and confusion. As I recall –

"I *think* – no intimacy ever with an adult. A parent. So *you* can't be intimate. No hugs gotten. No hugs to. *Give*. Woody. Strong like tree. Won't – *bend*."

"Will hug *Nat*," I mimicked.

"Will?" Here eyes flashed wide with hope, or something similar.

"Will. Won't kiss, though. Friend."

She chewed on the word *friend* like gum and then seemed to want to spit it out.

The problem with Nat being so drunk was that I had to drive the Buick to her house, which is about two miles from Aunt Zee's, and then hoof it on home, or maybe hitch. I wasn't that crazy about walking along Route 12, what with all the logging trucks and semis and whatnot, and hitching was always a little sketchy because likely as not you'd get some crazy redneck who'd be drunker than Natalie, as opposed to someone you knew. Normally I didn't mind rednecks, because I was pretty close to being one myself and I could speak their language, but the ones most likely to pick you up would be drunk, and the first thing out of their mouths would be *you got an older sister?* I swear I've heard that a dozen times, always from guys who look tough but who are lonely inside.

So I told Nat when we pulled in her long driveway, "Looks like I gotta walk home."

"'S good for you." And a burp, followed by a giggle.

"I could take your car."

She didn't even hesitate. "Yeah, take it. You can pick me up tomorrow."

"Your parents won't mind?"

She shook her head and seemed to gulp for another burp. "They don't mind. *Anything.*"

I knew that in advance, of course. Her parents struck me as kind of detached from her, and very relaxed about rules. "Well, if they do, you can tell them I thought the Buick might be burning oil and I offered to run it into Winkler's to have them check it out."

"They won't ask."

We got out by a stand of spruce where we wouldn't be seen from the house, and I gave her a big hug, just as I promised, as well as a little swat on the bum afterward. She was too loopy to try to kiss me, which was a break, so after the intimacies I watched her start to stagger back to her house, and then I hopped in the Buick and drove back to Aunt Zee's.

¤ ¤ ¤ ¤ ¤

It happened that it became extremely important to have Nat's car sitting in our driveway, right below my window.

I've told you I'm not a religious person, but I have a pretty strong streak of faith – in *something*, whatever it is that strings things together in the right way when you don't even know it. I connected the strings like this: Nat wants to take me on a picnic date, so she picks me up in her car. She wants to get a buzz, so she drinks and then gets too clobbered to drive home. I drive her to her house, and she takes pity on me for having to walk two miles, so she lends me the Buick. Suddenly, I have wheels I didn't expect.

I can say this *now*, looking back on it all. But at the time, that very night and the following day, there was so much going on that I wasn't exactly concentrating on how things got strung together.

It started when I popped into the house where Zee was sitting with her tray-table, eating chocolate cake and watching TV, and Ty was in the kitchen working on the dinner dishes. Zee didn't look up so I walked right by her to go help Ty, and maybe leak a little information about the picnic I'd just had. It didn't take long – she noticed my "new car," and I gave her an account of the afternoon's activities and Nat's yen for whiskey and the resulting problems with transportation. Ty allowed as how she was sure that rich girl had designs on me, which I knew to be true and wouldn't deny. It was flattering, in a way, but I shrugged it off. Otherwise, while Ty washed and I dried, her brow was crinkled and she looked worried more than usual, so I asked her about it.

"She called me Percy. Swear, if I look half as ugly as old Percy used to look, they better amputate me at the neck and protect me from the rest of my life."

Well, it gave me a start, since Percy was the maid Zee and Uncle Carl kept many years ago, and, judging by a photo I'd seen of her, Ty had a point.

"Might be a resemblance," I chanced, and Ty swatted at me.

"I'm sayin', Woody, if her mind's goin' so fast she thinks I'm Percy, I ain't the one to be workin' here."

Later at night when I was in bed, I gave that problem a lot of thought. I'd just gotten out of school for the year and didn't have much in the way of plans, but the plans I had didn't include trying to be a professional nurse for Aunt Zee.

It kept me up a bit. That, plus the usual dead quiet in the room with Tick gone and the wind not blowing. But in time I did fall off to sleep, just for awhile.

What woke me up was a far off noise you don't hear too often in Ogamesh. When my head cleared enough to make sense of it, I realized there was a blaring of sirens far, far off in the distance, the kind that fire engines use. And when I drew a breath, it was tinged with the smell of smoke.

FOUR

"Are you Woody?"
Those are the first words I heard Saturday morning, and the way the guy spoke them I wondered even then if they'd haunt me for the rest of my life. Things can happen that make you question who you really are, right down to your name, as I'll get to later. At the time, it was about nine in the morning and I'd woken up late – because of my general restlessness and the sirens the night before – and heard voices downstairs. Zee's voice, shrieky and defiant, and a man's voice I hadn't heard before. Fearing an intruder, I threw on a pair of shorts, grabbed my hunting knife and rumbled down the staircase two steps at a time with my heart pounding. I was too much in a sleep haze to understand I'd be no match for most intruders, even with the knife, but it was instinctual to grab a weapon.

When I landed in the hallway I saw that the man was a sheriff or a deputy and that Zee, leaning on her walker, was too confused to be of much use to him.

"Are you Woody?"

"Yes sir."

Zee seemed revolted to look at me.

"You come down here like a half-naked jaybird! Get some clothes on you!"

"You can put the knife down, boy."

"Yes sir."

"And get dressed, we got company!"

"S'all right, ma'am, he's decent enough."

It was a short debate because to avoid further wrangling I dashed upstairs, put the knife back, and grabbed a tee shirt. Zee has always been opposed to casualness of dress in the house, raised as she was to respect modesty, and her end-all limit was shorts and a tee shirt. When I got back downstairs, she'd settled herself into a chair by her card table.

This time, more awake, I got a good look at the sheriff's deputy. He was dressed to the nines with his gun and nightstick and handcuffs dangling from his belt, but he had a puffy, friendly face. I judged him to be about forty, based on the crow's feet wrinkles next to his eyes and some gray in his hair by the temples – otherwise blond, and cut short like a military haircut. The nametag said "Rawlins." In spite of his genial face, he was solid muscle head to toe and he did a fine job looking somber and serious.

It crossed my mind that having Natalie's Buick in the driveway was the cause of the visit.

"Son, I need to ask you some questions, if you don't mind."

"No sir, I don't."

I didn't steal it. My friend lent it to me. Ask her.

"There was a fire last night at St. Anselm's, where your brother is."

"Yes sir." Boy, did my stomach do a flip flop. "Was it bad?"

"The fire destroyed Magnolia House, which was his dormitory, and partly destroyed a service building next to it. We had a fatality. And we have two missing. One of the missing is your brother."

"Who's he talking about?" Zee cried out, but I ignored her just then because my mind was racing with a zillion questions and images.

"I don't understand," I believe I said.

"Well, the fire started in the basement and spread very fast. Children on the second floor mostly jumped out windows or took the back staircase. The one fatality seemed to be up on the third floor in an attic room that's off-limits to the students and here's my question to you, because I know you visited there several times."

"Attic room." I didn't know any attic room.

"Did Tick ever go up there? Did he ever talk about that room?"

"No sir, not that I remember."

"Well, did he ever talk about running away?"

"No sir, absolutely not." Tick actually seemed to like the place.

"Well, son, the fire was so severe that if he got caught up on the third floor it may take some time to get to the bottom of things. Sad to say. The whole building's just rubble right now."

He shook his head, seeming genuinely sorrowful. But I couldn't imagine Tick getting stuck in a fire. He was too wily to get trapped, and he'd jump from the third floor if he had to.

"Y'all sure he's missing?"

"We're sure. We checked hospitals –"

"He could've run to a neighbor's house or something. For *help.* If Tick jumped out a window to escape a fire, and twisted his ankle or something, that's just the kind of thing he'd do. He's a little disabled, in the head, and he wouldn't wait for an ambulance 'cause he wouldn't necessarily expect one to come."

"Well son, there was help at the school and their staff. Wouldn't he know that?"

"I'm *saying*, officer, Tick's head doesn't work logically, for the most part." It always saves time if people can figure that out sooner rather than later. Rawlins seemed a little slow to take it in.

"Well, we'll double check, but I 'spect our department's done a thorough job, checking with neighbors."

I added, feeling too dumb to think of anything else, "If I were Tick, I might do just that, I might just run off to a neighbor's." All I could think of was getting myself into the Buick and racing over to the school.

"Okay, that's helpful, I'll call that in."

"Be right back," I said, and raced back upstairs to put on my socks and sneakers and get my wallet. When I came back down, Rawlins was sitting at the card table with Zee, patting the back of her hand.

"We'll do our best, ma'am."

"Why was he there?" she asked. "*This* is his home!"

The deputy's radio blared at him, and he grabbed it and chatted for a minute or so, explaining where he was and then *yes, I'll tell them.* When he finished, he stood up and looked me close in the eye.

"Well, the other family's been notified, so I can tell you the other missing boy is Jupiter Strange. They hung out a lot together, so I'm told."

My head was in a spin, wondering so many things.

"Yes sir, that's true. They got to be friends."

More questions in my head and nasty images of the fire raging up to the third floor I didn't even know existed at Magnolia House. Jupiter and Tick missing.

30

"He was due for release next month, so it makes no sense, does it?" he asked me.

"What makes no sense?"

"That they'd run off."

"No *sir*, don't make any sense, not a bit."

"Still," he said, "word is, Jupiter's not as sensible as some."

"No *sir*, if they'd run off, Tick would come right here for sure, or go to a neighbor's house like I said, if he were injured. That's as far as he'd run off."

"Well, it's a sad business, in any case." He took a card out of his shirt pocket and gave it to me. "You call us if you get any information."

"Yes sir."

"And we'll do the same."

He turned to go, but paused for a second to look back at me.

"He's been a good boy mostly, hasn't he?"

"Yes sir, he has. Mostly."

"If you had a hand in raising him, I guess he has."

Well, that perked my ears up. It's not often a stranger makes a compliment like that, when he can't know much about you.

After Rawlins left, I needed to sit with Zee for a few minutes. She had milky blue eyes that usually liked to look off into the distance, but now they were darting all over the place, and it was clear to me she needed some talking to to try to settle her down. I told her what was as close to the truth as I could imagine it, knowing Tick and Jupiter. *A bad fire happened last night at St. Anselm's, where they've been living for a bit, and it looks like they got out okay but they've been slow to report back in and let everyone know they're okay. They might be off having a picnic or visiting friends.* She nodded as if she understood and her eyes stopped jumping around.

I could almost believe it myself.

¤ ¤ ¤ ¤ ¤

As soon as Ty arrived at the door and I blurted out the headlines, I blasted off toward St. Anselm's in the Buick. I didn't even call Nat to tell her. The Buick was a three-speed automatic, which sounds wimpy, but as I've said it had a Chevy three-fifty V-8 engine in it and a halfway decent carburetor so it had plenty of pep and torque between fifty-five and seventy. Unfortunately, the car smelled of whiskey, and sure enough I twisted around and saw the mostly empty bottle in the back seat leaking into a pile of trash. The cap wasn't twisted on right. I opened the windows all the way to try to air it out.

It's like she *lived* in this car. Sipping whiskey and enjoying the sights while driving under the speed limit.

To get to St. Anselm's you have to duck off Route 12 and go south, through a stretch of pecan groves, followed by cotton fields and some ramshackle villages that aren't really towns but just collections of trailers and old sharecropper's shacks, with their tin roofs and sagging front porches. No one ever paints these shacks, as if there's some law against it because they look prettier all gray and weathered. Or else, paint's too expensive. Black folks sit out on the porch in their rocking chairs or on top of a barrel, watching everything that goes by (it's the *world* that goes by, I thought – and you're missing it). Sometimes there will be chickens scratching in the dust in the front yard. It was hot this morning, and even though I was steaming along at a good clip I could hear the cicadas and crickets buzzing in the sun.

Black folks don't miss a trick. That's been my experience.

What happened was, I didn't stop at St. Anselm's. I drove right to it and slowly past it, but I didn't stop to get out and poke around. There were still fire trucks there with their lights flashing, and a bunch of firemen crawling through the rubble that was still smoldering and steaming, and police cars, and a van that said "medical examiner," and tourists and rubberneckers. I didn't stop mostly because what I saw was enough, but also because the smell was disgusting. It wasn't just woodsmoke, it was burning plastic and something with an awful sweetness to it that turned my stomach.

Darned if I know where all the kids were. It's a safe bet some of them got banged up jumping out of Magnolia House, breaking their legs in the fall and whatnot, and for sure all their belongings got burnt to a crisp, so my guess is they were hauled off to hospitals or to other places that could care for them.

After I moseyed past all the emergency vehicles, I found a dirt road going into the pine woods – well-traveled enough so it was possible somebody lived down there. Sure enough, the woods opened up into hayfields and some small gardens, with trailers and shacks spotted here and there. A couple of the driveways had sheriff's cruisers in them, so I figure Rawlins had called in my theory to the department – that Tick might hustle himself off to a neighbor's, nonsensical as it might be to do that.

Where Jupe had landed was anybody's guess. But he was even wilier than Tick, in spite of his moral pronouncements, and I just couldn't imagine that he'd let a fire get the better of him. Also, he was strong and athletic instead of blobby the way he used to be, so it was easy to see him busting through doors and windows and leaping off the roof to save himself.

The dirt road looped around to the right and into the woods again, and eventually popped right back out onto the same paved road. I recognized it, and turned left to head a mile or so into the little village where I knew they had a general store.

St. Anselm's was fairly strict as a home for troubled youth, but it was liberal enough to bus kids into the village once a week, with staffmembers close by their sides, to buy snacks or batteries or new socks or whatever. Mostly, the kids came to this store because it had a little bit of everything, including a big drum of hot water on the porch for boiling peanuts, so I decided to stop there and see if I could get my ear close to the ground.

Well, though it was mid-morning on a Saturday, you wouldn't know it. The place was empty of people except for a raggedy-looking family of a mother and her toddlers leaving the store as I walked in. An old black guy was tending the counter, and we nodded to each other, but I chose not to start up a conversation with him. He was so old and frail looking, I thought if he nodded more than once the effort might stagger him to the floor and kill him. So I just looked through the glass at a display of toy cars and trucks and a box of hard candy until he asked if he could help me.

Well, I had money and I was a bit hungry by now, but I had to debate if I wanted something I could eat fast or slow, to take in the car or enjoy on the front porch where they had some chairs – and yes, there was someone sitting out there by the drum of hot water but I forget who.

I decided on a slow food. "Believe I'll have a bowl of peanuts."

In the South, that means boiled peanuts because roasted peanuts come in a sack.

"Lorraine will serve you up outside."

I gave him the money and went back to the porch where Lorraine was sitting by the drum. She must've been his wife, or possibly even his *mother* she was so stringy and wrinkled with age, and it took her some doing to get the lid off the drum and scoop out a fair serving of peanuts for me. I thanked her and sat in the chair closest to her, watching cars go by and peeling off the soft shells to get to the gooshy nuts inside. I love boiled peanuts once in a while, especially if they're not overcooked and all the flavor's gone.

She watched me eat and said, "Smells like a storm coming." The voice was raspy with age, and her eyes crinkled as she sniffed. Now, lots of older people can smell a storm ten miles off, but so far it was just hot and sticky, the way Georgia often is in the summer months, and not a cloud in the sky. So I believed her nosebuds were hallucinating. Still, she had one of those old-people's faces that looked like it was storing wisdom in every crease.

"Yes, ma'am," I said.

"Passing through?" she asked.

"Yes ma'am, on my way to Waycross," I concocted on the spot. "Taking the scenic route."

"Fur piece," she said, and she was right, it was another hundred miles easily.

"Mm hm. I'm in no rush."

Well, we were trading looks, and she seemed quite interested in me and started yapping.

"Big fire here last night. At the juvenile home."

"Hm. Didn't know."

"Killed a colored boy. Nothin' left of him 'cept teeth, they say."

Some real old-timer blacks still say *colored,* and it always throws me.

"I'm sorry to hear that. Musta been a doozie."

Doozie was a disrespectful choice of speech, but she glided right over it.

"Word is, it got *set.*"

"Ma'am?"

"*Set.* That's the talk. Bad as you can be, doin' that, big house full of boys. There's one comes in here, shifty. They say he's missing and run off."

"Good peanuts," I said, not wanting to seem too fascinated. "They lookin' for him?"

She laughed pretty hard at this till I thought she might bust a seam somewhere. "Wouldn't *you*?"

"What's he look like? I'll keep my eye out."

"Halfway to Mississippi by now."

"What's he look like anyway?"

"Colored. Tall boy, built strong. Sheriff knows his name, I sure don't."

"Okay, I'll keep my eye out. You're right, it's terrible —"

"Always has this puppy white boy by his side."

"Puppy?"

"Looks like a puppy, acts like one too. Head ain't right."

"Oh."

"Say he's missing too."

"Mighta got burned up. They'd never find 'em. Just teeth, as you say, and what with all the piles of rubble — "

"Bet they ran off. Why else would you buy a map?"

"Ma'am?"

"I'm *sayin'*, last time they come in here, they bought a map of the whole U.S. Boys like them don't care about maps 'less you're gonna travel."

"Yes, ma'am."

"I know 'cause I sold it to 'em."

"'Spect you're right," I said. "Good peanuts, ma'am, but I believe I need to be moving on now."

She asked me to keep my eye out while I drove, and I promised I would, I'd watch out for both of them. Some days it's best not to make promises like that, the ones you don't intend to keep, because when you least expect it they turn on their heads and end up keeping *you*.

⌗ ⌗ ⌗ ⌗ ⌗

Every now and again people get a piece of mail, like a card or a letter, that has a stamp on it that never got cancelled or postmarked. This is nothing so special — I've had it happen several times, especially around

Christmas, and Zee's always asked for me to get out the clothes iron, fill it with water, and steam off the stamp so she can use it again and save a few cents. I don't know how the post office works with all its machines and whatnot, but from what I've seen in the world it's easy enough to make mistakes in business, so I figure the post office is no exception when they deliver a card or letter that they never postmarked.

Okay, it's nothing special unless it's that particular Saturday morning in June, and the postcard is a picture of the very general store I'd just come home from.

But I'm going to have to back up, because of a bunch of things happening at the house upon my return that made me clench my fists and prepare for battle. As I fleshed it out later with Ty's help, our front yard was invaded by reporters and photographers from different newspapers who'd somehow gotten Tick's name and tracked him down here. There was a Macon paper, an Atlanta paper, and even one from Americus, which is not so close as you'd think. Zee was inside certain the world was ending, Ty was on the porch fending off the attack as best she could, and what had fired up the newspaper guys more than ever was that Viola Strange, Jupe's mom, had come for a visit and had her face pressed up against the screen door, inside looking out, shouting *he was a good boy! A good boy!* as the flashbulbs popped. And Jupe's baby sister Saturna was at her side, holding back tears.

That's about when I arrived in the Buick, seeing so much chaos in the yard that I parked a few houses down on the street, then eased myself gently along the sidewalk toward the commotion. Ty caught a look at me and was about to blab my name, but I hushed her with my finger over my lips and stood just far enough away so I wasn't noticed. I didn't want to talk to any of those people. As if the saints had figured it out, right away a sheriff's cruiser swung down our street with its lights going, screeched to a halt in the middle of the street, and out popped two deputies who started yelling at the newspaper people, strongly encouraging them to get lost. One of them was Rawlins, and sure enough he spied me, and after the men had done their job to restore order to our front yard, he eased on down the sidewalk toward me, wanting a chat.

We sat on the curb, and as tensed up and itching for a fight as I was, I started to tremble when he got into his report.

"Woody, we found a boy who told us a fair amount about last night. I can't name him, so I'll just call him the witness. He lived in Magnolia House with the others. He tells us everything was fine and normal at the last bed count, which was around ten-thirty, but along around eleven-thirty he says Jupiter and your brother quietly rousted themselves up and got dressed. Well, the witness was curious, because it happens that from time to time some of the boys sneaked in a late night game of cards up in the third floor attic room. It was *poker*, playing for pennies in the dark with flashlights. Of all the things they could do on the sly, they pick poker. Anyway, one of the regulars, he said, was Jupiter, and as often as not Tick would join him. Another one of the regulars is a twelve-year old named Henry Jones, and he's the one that died in the fire. Now the witness says that Jupiter *insisted* there would be no game tonight, that he was just goin' down the hall for a pee, along with Tick, but it didn't sit right 'cause the boys got all dressed. Henry Jones got up, got dressed, and followed them."

"Maybe they were just going for a walk outside," I suggested. "It was a pretty starlit night last night."

Rawlins was shaking his head. "Son, we now know the fire started in the basement, which was full of old paint cans, kerosene and paint thinner and such – a regular bomb ready to go off. We can't tell yet if it was an accident or not – it could've been a boy down there smoking who got reckless. But what we're thinking now is, since the fire started a little after twelve, either those three boys were in the attic playing poker, or else they were up to something else and we sure as hell want to find them and talk to them. Henry, the victim – we suspect he was in the attic room, maybe waiting for the other two, and the witness tells us the door up there gets so sticky in the humidity it's damn near unopenable from the inside without making a racket. But the building's such a wreck now it's hard to know for sure *where* he was. He got caught somewhere, that's for dead certain. Poor kid."

"Tick's never cared much for fire," I told Rawlins. "Jupiter's the same way – some kids love playing with fire, but I've never seen that kind of thing with them." This was true. They didn't care about playing with fire any more than I did; they'd rather catch frogs or newts or in Jupe's case, borrow a car for a joyride.

"Woody, if they survived it and run off, we gotta find them."

"Jupiter and Tick do stupid things sometimes – that's why they were there – but they'd never do something as evil as arson, burn a building down and kill an innocent kid. Count on it, Mr. Rawlins, I'd swear to it."

"Okay son, I hear you."

"They're not built that way."

"Well, I know you're the man of the house these days, so I'm telling all this to just you, and you can pass it on to your aunt as you see fit. We'll sift that rubble for days, right down to shoelaces if we have to. But if they're alive and you ever have any contact with them, you gotta tell us directly."

That was about the sum of it. He appreciated my point of view, and I appreciated his telling the story, but it horrified me all the same.

If those three boys were playing cards up there and a fire started, Jupe would make *sure* they all got out safe. He wouldn't leave young Henry Jones all to himself to die in that room.

The reporters were gone now, but there was still plenty of fuss and fury to deal with inside the house, with Viola and Saturna near hysterical, with Ty trying to keep Zee under control, and now with the added surprise of Nat and her mother and stepfather pulling up in front of the house in their big car, unloading a whole party full of food. Casseroles, a chocolate cake, cookies for Zee.

I'd met her mom a couple of times, and the professor once, but you'd think they'd known me all my life, the way they hugged me and said how sorry they were and how we all had to hope and pray for the best. Nat wrapped me in the gentlest hug, and I could see from her red eyes she'd probably been crying. I invited them all inside, and I'm not going to be able to describe it well because it was an unholy racket of cheery Starke and Hawkins family and miserable everybody else, with Viola mostly in charge of the noise.

I escaped the confusion by going outside again to fetch the mail as an excuse. It usually showed up in the mailbox around eleven, and we were into the lunch hour by now.

That's when I found the postcard I mentioned earlier, unpostmarked. On one side was the photo of the general store. On the other was my name and address and a two word message.

Mal. Boo.

The writing was in pencil, but it sure wasn't Tick's handwriting, which looks loopy and carefully considered. All of the writing was in clunky block letters.

My head started to spin.

Now our mail, like everyone else's, tends to be in a certain order the way it's placed in the mailbox. The first class mail tends to be on top, and the trash mail underneath in its own stack, like the circulars from the grocery store and whatnot. Well, I almost dropped the postcard because it was on the very bottom, under the circulars, rather than with the letters on top. It didn't make sense that it got separated like that. Unless of course someone like Jupe or Tick stuck it in there much earlier in the day, or even last night, when no one was paying attention.

Mal. Boo. I knew just fine what it meant, considering it was Jupe who wrote it, and he couldn't spell to save his life.

FIVE

I was working on a plan, but things got so rushed the plan half-planned itself, without my knowledge of it, and it made things complicated.

For example, as they were leaving, Dr. Hawkins saw Nat's Buick down the street.

"Natalie should probably drive her car back," he told me.

"Well sir, she could, but the car's low on oil and burning oil from what all I can tell, so it wouldn't be good for the engine."

"Burning oil? Is that serious?"

"Well, yes it usually is, it could be valves but it's frequently a problem in the cylinders, meaning the piston rings."

"Oh dear."

"I know this 'cause a motorcycle I want to buy might have the same problem. Plus, I work some days at Winkler's."

Nat had come out with her Mom and stood beside him.

"But the one way to tell," I kept up at him, "is for me to get it to the shop and run a compression check on all eight cylinders. Now, I've worked on three-fifties before, and –"

"Three-fifties?"

"That's the displacement of this engine, in cubic inches. It's a Chevy small block and a very fine high-compression engine, so it should be running right, else it could seize on you."

Nat was giving me quite a look.

"I don't know cars very well," he admitted, which I could tell.

"Yes sir, that's okay. I know a few things, and I can run it over to Winkler's and do some diagnostics."

Nat was squinting at me, like: what am I trying to pull?

"Fine, though I'd think you'd want to be with your family at a time like this."

True, I should, but the plan was leaping ahead of me and I had to stay with it.

"I just want to make sure Natalie has her car in good working order."

It seemed to satisfy him. Before they got in their big car, Nat took me aside by the wrist and asked *what's going on here?*

I don't know yet I whispered back to her.

In time, Viola and Saturna evacuated our house to go back to their trailer, but only after we'd exchanged a number of sentiments that we're pretty squirrelly because no one knew at all if the boys were dead or alive. When they'd left, Ty assured me she'd stick with Zee while I took the old Buick down to Winkler's, which I did right away because they're open only till three on Saturdays.

Winkler's looks like the kind of shop where folks are amazed that anything ever gets fixed right, because of the mess. The front part is a big wooden building with four bays and half a dozen back rooms crammed with old car parts, and then there are five storage sheds out back for more car parts and long-term projects, like restoring old trucks and whatnot. I usually worked in the fourth bay, which had a lift for oil changes and replacing tires, with the help of Trey Winkler, who was one of the two brothers. Trey was the biggest player ever in the history of Ogamesh football, and for his size and probably his pink skin he was known in those days as Hawg. Plenty of people still called him that twenty years later, in spite of his gentle encouragement that they remember his given name, which he preferred. He was as friendly and slow-witted as they come, but a finicky mechanic who'd take twice as long on a job as normal, just to make sure he got everything right. He was even fussier as a teacher for me, and I could get pretty frustrated sometimes with him leaning over my shoulder while I worked. But it was obvious that he liked me and appreciated my intelligence and good spelling, when it came to writing up a bill or a purchase order for new parts.

The other Winkler was Dave, Trey's older brother, who managed the office on those days when he was sober. He had problems with his liver and could be so irritable you wouldn't want to risk saying hi. Today, only Trey showed up, which made things simpler.

He's always quite a sight, and I swear I never get used to it – that enormous three hundred-and-something pound hulk squeezed into a muscle shirt, all soaked with grease, and orange hair sprouting all over his body, keeping company with a sea of freckles. He's married to a very attractive woman from Macon, and has two toddlers, so he's living proof that some women are very forgiving of a man's appearance in favor of his inner character. Trey was about the most sweet-natured guy I knew in Ogamesh.

As soon as I pulled the Buick into the bay and hopped out of the car he stopped fiddling with the voltmeter under some car's hood, came over to me and proceeded to gush his distress about Tick, hoping the Lord would see to it either to admit him into heaven or find him alive somewhere, one.

I had to nip his sorrow in the bud.

"Trey, I believe he and Jupiter are safe and sound, and on the road, and I can't tell you why and you can't breathe a word of this to anybody. But that's why I'm here with Natalie's Buick, as I'll explain."

Sensing the conspiracy in my voice, he drew me deeper into the bay, out of sight from people walking by on the road.

"Tell it nice and slow, Woody."

Well, I started to, but my tongue got ahead of me. "I need this favor from you, and it's a big favor and I'm prepared to pay for it. The car's gonna need a ring job, but not really, because I'm gonna need it to find Tick. It's got almost no compression in the number five and seven cylinders, but not really, 'cause to take the engine down and do a ring job on two cylinders I figure could take three weeks or so, depending how busy y'all are, and that's the kind of time I need to go find him, while you keep the Buick in one of the sheds locked up tight, but in fact while I'm driving it."

That may not have been exactly how I said it, but that's how it struck him because he was more addled than I was, which is saying something. There were just two people I could trust to keep a secret like this, and Trey was one. Nat was the other, if she didn't get herself drunk. In time, Trey and I sorted it out. The idea was, he would write up a repair order for an engine overhaul, provide an estimate, and alert them it could take three weeks or so because Winkler's was so busy this time of year. Nat would be in on the secret, so she wouldn't pester him for a car that wasn't there; neither would her parents, because they were so liberal with her and it was her car, after all.

To a degree, Trey didn't like the plan, partly because I couldn't tell him where I was headed or for exactly how long. He could be big-brotherly with me sometimes, if he thought I was behaving in a mis-guided way. But the main reason he was twitchy about it had to do with the sheriff's department.

"If you take off," he said, "they'll know something's up. And they'll ask me, 'cause you're my employee. That's plain common sense."

"Yes it is, and you'll have an alibi for me that I haven't invented yet." Which was true, but I was already working on it.

"Better get to it," he said.

"You know a deputy named Rawlins?" I asked.

He thought for a bit, then nodded. "Went to school with him. Good man. And smart."

"How smart?"

"If the fox wants to get in the coop, it will."

I offered him five dollars a day for storing the Buick in the far back shed, the only one with no windows in it, but here again he got con-fused. If you're not really *storing* it, why pay for it? I told him we both had to pretend in an almost real way that the car was back there being worked on, and therefore it should cost something, especially to keep the shed locked up tight away from prying eyes. Trey said whatever the amount should be, he'd just dock it from my pay when I got back.

I told him I'd bring the car by on Monday for the ring job, and he still didn't get it because he was shaking his head as I drove off.

⬚ ⬚ ⬚ ⬚ ⬚

I tried to imagine being Deputy Rawlins and having his job right now. Rawlins struck me as more than smart, he was more-than-average eager to uncover the truth of the fire and the fates of Jupiter Strange and Tick Elmont. The witness-kid he found at St. Anselm's gave him plenty of information to heighten his belief in two totally opposite things: that Tick and Jupiter died in the fire, and that Tick and Jupiter had some-thing to do with starting it and were now on the lam.

It was challenging for me to wrestle with the problem of keeping my secrets from him. I had his phone number in my wallet, and I could call anytime and inform him *well, they bought a roadmap of the United*

States last week and then sent me a misspelled, unpostmarked postcard saying Malibu, which might be their destination. But it didn't seem as much like information as sheer guesswork, and I wasn't likely to sweeten the pot and tell Rawlins that Tick had been obsessed with surfing at Malibu before he could count to seven. It was still pure guesswork.

Zee was napping when I got home from Winkler's. I went straight up to our room, tore off all the surfing pictures and posters and the letters that spelled out Malibu, and stored it all as best I could in our closet, behind the rest of Tick's junk.

Then I sat down on my bed with my hands over my ears to try to *think.*

My first thought was, *this would be a great time to have a parent.*

I'm just sixteen; I don't know enough. Damn it, why do good men leave good women? Worse, when they're pregnant and have a three year old.

The thoughts started piling up, and I tried to keep them orderly.

Tick has no money, and never has. Jupiter must have money. They wouldn't be hitchhiking, a big lanky black kid with missing teeth and a sawed-off white scamp traveling together. It looks too weird, they'd get reported.

They'd take a bus. Jupe wouldn't risk stealing a car.

Unless somebody lent him a car, or gave them a ride.

The nearest bus station would be ten miles or more from St. Anselm's, most likely in Nortonton, to the south. Ogamesh didn't have buses; the nearest to us was Hartwell, kind of northerly. But if someone on the outside gave them a ride, they could end up at almost any bus station in Georgia.

They didn't start the fire. But they were there in the dormitory at bed check, and according to the witness kid they were up and dressed at eleven-thirty. The fire started after midnight.

They didn't start the fire, but it was too much of a coincidence that the fire started soon after they were up and about, ready to go somewhere. There could be a connection, of some sort.

Did they mail the postcard two or three days before that? Or did they plop it into our mailbox sometime really early Saturday morning?

It's twenty miles from St. Anselm's to Ogamesh. That's about six or seven hours walking – it would take too long, and they'd be spotted on the road, what with all the fire engines and lawmen. If they stuck the postcard in our mailbox, they had a car.

Which told me, yes, they'd be planning this for awhile, like buying the roadmap. Jupe had set it up with a buddy on the outside.

But all these ideas started to buffalo me, because they were tricky and the questions had no answers. The *other* ideas were simpler and fewer and didn't buffalo me at all:

They'd planned to run off to California, and they'd mailed the postcard a few days earlier and the post office didn't postmark it.

And they got caught in the fire somehow, in some way that really trapped them, and they died.

¤ ¤ ¤ ¤ ¤

Zee kept napping, and while she snoozed I kept planning and coming up with a scheme that seemed least likely to fail. I did this by getting out of the house, hopping on my bike, and cruising the streets of our neighborhood. Past Ty's house, John Dandridge's house – the older man and friend of Zee's who watched her while Ty and Tick and I were at the hearing – past all the houses till the road turned to red Georgia dirt and led out into open farmland of peanuts, soybeans, and farther along, Jameson's cotton fields and the Strange residence, with just a glint of their old trailer peeking through pine trees. I like farmland because you can actually see things and get a sense of the sky. Hot and greasy weather all day, but changing, with the air thickening. Off to the southwest, it looked dark and grim. I remember Lorraine, the old woman at the general store, warning that she smelled a storm on its way.

An open sky helps you plan because you get a sense of how *big* a plan can become. A storm coming also helps temper your enthusiasm for the plan, because it warns you how fast things can change for the worse.

Sometimes Tick would come out here on his bicycle and just sit. He'd do it by riding into the peanuts or cotton, then he'd dump his bike and squat in the bushes so no one could see him (like me, who'd be trying to fetch him).

I chose to be him for a second, ducking into the cotton field and sitting.

45

When I was around, he was hard to shake. When I wasn't around, Tick could be as happy as a hermit. If Jupe said, let's go to Malibu, Tick wouldn't be able to contain his glee and it might be three or four days later, somewhere in Oklahoma or Texas, before he might ask about his older brother or his aunt Zee. The kid had a singular focus like no one I knew, though it got heavily relieved now and then by distraction or daydreaming.

Jupe had told me in so many words at St. Anselm's, Tick was in training for surfing. When he'd said that, I should've jumped on him to get his true meaning and judge how much he was kidding, if at all. Jupiter Strange will drop little bombshells like that without batting an eye or cracking a smile, and there was no way to gather the truth of it.

Why would he run off with just a month to go?

I got my head back into planning as I hopped on my bike again and continued riding, turning left on an old county farm road that would dump me out on the back edge of the Starke/Hawkins estate, some two miles west. The sky looked nasty through the tops of the trees.

Summer here in the south is sun in the morning, thunderstorms in the afternoon. Not every day, but most, and you have to adjust to it if you're not from here. Some of the storms can be bone-trembling in their behavior, and the best way to keep yourself safe is watch the sky and listen to what kind of thunder you hear. Zee, when her head was right, had summer thunder figured into three types, and she'd announce it to us. The least was the Boomer, or "just a Boomer," which boomed and then faded. Most storms had Boomers, with lightning of course, and there could be high winds and downpours, but generally they weren't so bad.

Next were the Rumblers, which came in groups and sometimes exploded. You'd probably get some hail with these, and plenty of wind with trees coming down.

The worst were the Rollers. I'd experienced them maybe four or five times that I can remember, and they send you scurrying for the basement because the thunder never stops, it's like a huge freight train roaring along with more freight trains right behind it, and the sky gets *white* in front of the dark bruised sky, an enormous boiling blast of noise and hail and often tornadoes. The air feels weird and full of electricity, and your hairs stick up on your neck and arms and you just *pray* it goes away fast, but as I recall it hangs right over you and keeps on rolling and dumping oceans of rain on you, with lightning.

What I sensed about the storm brewing to the southwest: somebody's in for the Rollers. But it looked like it would stay south of Ogamesh by a good ten miles or more, and miss us.

I rode on to Natalie's place, through the woods. In those last ten minutes or so, I did the best of my planning.

☒ ☒ ☒ ☒ ☒

I found her out behind her barn sitting in the grass and writing a letter to me, which she promptly crushed into a ball, saying she could tell me now in person. I said, *it can wait, let's go for a walk,* which we did – along the fenceline of the horse pasture and farther along into the old pecan groves, then out into open hayfields.

Riding over, what I'd struggled with was, *how much can I lie to her?* If I lied just a little, I'd probably get caught in some small mistake. If I totally lied, I might get away with it but I'd lose an ally back here in Ogamesh while I was on the road, and the fact is I needed Nat to keep her eyes and ears open. But mostly, I determined I couldn't lie at all because of how it would make me feel.

So I swore her to secrecy as best I could, and then spoke to her of the necessity of what I was doing.

"There's a nasty storm to the south of us, and it creates challenges that have to be faced," I told her, feeling momentarily poetic. "Right now, *I am in the middle of a storm of necessity,* and there are no choices but to fight right through it."

I need the car for a couple of weeks, maybe three. There's nothing wrong with the engine.

She was nodding, letting her jaw drop down a bit.

I need to find Jupiter and Tick, warn them they're being hunted, and fetch them back.

She kept nodding, not speaking.

I need to believe they're alive. I could be wrong, but I doubt it.

She was nodding and biting her lip at all these necessities.

I need to create a diversion, so I can get a good long head start on this man Rawlins, who's seriously determined to get to the bottom of things.

47

The Rollers opened up, far to the south. Some town down there was going to get clobbered – it might have been right near St. Anselm's. While I was staring off at the storm across her hayfields, she blind-sided me and laid a kiss on my cheek.

"Hey Nat, c'mon."

"You are a poser, Mr. Elmont. Can't figure you."

She was tarting up her voice with a phony southern drawl.

"Anyway," she continued, "I wanted to kiss you – before you race off to parts unknown. As if you can tell me where you're going."

"I can't. As they say, the less you know, the less you can blab."

"I'm not a blabber."

"No, but whiskey is, I've seen it firsthand."

Well, she reared back to take a swat at my face but I dodged her just in time. It wasn't going to be much of a slap, but I've never been partial to pain, no matter how slight. Having missed me, she gave me a shove.

"That's unfair."

Well, I bit my lip to consider it, and she might have been right. It was a weakness she had, good old southern bourbon, and I don't like picking too much on other people's failings.

"I apologize," I said. "I mean it."

"If you take my car, you keep my trust."

That seemed fair, but I still clamped down on mentioning my destination. Rawlins could come swooping down on her at any time and she'd have to fess up what she knew. But she couldn't confess what she didn't know.

Still, she pressed me on the details of the trip, in a motherly kind of way. Where to stay? I told her I had some old camping stuff in the basement, including a pup tent with just a couple of holes in it, and some cooking gear. Money? I had two hundred and eighty dollars in a shoebox under my bed, and ten dollars in my wallet. It was all going for the Honda, but the bike would have to wait. Driver's license? I'd have to be very law-abiding and not get stopped. First Aid kit? I didn't have one, so she said she'd throw some stuff together from her house.

She offered me extra money, too, but I declined. I didn't need to be more in her debt.

Man, the Rollers roared away! Just like kettledrums pounding away in an orchestra. St. Anselm's was down there somewhere and Magnolia House, what was left of it.

¤ ¤ ¤ ¤ ¤

Anyone who happened to be asleep all weekend got plenty of news in the papers on Monday about the fire and then the storm, with photos of Henry Jones and Tick and Jupiter plastered on the front pages – *one boy dead, two missing.* The pictures seemed to be taken at St. Anselm's, probably when they were signed in, on account of all the faces looking glum and ashamed. The papers said the storm dumped hail and six inches of rain in the area, along with what they thought was a tornado because of the damage, though nobody saw it. I gathered it didn't hit St. Anselm's directly, but close enough to make a mess of things including, as the sheriff was quoted as saying, *stroodling the fire rubble around like jackstraws.* The rain unleashed a flood of thick Georgia mud that oozed into the basement of Magnolia House and swamped it full.

It makes our job almost impossible, said the fire chief. *Looking for remains.*

I skimmed down a bit till I found the sheriff again saying *if they're alive, they are people of interest and we want to find them.*

Then,

We just don't know.

SIX

To hear people in Ogamesh talk about it, you'd think Mississippi was a kind of hell on earth, ugly to look at and as dumb as a state can be. You get a sense of a strong rivalry among southern states that goes way beyond college football, and wherever people came from – whether Alabama, South Carolina, Florida or Georgia (these are the only states I'd ever set foot in, by the way) – Mississippi was always taking it on the chin for being backward and unpleasant. I had to disagree. The people I met were kind enough to me, as soon as I crossed the line and needed some more ice and a cold pop, and for a pretty landscape I had no quarrel with it. Where I was driving now, about halfway through it, the land was wide and flat and open, with a beautiful sky to the west. Cotton, soybeans, sometimes corn, and some fescue sod farms.

I drove in such a way that it took a fair amount of discipline before it became second nature to me. First, I kept the Buick at about five miles an hour over the speed limit instead of my usual ten or fifteen, which forced other cars and trucks to pass me, sometimes with an angry beep. Second, I had one eye on the rear view mirror as often as was practical, with the sense that *anyone* behind me could be a source of trouble. Getting caught without a license would end it, for sure.

Starting the trip in a paranoid way, I thought, might make it less paranoid as I moved west. The idea is to start scared, then breathe a little easier as you go. The way I'd planned it, I seemed to be in good shape so far.

I sat down with Tychander Sunday evening on our front porch and told her what I was up to.

"The Forest Service?"

"That's right, it's volunteer work, but if I'm good at it I might get a real job next summer."

"What they want you for?"

"Tagging trees, bush-hogging and whatnot. It's just for two weeks."

She gave me one of those looks that suggested I was nuts.

"In *Arkansas?* Couldn't you find some trees closer to home?"

"That's where the program is. We start in Little Rock, then move up to the Ozarks."

In fact, there was such a program for teenagers like me, I'd seen it on our school bulletin board back in the spring and grabbed the brochure. I handed it to her on the porch and she furrowed her forehead while she read it.

"Federal government," she said.

"Yes."

"You pick a fine time to be goin' off into the *trees.*"

I explained as best I could that as long as my brother was missing I felt like a cat in a cage hanging around the house, and just being there wouldn't bring him back any faster. This was true. I could have added that it actually hurt my stomach to think of him, which was also true, but I didn't want to pour it on too thick.

"Ty, it's like *therapy* for me. I can't worry myself to the bone staying here. But being in the woods —"

"Like, I'll need to move in with Zee. She's the one who needs the therapy."

She correctly accused me of being selfish and not thinking of others, and moaned about the upheaval it would cause her to move in, plus having to sleep on the couch so she could hear Zee in the middle of the night, whether it be farting or a call for help. But I knew Ty liked the money, and being there round the clock would fatten her purse more than usual. I'd write her one of Zee's checks in advance.

Still, with me on the road she'd be pretty stretched, so I informed her I'd had a brief chat with John Dandridge a few doors down the street from her, to see if he might want to help out.

"He all *old,*" said Ty, which was true, but he'd been a friend to Zee for years and in fact was sweet on her, I judged. They enjoyed cribbage and gin runny together, and he'd visited enough so he knew the ins and outs of the house. He could walk upright, he had his brain intact, and he allowed as how he'd be delighted to pay some visits as needed. He was crusty looking, but a fine man on the whole.

Burdened as she was, Ty seemed to adjust to it all, but wrangled with me for quite awhile when I asked her to give me a ride up to the bus station in Hartwell first thing Monday morning. I'd have too much stuff in duffel bags to hitchhike, and didn't want to risk missing the morning bus to Mobile, with a change for Little Rock.

It was all of a fifteen minute ride in Zee's car, Ogamesh to Hartwell.

She got a five dollar tip for her troubles. The tip was courtesy of Natalie, who called at the last minute wanting to join us.

The Buick was stashed in the parking lot next door.

It was stashed there thanks to me and Trey Winkler late Sunday night. We caravanned up to Hartwell and he favored me with a lift back home in his truck.

All the hugs good-bye at the bus station were real and heartfelt enough (even Ty gave me one), as was the tear in Natalie's eye, maybe while the other eye glanced over at her car parked next door.

Freedom is that expensive, with so many thanks to give and debts to pay.

They watched me stagger into the bus station with all my duffels bulging with pots and pans and other gear, and I hung around long enough in the line at the ticket counter to see them hop back into Zee's car and pull out into traffic, heading south. Then I staggered back out again, across the lot, heading for the Buick.

☒ ☒ ☒ ☒ ☒

I'd forgotten how the Buick sucked gas.

Dave Winkler, on one of his sober days at work, told me the story of this old geezer who pulled up to their pumps years ago, in and old jalopy, and said he had to keep the engine going because of a starter that was going catawampus on him. Dave was a boy then, learning to be a gas jockey. He stuck the nozzle in the filler pipe and cranked on the gas and turned the pump on full, but after about five minutes and a hundred gallons later he yelled at the guy, "Turn the engine off! She's gainin' on me!"

Well, of course it was a joke, but the Buick could've been a candidate for the story instead of the old jalopy. Doing the math when I filled her up, I figured she was getting about eleven miles to the gallon. That usually signals a problem with the carburetor, which is just beyond my mechanical know-how.

And she used oil, too, about a quart every fill-up. I didn't spot any blue smoke coming out the tailpipe, so she wasn't burning oil as such, she was just using it or leaking it through a gasket. Either way, though, it would cost me.

When I wasn't worrying about gas and oil consumption or some guy chasing me, I tried to picture Jupe and Tick heading west to Malibu, then arriving to go surfing (they'd have to borrow somebody's surfboard, obviously), then wondering what the hell to do *next*. You can't surf week after week without eating or sleeping, and I bet they don't let you camp out on the beach there in front of all the movie stars' houses. Plus, they'd eventually get caught, shipped back to Georgia, and slammed into the Big House, as they say, which is juvenile detention, without even a how-do-you-do.

So the things to worry about piled up instead of going away.

On the rare occasions when I actually passed somebody, I'd chance a look at them to ascertain that they weren't Jupe and Tick. Always, they weren't. My strong suspicion was they wouldn't risk driving, but would take a bus instead. Which meant Jupe had gotten a chance to hoard up a bunch of cash somewhere.

Buses can take a southern route, through Mobile, New Orleans, then Dallas, or a route more northerly like Little Rock, Oklahoma City, Amarillo, then Albuquerque. This was the best guess I could make, looking at the map. Either way, they'd take the interstates and make pretty good time.

I needed to stay on the smaller roads. Once Rawlins dug into my story a little bit, he'd figure it out and I'd be wanted by the law as an accessory of some sort, so the interstates wouldn't be safe.

Here's what I had in the trunk:

Frying pan, two pots, utensils from the basement (from the year I was a Boy Scout)

Ten books of matches

Poncho, for use as a ground cloth

Pup tent with some holes, tent fly, poles, tie ropes and stakes all in a carrying bag

Sleeping bag

Fishing pole with catfish lures, pole disassembled

Flashlight with new batteries and a battery lantern

Clothes: five tee shirts, two shorts, two jeans, five pair of socks, five pair underwear, hiking boots, swimsuit (for Malibu), neckerchief, one sweater, one rain jacket, one leather jacket

First Aid Kit from Nat: bandages, aspirin, petroleum jelly, Ben-Gay for muscle soreness, gauze, iodine, needle and suture thread

Toilet paper roll

Toilet kit with usual stuff like toothbrush and deodorant and razor (two extra blades)

Tools for car: jack, vise grips, socket wrenches, pliers, baling wire, duct tape, screwdrivers, crowbar, jumper cables, towing rope, WD-40, coolant, spare tire, fuses, extra electrical wire, electrical tape

In the back seat:

Paper towels

Hunting knife with sheath, pocketknife

Address book with phone numbers (like Natalie, Winkler's Garage, Ty's home phone) and Rawlins' card

Extra tee shirt

All these were in a small knapsack. I also had —

Grocery bag with bread, crackers, banana, cereal box, one Moon Pie

Front seat:

Small ice cooler with two peaches, jack cheese, jar of pickles, three cans Dr. Pepper, loose ice

Canteen with water

Small gunny stack stuffed with change — about ten dollars worth — glove compartment

Map of U.S., Forest Service volunteer program brochure, wallet with $290, sunglasses, photo I took of Tick when he was twelve in envelope

The extra razor blades will tell you something. I was kind of a late bloomer as an adolescent, and didn't need to shave till about a year ago when the brown fuzz on my checks started to thicken up a bit. Being a kind of penny-pincher, I ferreted around the bathroom closet upstairs and found Uncle Carl's old shaver and some injector blades. These were cheap blades and seemed to be good for only two shaves before they got dull, but at the most I shaved only once a week or so. I didn't think I'd be able to buy injector blades anywhere, on account of they're antiques by now, so I brought two extra, which shows you I was planning for a six-week trip at the outside.

I sure hoped it didn't take that long. I'd be reported as missing, for sure.

Tick had a leg up on me, becoming adolescent at thirteen. The last time I saw him at St. Anselm's, he'd popped up an inch or so and his voice was starting to croak. I don't think I'd call him a squirt any more (though I did earlier), even if he was a little short for his age. He gave an impression of being powerful, what with his wide shoulders.

Of course I frequently wondered what all Milton Clayne would think if he saw his children today. And my mother, too, if she'd had the strength to keep living.

✕ ✕ ✕ ✕ ✕

The best place to camp if you want some privacy is not at one those KOAs that are so popular, though I expect they're generally okay, but rather whenever you run into a small homemade sign tacked to a tree that says "camping, fishing, fresh bait, ice." Or they might add, "RV hookups." These are private country residences where the guy happens to have a pond and some cleared land where you can pitch a tent and where he can make some money. The one I drove into was priced right, just three dollars for the tent site, and it sat near the edge of a small pond, which was scummy with algae and spawning mosquitoes by the millions. I was all by myself except for some other guy nearby with an old beat-up trailer that looked just big enough for a man and a dog.

Well, it happened it was big enough for a whole family: a grizzled guy in his fifties, I judged, a girl who couldn't have been a year older than me, a boy toddler in skivvies, *and* a dog, a German Shepherd. They'd set up three campsites away, but now and then they'd mosey closer as if to get a good look at me, maybe to test my sociability. I gave them a nod once – to the girl – and a bit later, after I'd pitched my tent and unrolled my bag in it, the man ambled forward.

I have to say, I didn't like the looks of him from the start. He reminded me of some of those old carneys who travel place to place, raw and wiry because they're underfed and overworked. This guy approached me with a hatchet in his hand, and I've never seen a man's arms so thick with veins as I did then, when he stood before me. I shrunk back a bit, respecting both him and the hatchet.

"Got wood?"

I shook my head. "But the owner's got bundles for sale —"

"I *know* he's got wood for *sale,* son, I'm looking to be favored, not robbed."

"Yes sir, unnerstand. I'm not carrying wood."

"Picked up every last twig for a hundred yards around, sumbitch."

"'Spect he did" I said, agreeing that the grounds around the campsite were pristine.

The girl and toddler and dog had strode up behind him to get a closer look at me, and something set the little boy off because he started howling. Maybe a bug bite.

"Shut him up, Lindy!" the man growled.

"You do it, Irv. I'm tired."

"Do it with my *hand*," said Irv, and he made a motion to swipe at him, but the boy was fortunately too distant.

"He didn't mean it, Max," Lindy said, picking the boy up and bouncing him. Judging by the sound and pitch of his squalling, he was well-practiced at being unhappy. Lindy may have gathered that skweets were his problem, because she took out some bug repellent from her pocket and started rubbing him with it. This appeared to soothe him as the shrieking eased off somewhat.

"On the road alone, son?" Irv asked me. He'd tucked the hatchet into his belt so I stepped toward him a little, to be friendlier.

"Yes sir, on my way to Little Rock."

"That's just four, five hours off, depending on your car."

"Well, I'm in no rush, really," I said, and then lapsed into feeling philosophical. "Also, if I'd kept on going, I wouldn't have met y'all."

He kind of smiled at that, then extended his big paw. "Name's Irv. That's my wife Lindy, our boy Max, and the dog is Oozie."

It might have been *Uzi* instead, like the machine gun. But Oozie was more appropriate, judging by the open sores on the dog's back and legs.

"Pleasure. I'm —" and it just came out of me "— Orville."

I have to say, Lindy was the youngest-looking wife I'd ever seen in the flesh for a man of his years, unless she was exceptionally well-preserved and he'd been horribly aged by a bad event or trauma. He could've been her grandfather, on most days.

"What all's in Little Rock?" he asked.

"Well sir, I'm volunteering for the Forest Service, tagging trees, bush-hogging, clearing kudzu, that kind of thing."

You'd think I'd told him I was an alien being.

"Doing all that for *no pay*? Why on earth?"

"Well sir, it's a program for teenagers."

"The word *program* don't make it sensible. *Guvment* program at that. Expecting something for nothing."

"It suits me fine. I want to learn about forestry. It's my passion, I believe."

Lindy, Max, and the dog were heading back toward their trailer, where they had everything set up for a fire, but without campwood. I had Irv all to myself, which was less pleasure than I wanted.

"Y'ever drink?"

"No sir."

"I got beer in the cooler. Why not come join us after your supper."

"Well sir, I don't drink, and beer is included in that. I appreciate it, though."

"It's just *beer*."

Some people keep on pushing the dumbest little thing.

"Thank you anyway," I said.

"You never tasted beer or liquor?"

"Yes I have *tasted* it, but it's not my favorite thing, and maybe at my age I should start workin' on it, but if it don't taste good why irritate yourself? I just don't cotton to it, I guess."

He eyed me with suspicion, then turned to look back at his family at the campsite. They were struggling with a can of Sterno or some such thing, prying it open.

"Get that thing *lit!*" he shouted at them.

Tryin', she called back to him.

"We're going to Florida, my cousin's place. He's got an extra acre for us."

"That sounds fine. I've always like Florida."

"Sure you don't want a beer after supper?"

Boy, he had a one track mind.

"I'm sure. I'm having pickles and a cheese sandwich and some Dr. Pepper, and then I'll be tired, so I'll probably turn in early."

I wanted to say, *if you're the kind who hits your kid, I can't socialize with you for more than a minute* or some such thing. I'd seen how he'd raised his hand against him, and it hurt me to imagine that he'd already walloped Max with that hand, and I could better appreciate why Max tended to howl. Any second of the day, for a boy like that, could be the last one prior to a whupping. I'd howl, too, if I were him, living with that kind of suspense.

While I ate, I could hear them lighting into each other. I couldn't discern what their fuss was about, but their voices rose in anger and whining a few times, Lindy and Irv. She would whine and he would shout, then she would shout and he would whine. If a shout was extra loud, the dog would chime in with a howl of his own.

After supper, just when it was turning dark, I went to fetch my sack of change from the Buick to make a call to Natalie, from the pay phone that stood outside the camp store. While at the car, it occurred to me that if Irv and Lindy were thieves, the Buick would be an easy target because it was unlocked and the windows were down to air it out. Also, the pay phone was stationed on the far side of the camp store and out of sight of the car.

What most people would do, of course, would be to wind up the windows and lock the car, but while I was fetching the sack and straightening up the front seat I could tell they were watching my every move as they drank their beer, and they'd feel insulted if I did those things. They were the only other campers here, so they'd get the message that I didn't fully trust them.

I retrieved my wallet from under the seat and stuck it into my back pocket. Otherwise, I left the car wide open, as a sign of "trust," and to keep the peace.

Boy, did I take chances!

When I called, I got Nat instead of her mother, which was a break. But it was obvious her mother or Dr. Hawkins was nearby because of her lah-de-dah tone and referencing of the Forest Service. Was I all right and where was I? I told her, northern Mississippi and I'm just fine. Then she gave me some news that made every tiny cell in my body stand up to attention.

She'd dropped by our house in the afternoon and spent a little time helping Ty with Zee. While she was there, deputy Rawlins telephoned, with Ty taking the call and Nat hustling upstairs to grab the extension in Zee's old room. Here's how I managed to piece it together:

He wanted to know if I was there.

Off with the Forest Service, said Ty. *In Little Rock.*

Nat announced herself to him on the other line, as Woody's close friend. *He's been planning it for some time, and he needed to get away briefly during this difficult time.*

Well, Rawlins was chewing on the statement, for sure. He wanted to know how "brief," and Ty and Nat both said "two weeks."

He plans to call every day though, Nat added. *Either me or Tychander, if he's got access to a phone.*

Rawlins wanted to know my mode of transportation, which of course was by bus, from Hartwell. Ty had driven me up that morning to the bus station, along with Nat.

The part that stirred me up, though, came from Rawlins and further investigation at the fire scene. Even though the nasty storm had flooded the place with mud and strewn much of the wreckage around, they'd discovered some things that were very informative.

They found a chunk of the door from that attic room where they thought Henry Jones had died, and maybe Jupiter and Tick as well. It was all buried in the mud. What they found was the door lock, a simple deadbolt, in the locked position with a charred chunk of the door jamb. They knew it was the door to the attic room because on the same piece of wood was an old metal plate marked A-1, which signified the attic room.

As you'd expect, the deadbolt could only be operated from the *outside,* and it was customary for it to be locked, according to St. Anselm's custodian. Kids could easily go in there simply by unlocking the deadbolt – there wasn't any key to that door – and often they did, to play poker and whatnot. But because the deadbolt was closed it indicates nobody was inside at the time of the fire.

Unless somebody was super mean and wanted to lock Henry Jones in there as a joke, which was highly unlikely because they *also* found his chain bracelet in the rubble and his cloverleaf charm on it under the rubble from the attic, tangled in bed springs.

So, Rawlins concluded, lacking any other evidence, they believed no one died in the attic and therefore it was a bit more likely than before that the two missing boys were alive and on the lam. Which would lead to a lot more questioning of family and friends. *Why would Jupiter run off with Tick?*

Ty noted to him, *they're both crazy as loons.*

Nat told him she wanted to know if they still thought the fire was set by somebody.

We've got two persons of interest – the two boys. But from what we've learned there's likely more.

That was like another zing rushing through my body.

Rawlins couldn't elaborate, owing to the nature of the investigation. But, she noted, it seemed odd to her that he appeared "emotionally involved" in this affair, judging by a catch or two in his throat when he talked. Not like the tough, strong man she'd expected.

Of course he wanted to know if he could reach me, and Nat claimed she'd do the best she could to handle this problem. She informed him, Woody gets to Little Rock sometime Tuesday and I'll pass on the message.

He asked, is there a number there?

She said *it's on the brochure, I'll have to go find it.*

There followed fuss and bother about the brochure, which Ty and Nat couldn't remember if I had with me or not (I did), but Rawlins allowed as how he'd try to track down the number himself.

I'd like to talk to him.

That was about it. I said goodbye to Nat and hauled myself back to my campsite. I didn't even check the car to see if everything was intact, I just rolled into my tent and prepared to go to sleep. After an hour or so, Irv's family settled down and piled themselves back into their tiny trailer. Quiet slowly enveloped the woods and the pond, except for the bullfrogs and crickets and cicadas expressing themselves.

SEVEN

I'd had half a notion to drop in on the Forest Service office in Little Rock, just to beef up my alibi a bit and maybe register as an applicant for the program, but it seemed ever more foolish to do so. I expected the application deadline had passed, and they'd think me pretty irresponsible just to show up and hope for a slot on the team. Also, the idea wasn't to fool Rawlins forever, it was just to get a heck of a head start on whoever might be chasing me, whether him or some other lawmen working from an all points bulletin. *Plus,* stopping in at Little Rock would slow me down a couple of hours, and I believed I was trying to catch up to a cross-country bus on the interstates, zooming along at seventy.

I skirted well south of Little Rock, heading west for Oklahoma.

A couple of years ago I'd chanced on that book by Steinbeck about traveling around America with his dog. The book was stuck into Zee's small library of novels and romances and mysteries. The inside flap was scrawled "M. Clayne," and after reading most of the book I could see that it suited my father perfectly well, roamer that he was. Anyway, Mr. Steinbeck was the same kind of roamer in lots of ways, and he has much to say about motels and restaurants along the highways, and not all of it very kind. He noted that motels in particular were over-sanitized, as if the flow of people through them was something like a spreading disease. But in spite of his ill-humor, he and his dog seemed to have a good time, on the whole, and they mostly enjoyed the romance of traveling across country. The dog's name was Charley.

I felt similar in the Buick, crossing into Oklahoma and feeling for the first time that I was edging into the Wild West. As a name, "Oklahoma" has a wild, outdoorsy ring to it, like the wind blowing free, and of course I knew the song and started to sing it while tapping the steering wheel.

But this was just eastern Oklahoma, so it looked more or less like western Arkansas, with no waving wheat or hawks making lonely circles in the sky. Instead, it featured nice rolling pastureland dotted with trees as if somebody'd laid down a green blanket and didn't quite get all the folds out of it. It smelled lush and warm, and horsey – those times I drove past horse farms with their neat white fences.

Damn! Flashing lights behind me, and there was a cop car closing in on me.

I was seven miles over the speed limit.

Now I've never been stopped before, but I know kids who have, and rule number one is, pull over right away. You don't outrun cops, no matter what sports car you're driving. They'll just radio ahead and set up a roadblock or something.

I say this now, but at the time I was plenty terrified and, with all my trembling, could barely manage myself to slow the car down and pull off on the shoulder. My heart was hammering away in my chest like hoofbeats and I felt a cold chill pouring all over me. I got the car over to the edge of the road and turned the engine off.

They also say, *stay in the car,* which I did.

The cruiser was a local cop car, the usual black and white, and it halted about two car lengths behind me with its lights flashing.

I had to think.

I lost my license.

No, they'd call my name into the dispatcher and check it to see I'd never gotten one.

I have no excuse. I'm going to see the West. My friend Nat loaned me her car.

The guy was out of the cruiser, strolling slowly toward me. He looked young, and scrawny also, which alarmed me because the skinny ones – at least in Ogamesh – are the nastiest, trying to make up for their skinniness with harsh talk. It was a skinny cop who nailed Jupiter when he went on his joyride, and though some folks thought the guy was bigoted against blacks I believed it was his caved-in physique that made him so contrary.

He got to the Buick and peered in the back seat, then came to the window.

Forest Service.

"Afternoon," he said, all pleasant and deceiving. I judged him to be just out of college, which suggested he'd stick close to the book.

"Yes sir."

"You been camping?"

"Yes sir, I have."

The back seat didn't have much camping stuff in it; maybe it was my grubby appearance that tipped him off.

"Georgia, hey?"

"Yes sir." Smart guy, he could read license plates. I have to admit, I felt some hostility toward him because he wasn't getting to the point, rather preferring to play cat and mouse.

"Where you headed?"

"West, sir," and then it garbled out of me. "Albuquerque – National Forest Service, a training program for teenagers, tagging trees, bush-hogging and whatnot. It's a two week volunteer program."

He listened to this and gave a little nod.

"Taking the back roads," he noted, as a statement.

"Yes sir, I enjoy seeing towns and farms and such."

"Well, you need to be more careful with your equipment," he said. "Looks like you got a tent rope dangling out of your trunk."

"Sir?"

"You can step out of the vehicle, please."

He opened the door for me and I stepped out.

"It's not hurting anything but it's bouncing all over the pavement and could be a distraction to other drivers."

"Yes sir, I gather."

I went back to the trunk and sure enough one of the tent ropes never got stowed right and was frayed at the end from all that bouncing along the highway. I popped open the trunk lid and tucked the rope inside.

"What's your name, son?"

It's truly weird having a guy five or six years older calling me son.

"Archie."

Yes, it was risky, since the social security card in my wallet said Woodrow, but I felt he was way past wanting to see any ID.

"I'm Dell. You're my first Georgia pull-over. You were going eight miles over, which is right near my discretionary limit, but it was the rope that caused me to stop you."

"Yes sir, Dell, I'm grateful you did. I'll need that rope later, I don't want it all frayed and –"

"You drive slow and safe, have a good trip."

When I was back in the car I waited till he'd peeled out onto the highway and gone ahead of me, while I pretended to fiddle with stuff in the front seat. I didn't want him to see me bent over the steering wheel taking deep breaths and thanking my lucky stars.

I also allowed myself a cocky thought: what a jerk! *I'm Dell*, as though he wanted to be pals or something. Cops are tricky, I've learned. They can get all cozy with you and then blindside you with their power, which is considerable.

The exception might have been Rawlins, who seemed to stick to the book while treating you as an adult, more or less. Also, if Nat had heard him right, he had emotions about the St. Anselm's fire, and couldn't completely hide them.

I was on the road again, at *exactly* the speed limit for a half hour so until it felt unnatural for the road conditions and I pumped it up by four or five miles over. The time Jupiter got caught borrowing his neighbor's truck, he was doing *thirty* miles over and didn't seem to slow down obediently enough to suit the skinny cop who nailed him.

Thirty miles over the limit at age thirteen!

He was a funny kid back then, generally very amusing but often moody and as quick to shift his attention as a gnat. He *did* talk up a storm about getting out of Ogamesh and traveling freely, striking it rich somehow so he could stay at fancy hotels with swimming pools and room service, but aside from his fast mouth and extra-bowl-of-Wheaties energy I didn't see a talent or skill within him enabling him to strike it rich. Someday, he told me, he'd do something important, he just didn't know what it was yet. In the meantime, as younger kids, he and I would go to the river and swim, we'd climb trees and sometimes wrestle, catch baby snapping turtles, that kind of thing. Fire was never part of his interest, aside from sneaking an occasional cigarette from his mother and lighting it.

He always got a hoot out of Tick, who of course would be attached to me most of the time. He'd laugh at him when Tick said something innocent or dumb, then apologize and ruffle his hair when he felt hurt by it. Of course, Jupe knew I was protective of my brother, by and large, so he tended to minimize his abusing treatment in my company.

Knowing Jupe as I did, it didn't totally amaze me that he might light out of St. Anselm's with just a month left of his term, to go surfing with Tick in Malibu. It was a stretch, for sure, because it was completely non-commonsensical and self-injurious, but Jupe never stuck too close to the rules of common sense. Also, he had a switch in his brain, I'm sure of it, that shut off access to any thought of the *consequences* of his deeds. Stealing the truck and joyriding was a fine example of that, because it all seemed totally harmless to him. The neighbor – I forget his name other than Earl – was a retired fellow who'd known the Stranges for years, and didn't seem to mind missing his truck since he didn't press charges. It was the speeding and resisting arrest that made life tough for Jupe, back then.

My driving route was going to take me south of Oklahoma City, which I wanted to avoid for traffic reasons. In fact, I wanted to stay away from cities altogether for this reason, so I wouldn't get caught in their snarl. Maybe on the return trip, assuming Jupe and Tick were with me, we could stop in a city now and then to see some of the sights, if we had any money left.

I was down to two hundred thirty-seven dollars. Gas was the main culprit, oil and food a close second. I hoped they had money, because coming home with the two of them would be costlier and I'd want them to contribute their share. Somehow, Jupe latched onto a wad of cash to finance his trip and to finance Tick, who was poor as a churchmouse but ate like a horse.

It made no sense.

I kept saying that from time to time about their journey to "Mal Boo," until the sentence itself made no sense.

But it made even less sense they'd be dead. It kept playing through my brain –

They were up and dressed at eleven-thirty.

The fire started soon after midnight.

If they'd hoofed it through the woods, they might have made two miles before the fire started, and another mile or so before the fire engines started blaring and the smoke pouring into the sky. They'd figure *something's wrong, there's a fire. Maybe at St. Anselm's.*

If they'd had a person on the outside snatch them by car, they could've been thirty miles away before the fire was noticeable to anybody.

To this day, to this very *minute,* they might think everything's just as fine and dandy at St. Anselm's as it could be, with Magnolia House sitting neat and pretty, just minus two boys.

¤ ¤ ¤ ¤ ¤

That evening I settled into another cozy private campsite, this time in the back yard of a little farmhouse not far from a town. There were no woods or pond, just a grassy lawn sandwiched between a clothesline and a pig barn with a couple of trees for shade. The lawn had room for maybe six pup tents and two RVs, but I was the only one who arrived there, so it seemed broad and airy, and fragrant too, being so close to the pigs.

On the map, I'd crept into the western part of Oklahoma and the scenery had changed. You could see a lot farther out here, across miles of shin-high corn and dark green grass that wasn't grass at all, but wheat that hadn't turned yellow yet. You'd see silos far off, and boxy looking buildings that suggested a large town, but were actually grain elevators.

The proprietor where I camped was a farm woman with two chubby kids, a boy and a girl, who might have been mute because I never heard a peep out of them. I didn't see a man of the house. In any event, before supper, I wanted to call Ty or Nat to check in, so I asked her if she had a pay phone, which she didn't.

"Where you calling?" she asked.

"Home, in Georgia."

"Use the hall phone. Since it's Georgia, just leave two dollars on the table for the toll."

"Ma'am, I could drive into town and find a pay phone, it's no trouble."

"You *could,*" she said, "but the only pay phone I know in town sucks quarters like a Hoover and you're not likely to get 'em back, so I'm offering you a discount here, if you don't mind not having much privacy, because the kids'll want to watch."

I wasn't going to argue, and thanked her. Sure enough, the chubby children (in truth they were *fat,* but it seems an unkind description) hung in the living room doorway facing the hall and watched my every move.

I chose to call Tychander, mostly because it was logical and appropriate. If Rawlins were sniffing around my circumstances, it would set off alarm bells if I only called Natalie at her house.

Ty's big news was that she and John Dandridge had worked it out to hire both a day nurse and a night nurse to come attend Zee, to take the pressure off themselves. Zee's insurance would cover most of it, and her pension checks the rest. I told Ty,

"If I just had one or two more days there, I could've taken care of that myself. I'm sorry for that, and I appreciate it."

"Had to get off to the damn *woods*."

"Yes, they had a schedule. I'm glad y'all've done that, and I'm relieved."

"How can you be *relieved*," she sang at me, "when you paid it no never-mind from the gitgo?"

Well, I didn't want to tussle with her over this, because I'd always thought Ty would be happy to stay in our house for *years*, for the money she was making. Now I gather this wasn't quite the case, and she was ready for a break.

I swear the chubby kids heard her voice soaring over the phone line, judging by how their eyes widened. Ty's voice carries a couple of blocks back in Ogamesh, and would be suitable on an opera stage if she could sing.

"Deppity Rawlins sure ready for a phone call from you, whatever it is that's on his mind."

I acknowledged that, and before hanging up asked her to give my regards to Natalie, and also to Zee.

I put two dollar bills on the little table, then turned to the kids.

"One more call."

The boy, who was seven I guessed, stuck his thumb in his mouth. And now I got a full flood of cooking smells from the kitchen – it was about six o'clock, and dinnertime – and my appetite ratcheted up about four notches. I assumed it might be apple pie, or something similar.

Now to Deputy Rawlins.

I figure I *could* have called him the night before, in Mississippi, to quiet down his suspiciousness, and maybe I should have, but it was getting late at that campsite and I was a bit unsettled about Irv and Lindy and all my stuff in the unlocked car. Also, if I'd jumped on a call to him right away, I might look overeager as someone with a pretty odd alibi that needs bolstering up, or I might appear too anxious to hear about some other "persons of interest." So, I guessed waiting one night wouldn't hurt.

I got his card from my wallet, plucked two more dollars out to put on the table, and called him at his house number. He answered,

"Charles Rawlins."

Well, now I had a first named attached to the last. Funny, he didn't strike me as a Charles, more like a Clint, Jake, or Bart – one of those more macho sheriff-y names.

"Hi, it's Woody Elmont."

He seemed to draw a breath. "Hoping to hear from you last night."

"Yes sir, I'm sorry, I was in a campsite too far from the car, which was unlocked, and some weird people nearby –"

"Woody, listen, we've stopped looking for their remains. You've had no word from them, isn't that so?"

"Right, I've been on the road to Little Rock."

"Woody. Why did you go off to Little Rock at a time like this? I gotta tell you, I don't get it."

I was ready for this one, I thought. "Well sir, I've been planning to volunteer for some time, since the spring really, and the session started today, and to be honest I'd suffered some, those first couple of days after the fire, and debated with myself if I could stand to stay in Ogamesh, and as you can see, I couldn't. It's been difficult with my aunt, and then all the confusion with the fire, and my brother and all, possibly being dead. I'll be out in the woods tomorrow with the crew, away from it all, and that's what I need for a short while."

"Two weeks," he said.

"Yes sir."

I could hear him breathing in the phone, in a way that struck me as agitated. I decided to jump into the empty space.

"The group leader tells me the cabin where we're bunking for the night has a phone. I don't have the number yet."

He just gave a whimpery *uh huh*, which I couldn't decipher.

I continued, "Natalie said something about other persons of interest, or similar talk like that. Meaning, the fire."

"We're working on it."

"Well sir, Jupe and Tick didn't set it."

"Maybe not," he said, and I felt a small lightening to my body, mostly in my shoulders. "Maybe so," he added, and the weight came back. "The department's treating them as suspects, and they're at large. People who knowingly help them are accessories. You understand."

"I do," I said.

"Woody. I *think* I got the right Forest Service in Little Rock, but when I called them, darned if they didn't draw a blank on who you were. They went through some rosters of volunteers, but they didn't have Elmont anywhere. Not to say you're being dishonest with me, but you can help me here if you want."

It was bound to happen. I just didn't think he'd be so quick on the draw, to call them so fast. I had a quick reply for this, too, though maybe not as convincing as if I'd rehearsed it a bit. He sprung it on me too fast.

"Well sir, it took *me* a little while to find the right office, too, and when I did I've never seen such a disorganized operation in my life! I could've signed in four times, they still wouldn't have me down right. Elmont, *Al*mont, *Du*Mont. Guess that's the way it is these days, with government. Catawampus."

He chewed on it a second.

"Woody. I have a need to tell you something."

"Yes sir."

Again, he left a gaping space with just his breathing in it.

"But now's – I got a radio call. I need to get off the phone now."

And I heard a kind of *chirp* that sounded like his voice losing control or giving way to a hiccup, and the line disconnected, leaving me with a dial tone.

Darn the luck! He had something big to tell me, and his radio goes off.

I started to see Rawlins as a person, more than a muscly guy in a uniform. Why are the scrawny cops, like Dell, so icy cool you think they've got no heart, and the big beefy ones, like Rawlins, so touchy that they'll burst into tears for no reason at all?

I couldn't figure either of them.

EIGHT

The next morning, the main radiator hose going into the engine block sprung a leak through a tiny crack, right at the intake. A good rule about cars is, *if you smell coolant, stop the car right away and check it out, else you're up a creek.* So I pulled off the road right by a giant feed lot, where they were fattening up hundreds of cows for market, opened the hood and found the leak.

I have to say, the air stank from the cow manure much more than coolant, and it was all I could do to keep my stomach under wraps while I made the repair. I wasn't but a hundred feet from the corral, where cows jostled for room at a feed trough to eat themselves silly, then get slaughtered. It seemed sad to me their last days had to be in such cramped filthy quarters, rather than out on the range where they at least had the illusion of freedom. I gave them my best *moo* in sympathy, but no one responded.

It was a lucky break that the hose cracked right by the intake. All I had to do was undo the hose clamp, use my hunting knife to carve off the last inch or so of rubber where the leak was, and then reattach it and clamp it tight. Evidently, car manufacturers are smart enough to give you an extra few inches of hose, just for this reason. According to Trey anyway.

I was off again, heading for Texas.

The land had been rising up in a kind of gentle way, all through Oklahoma, and now I came up out of a dip and onto the most sprawling far-off flatness of land I'd ever seen. Wheat, prairie grass, and rangeland, as huge and lonely and treeless as you could design it. I could spot a cluster or two of grain elevators far to the north, but otherwise the blue sky settled down *flat* on the horizon like an upside down lake on a windless day. You couldn't help but feel awed by the space, and a bit unnerved, too, since it seemed there was nothing to hold the ground in place except the sky.

Or the people on it. There *weren't* any, except for an occasional semi going by, or a motorcycle or two.

When I crossed into Texas, they advertised it as "The Lone Star State," just as you've heard. It was only the third day of my trip, so I was pleased with myself for making such good time – about five or six hundred miles a day.

✠ ✠ ✠ ✠ ✠

It had heated up on the plains and even though the air was pretty dry I wished Natalie had spent a little more on her car by installing air conditioning. I'd been lucky driving through the south – it hadn't been that hot, for June – but here on the plains I must have blasted through a warm front of some kind, because just within a few miles the temperature shot up noticeably. It was plenty toasty. You could see the heat as a kind of shimmer across the prairie, with the effect that the distant grain elevators looked like tiny houseboats floating on the water. That's the way it seemed to me.

I had some funny notions about this trip that started popping into my head. I started with this goal, which was to meet Jupe and Tick on the beach at Malibu, tell them everything that happened, then snatch them back to Ogamesh in the car with the hope that if they returned voluntarily their punishment would be light. More and more I believed the goal could be over-optimistic, and I might come up empty-handed. *Anything* can happen on a trip this long, and they might be stuck in the middle of Alabama for all I knew, especially if Tick had reverted to his shoplifting habits. So I started to envision myself roaming the beaches of Malibu for a few days with no sign of them, and then turning around to head back home alone.

If it happened that way, my trip would be just a trip.

Fine by me if it were just a trip. I'd met interesting people and would meet some more. I was seeing unknown country I'd only seen in pictures. I was learning what it was like to be a little bit afraid, all the time, as a means of self-defense. It felt right, and strengthening somehow, to be a little bit afraid.

They had anti-littering signs posted here – "Don't Mess With Texas." It sounded kind of swaggery to me, and a little ornery.

Around noontime I stopped at a roadside store to buy food for lunch. It was usually cheese and some cold cuts, maybe a Moon Pie and a pop, but today I grabbed three loose carrots, a bag of pork rinds, an apple and some chocolate milk. There's no predicting what all your stomach will tell you to buy, you just go with your craving, and for some reason carrots were high on the list. I also bought more ice to throw in the cooler.

I'd been driving so hard I wanted to take an hour or so and have a picnic somewhere, and maybe mosey out into the prairie to look for signs of arrowheads. Back in Ogamesh, my arrowheading buddy was Jake Culpepper and in the spring we'd follow along behind his father's tractor while he plowed the field for soybeans and sure enough, Jake and I would each snag three or four good unbroken flint points, right behind the tractor. It was guaranteed. But the very best arrowheading was a day or two after plowing when it rained hard. The treasures would poke up out of the mud with a pearly gleam to them – you couldn't miss them.

At Jake's funeral after he killed himself, I went up to his casket in the church and put my favorite arrowhead on top of it, wanting it to be buried with him. The pastor said he'd see to it.

I have to say, since I was just twelve at the time, I didn't have much understanding about his suicide, and it was a thorny knot to try to explain it to Tick. My only guess was that Jake's father was tough on him and wanted him to be more of a man than Jake was ready to be at the time, teaching him boxing and such. Jake liked to draw with colored pencils, and was very good at it. He didn't care about boxing or sports or cars, and at various times you could see the disappointment in his father's face when Jake would go off to draw, or help his mother in the kitchen making biscuits or pies. He wasn't manly, but he was one of my best friends anyhow.

I drove until I saw signs for a rest stop up ahead, which turned out to be a pleasant shady area off the road with a couple of picnic tables under an open roof, like a gazebo, and I had it all to myself. It was set off the road just enough so it felt private and not too loud when a semi roared by. I parked, unpacked my food, and had a nice peaceful lunch in the shade with my roadmap unfolded in front of me so I could speculate on the most enjoyable route through the Texas panhandle and into New Mexico.

The land beyond it was unfenced and looked inviting for a stroll – which is to say, perusing the ground for signs of Indian activity like stone chips or old hearthstone. There were tufts of dried prairie grass scattered about, but otherwise the land was a mix of coarse sand and crumbly rock. Most intriguing to me was a gently rising mound about a hundred yards off that would have appealed to Indians, who tended to favor elevated areas so they could spot game or approaching enemies. I put my lunch stuff away and proceeded to load up my knapsack with some essentials: canteen, unfinished apple, hunting knife, sunglasses. In addition, I knew I should lock up the Buick while I was gone, so I fetched my wallet and threw it in the knapsack, locked the car and sauntered off onto the prairie.

You can probably tell: I wouldn't be giving you this sort of detail for no reason.

I was aware that I was in the kind of landscape where you might roust out a rattlesnake or scorpion, so I was extra cautious stepping over rocks and large tufts of grass. Fortunately, there was nobody like that to bother me and soon enough I got to the mound and clambered up on top hoping for clues to historical Indian presence.

Well, there wasn't any. I did a thorough survey of the mound and the ground around its base and told myself Indians never stopped here except maybe to chew on cactus root or to pee. I chose to rest a moment. I shed the knapsack and took a swig of warm water from the canteen, then sat with the sun behind me as the heat started to cook the back of my neck.

Because I was on the far side of the mound I couldn't see the Buick and anyone who might be there couldn't see me, either. But while I sat in perfect peace I started to hear a kind of banging or thumping back at the rest spot.

I eased around the side of the mound until I could see someone pounding the door of the Buick, on the passenger side. It was a man, from what I could see through the trees, wearing one of those muscle shirts with no sleeves. The pounding didn't seem angry or violent, more like a testing of the strength of the steel in the car door. Whatever the reason, it looked nuts to me, and possibly hostile, so I started hoofing it back to the rest area, and shouted out a *Hey!*

He stopped pounding the door, stood by the car and waited for me. I pulled up short, at the edge of the rest area and on the far side of the picnic table, so I could get a good look at him and also make tracks if he tried anything funny.

The guy was thirty, maybe, lean and wiry as they come, and painted liberally with tattoos on his arms and shoulders. He stood with his hands in his jeans pockets and smiled at me. At his feet was a beat-up old army duffel of some sort, not very full.

"Yours?" he asked, meaning the car.

I nodded, lying. "Why were you beating on it?"

"*Shit,* bet it's got a three-fifty, don't it! Or a three twenty-seven."

He knew his engines; they were both Chevy small blocks and good performers.

"Yeah it's a three-fifty. Zero to sixty faster'n you can spit."

"I bet. It's a sweet machine."

"So why were you hitting it?"

He didn't rightly answer me. "Man, that's good steel! Oldie but goodie. You got good taste. What's your name?"

I thought, *his brain works like Tick's,* which is to say jumpy and insensible. He was also creepy, on account of his dropping in here with no car, out of the blue, so my tongue got tied and wouldn't reveal either my real name or an alias like Archie and Orville.

"Okay, so you don't have a name, that's fine. Mine's Vic. For Victor. For *victory!* Victory over adversity! Whatever obstacles may come, I subdue them in pursuit of my goal, which is everchanging like how the wind blows. Always in motion, smelling the air. So why the *fuck* doesn't it have dual exhausts, with a mill like that?"

The curse threw me, coming as it did in a flurry of poetizing. I had no answer for his exhaust question, which was a good one, since high-performance V-eights should have a separate exhaust system for each side of the engine to reduce back-pressure through the valves, which will rob an engine of efficiency.

"Never did," I said, holding my ground. But I was loosening up the tiniest bit, feeling this guy was as strange as they come, for sure, but possibly not a danger to me. He sidled away from the car and approached the other side of the picnic table.

"Y'ever see the Grand Canyon?"

"Nope, not yet."

"Nebraska sand hills?"

I shook my head. "Didn't know they had 'em."

"Well my young friend, an experienced guide like me could show a *tyro* like you, meaning a little wet behind the ears, a sight or two. Maybe grab a beer, shoot some pool, check out some skirts, if that's your inclination. What say? You got an extra day or two?"

His congenialness was a little pushy for my taste, and no, I didn't have an extra day or two.

"I'm kinda on a short tether," I told him. "Don't think I can."

Well, that tightened up his smile. He grit his teeth.

"All right, let me just spit it out. I've been hitching, and a ride dumped me here at my request, 'cause I saw the old Buick and believed whoever the driver was must be some hip dude, like yourself, and I wanted to meet him or her. Well, it's a *him,* which is fine, because a ride's a fuckin' ride, right? Where I need to go, I'm headed for North Platte."

"Where's that at?"

Okay, bad grammar, but now and then I slip into it depending on the company I'm keeping, and it was a good match for him.

"Nebraska. Due north. You cool with that?"

"Well, I'm going west."

"West is fine, for a few miles, till the next state highway. You got anything cold to drink? I see a cooler in there. Fuckin' *dry,* man."

"Might have an extra RC Cola," I said. I bought three in Oklahoma, and believed there were two left.

"Suits me fine."

"Sorry I can't give you a ride, though. I'm travelin' alone."

What I just said was one of the tougher statements I ever spoke to anyone, and it looked like he wanted to take a new measure of me. He was a vagabond, obviously, and a hard man with an aggressive neediness to him (basically demanding a ride and a cola). His eyes got steely as I edged around the end of the table, took the keys out of my pocket, and headed for the driver's side door – which put the car between us.

"My Mom's in North Platte," he said, as I opened the door to fetch the cola can. "She's pretty sick right now."

"I *am* sorry to hear that," I said, not knowing if I should believe it. "But people *do* give rides out here. Semis and cars go by here all the time, I've noticed. Shouldn't take you long."

I closed the car door and, when he was ready, tossed him the can over the hood of the Buick. Not a thank-you or a fare-thee-well. He glared at me, popped the can open and guzzled half the can down without a breath, his neck all bobbing Adam's Apple and straining tendons.

When he was done he slammed the can down so hard on the table I jumped a foot off the ground.

"*Damn you,* you stupid shit! How fuckin' *pleasant* do I have to be?"

I stayed by the Buick driver's door and held tight to the keys.

"You're not even old enough to *drive!*"

I could hop in and drive off, but my knapsack and wallet were still out by the mound.

"Just a boy."

I could drive off, come back an hour later and fetch them.

It was useless to sort things out and make decisions because he was headed for me.

"You need to gimme a ride," he growled, "or I'll take it myself."

"Nothin' doin', Vic. *My* car."

"Gimme the keys, boy, you're no match and you know it. I'll bust your head or break your arm or choke you silly, one way or 'nother I'm drivin'."

The smart thing to do was to give it up and save my skin, but I was so attached to the car and my mission that I wasn't thinking right, and I made an attempt to pull the door open and dive into the seat, but he grabbed the edge of the door and yanked it wide open, pulling me with it. Knowing I was in a mood to resist, he tossed me into the dirt and beat on me. He whaled at my face with his fist till my head rang, shouting *gimme the fuckin' keys!* as he did so, but I managed to hang on to them tight, and I tried scrabbling away on my knees, which was stupid because I was an easy target for a swift kick, which he delivered to my side, near my stomach, and I swear he snapped a lower rib or two because it felt like a hot knife in my gut. I had to endure his foul-mouthed insults along with the pain, but I must have gone slightly deaf from the beating because his voice trailed off into a kind of distant hum. I felt him pile on top of me and crook his arm around my neck in a chokehold while he bludgeoned my face with his fist, over and over. *Man,* he closed my throat so tight I couldn't suck a thimbleful of air, and kept beating on me at the same time. Whatever it was that got me, getting choked or clobbered, I can't rightly remember, but either way he was way too much for me and soon enough I blacked out like a landed catfish.

But of course my senses returned to me, and it wasn't more than a couple of minutes later because I could still smell the exhaust fumes from the Buick.

I lay there in the dirt and started hacking stuff out of my lungs. When I got the coughing under control, I groaned for a bit because my head felt like a firecracker had gone off inside it, and my throat hurt like he'd half-squished it. I also couldn't move much, or take in a deep breath, without getting stabbed in the gut by a chunk of rib bone.

I heard quite a few cars and trucks go by over the next half hour or so, and wished someone would've had the civility to need a moment or two at the rest stop. But nobody needed a rest, and they couldn't see me from the highway.

I twisted around enough to ascertain that the car, for certain, was long gone.

I managed to get to my knees, which is when I saw spatters of blood on the dirt under me. I must have been swelling up around my left eye because it hurt to open it. In fact, it was pretty well slammed shut. Of course, I couldn't see myself, but I had plenty of evidence that I was pretty well trashed by good old Vic.

I cursed a bunch as I struggled to my feet. You may have gathered, from my description of living with Aunt Zee, that things ran fairly proper in her house, so it's no surprise that both Tick and I were brought up in respect of polite English. *Goldang* was about the worst we could get away with in her company, and so the habit stuck with us, even in school. So using the language that I did was a refreshing novelty and helped ease the pain a bit.

The car was gone but my knapsack – canteen, knife, wallet, apple, sunglasses – should still be out on the prairie beyond the mound. I lumbered off to it, taking it slow because of the rib problem, and all the while feared the worst, that somehow Vic knew it was there and went off to retrieve it while I was in my black sleep.

He was one nasty duck, no question.

But evidently he didn't know about my knapsack and sure enough it was right where I left it, with all contents intact. I grabbed the canteen and sipped water till I felt slaked. Guzzling wasn't an option, because of the condition of my throat.

I polished my knife blade against my jeans and then held it up to use as a mirror. From what I could see, I didn't bear much resemblance to the Woody I'd always known, what with the left side of my face mimicking an eggplant.

I managed to get back to the rest area. I poured out what was left of Vic's RC Cola, being careful to hold the can by the rim so as not to smear whatever fingerprints he left, and put the can in the knapsack for safekeeping. Then I limped out to the highway to hitch a ride.

It was going to be tough to get a ride, looking as battered and pulpy as I did.

NINE

Over the next hour or so, there might have been twenty cars and trucks that went by, which is not what you call heavy traffic. I tried to guess the reasons, the main one being that this was not a well-traveled road even on the best of days, since it was a "C" road, which meant "County." I guessed it was a short cut from one state highway to another, but since I didn't have my map anymore I started to forget where it came from and where it went to, except that it was headed more or less toward Amarillo to the west. Also, it was a Wednesday afternoon and I gathered folks did most of their errands in the morning. In any case, it seemed peculiar that Vic and I happened to collide on this waste-of-pavement piece of garbage road that I wished I'd never taken.

A couple of people looked like they might pick me up because they slowed down a bit to get a gander at me, and that's where their sense of humanity got stretched too thin, since they floored it and drove on by when they saw my face. Possibly they believed I was deformed, and they weren't ready to engage in awkward conversation. Or else they knew I'd been in a fight, and I might be ready to pick another one. Like they say, *don't mess with Texas.*

It wasn't much of a fight, you can count on it.

A storm was cooking up to the southwest, dark and angry looking. But where I was the sun was still beating down, and didn't help ease my pain.

Generally while I was hitching, I stood up. But every few minutes I'd feel weak and tired and I'd sit in the grass by the road's edge, with my thumb still out. Every heartbeat I had banged in my head like a slow-motion jackhammer, it hurt that much. If I winced, it hurt even more because the blood had turned crispy around my wounds. I almost forgot about my busted rib, unless I took too deep a breath.

I hadn't felt so alone since God knows when. I gave Tick and Jupe a mild curse, being the cause of all this.

About the time that the front edge of the storm clouds swallowed up the sun was when I got my ride. It was a shiny new one-ton pickup with a young guy driving and a teenage girl next to him. She opened the door for me and kind of yelped to see my face.

"Sheez, boy, you run into a bull?"

I shook my head. "Guy hit me. More than once."

"Get in," she said. "You need stitches, ice and maybe some meds."

Her name was Lacey, and the guy driving was Cade – I guess that's the spelling, though it could have been Kade or even Kaid – who was a quiet sort that turned out to be her boyfriend. I told them I was Archie Wetherall, grabbing the last name from a basketball player in Ogamesh who was a bully. At first, Cade suggested I ride in back on top of the tool chest, but Lacey would have none of it because of her concern for my wounds. It happened that they were coming from a baby shower and were driving back to Amarillo, where they lived. Sitting next to me in the middle, she had a fantastic view of the left side of my face and felt the need to dab at it with moist towelettes, some water from a bottle, and Kleenex, and it was all I could do to keep from bellowing, but I stayed quiet.

In time, Cade asked, "Why'd the guy hit you? You insult him or somethin'?"

"Tryin' to rob me. While hitching."

You see, I'd decided as soon as I got my senses back, lying there in the dust at the rest stop, that I'd just have to let the car go. If I reported it stolen to the police or a sheriff, the whole story would come unsnarled and my mission to Malibu would be over in a flash. I twisted the truth around: *I* was the hitchhiker and Vic was the driver.

"He *did* rob me, too," I said, clarifying things. "My camping gear, clothes, food and whatnot. But I kept my wallet."

"He took all that shit but not your wallet?"

"Yeah, he thought it was in my duffel, but it was in my knapsack."

"Weird," said Cade.

"We're getting you to the clinic," Lacey proposed. "There's a good doctor there who's friends of my daddy's."

"I don't have much money. You see, I'm volunteering for the Forest —"

"We'll get you fixed up and you can worry about money some other time. Don't want to lose that eye, assuming it's still in there."

It had been squeezed shut for so long I forgot I had it.

"'Spect I don't."

She wanted to know my age, so I told her sixteen, which I gather surprised her. Unless people know me, I can be misinterpreted for fifteen or even fourteen, which is annoying to me. I was glad to be through with those ages, like most kids, and would just have to wait for nature to age me in a proper manner.

We were about an hour from Amarillo. The truck's engine and the quiet music they were playing on the country music station got to me pretty quick, along with Lacey's gentleness and friendliness, so without knowing it I dozed off for much of the ride with the healthy side of my head leaning against the window.

¤ ¤ ¤ ¤ ¤

At the clinic, Lacey took charge in such a way I figured her daddy was one of the local bigwigs. *Help this poor boy as fast as you can,* she commanded, and from all the commotion it stirred up I judged they were in the mood to obey. I had *two* doctors and a nurse working me over in a little room, shooting painkiller into my cheek and head, swabbing me with iodine or some such thing, then stitching up some flaps of loose skin near my eye and upper cheek. The shot was so painful I leaked a little howl, but then they'd warned me it would be a pretty strong "pinch." Lacey was in and out a few times while Cade waited on a couch, and they called her "Miss Calder." She took an interest in me that was the exact opposite of a fellow like Vic, and it was gratifying to me, and somehow warming.

There wasn't anything they could do about the ribs, they said. At least two were badly cracked, apparently, and they were nipping at the bottom of my lung, but in a few weeks' time they allowed as how it would heal pretty well.

"Looks like you got the right people to pick you up," said the nurse to me as she held an icepack to my face. "Lacey can spot an injured bird clear across the county."

I nodded.

"You're in good hands, Archie" she added.

"I'm glad. I don't need no more bad luck, like the man who tried to kill me."

"I'm guessing," she went on, "you're a good boy. Something on your mind, though."

"Yes ma'am, I'm trying to get to Albuquerque to volunteer for the Forest Service. It's a program for teenagers."

"Something else," she ventured, and I fell quiet.

In fact, she was right. When she left the room and I had to wait awhile for the head doctor to come back and check me out, the pain eased out of me enough for my head to get clear. Or at least become less muddled. And what was eating at me was the question of the whole trip.

I was half-wondering if I should keep going.

The police would *never* find Jupe and my brother, unless one of them called home and fessed up where they were. That could happen, but I doubted it because of Jupe's noticeable lack of common sense, and Tick's *complete* lack of any sense at all. So with no clues for lawmen, Tick and Jupe would just slip through the shadows and be forgotten, or else be presumed dead in the fire, one.

From what I'd read, the law wasn't so good at finding runaway kids.

If I didn't keep going, those two nutcases possessed just enough instinct to land on their feet and stay alive, even if they ended up with a short surfing career. They were half-charming, in a truly offbeat way, and adults commonly took a shine to them, so some movie star might half-adopt them and feed them and give them a bed.

If I didn't keep going, they'd probably be okay, and eventually, in a few weeks, they'd call me or Viola at home, asking for money to get back to Ogamesh.

And Charles Rawlins would be all over them.

For certain, if they didn't turn themselves in, they'd both end up in juvenile detention. Jupe might fit right in, which would be okay, but Tick wouldn't understand the place.

More and more, it made sense those two doofuses had no idea about the fire, else they'd feel a lot of pressure to call home and announce that they were fine, and off on an adventure.

If I *did* keep going, I could give them all the news and insist they turn themselves in so Tick wouldn't go to jail. He was just thirteen, and innocent of all serious crimes except for running away from St. Anselm's.

If I *did* keep going, I could help keep them out of trouble in California, buy them a decent supper and maybe a motel room.

As always, I boggled myself with all the ifs.

TEN

I'm going to start this part with the phone call I made to Tychander that same night, in a back room of the Calders' house outside of Amarillo. I'd told Lacey I needed to call my home, but didn't want to make a big fuss about it with her family (I'll get to *them* in a minute), so it had to be kind of on the sly. At the right time, she herded me down the hall to this little study or den, and told me to dial away and don't worry about the charges. I thanked her and eased the door closed.

Ty's first words were,

"Y'aint in the *woods,* are you?"

"No, I'm not, but –"

"That story holds water like a *sieve. Forest* Service, sheeee! And Rawlins, he *on* to you now like paint."

"Ty, gimme a second –"

"No, gim*me* a second, 'cause that boy Jupe checked in with his mama this mornin', on the phone, and they both scared each other half to death. He scared her, because she thought it might be a call from the *grave,* and she scared *him* when she said if he was truly alive he was in deep doo-doo with the police as a prime suspect in the fire. *Fire,* he says, *what fire?* Might explain a lot."

Hair rising on the back of my neck, even with the pain killer I had, which tended to numb my senses. All I could say was,

"They're okay – Tick's okay."

"They *fine,* so they say, but wouldn't say where they were, but they're eating and sleeping and camping out *somewhere,* Lord knows. So says Jupe. But the way Viola tells it, Jupe now thinks he's a suspect in a fire he didn't know about, and he's got a bug up his butt to get movin' and stay away from the law. That's the sorry truth 'cause just this afternoon the sheriff got a confession out of one of the St. Anselm's grounds workers, who was dallying in the basement with his honey that night, and they dozed off and a cigarette she was smokin' fell into some trash and the rest is what we know, meaning they got out okay, but Henry Jones didn't. After all this time they fessed up, finally feeling guilty. Where *are* you, anyway, Woody? People want to know."

It took me a minute to tell her, *I'm fine.* I couldn't tell her *where* I was fine, though. My sore old swollen head was filling up with all new manner of things to wrestle with, and it addled me some.

But I wanted to know: "Did Tick get on the phone?"

"Don't 'spect he did, talkin' to Jupe's mama. Now it's plain to me what you did. You're going out to fetch them, that's plain as day."

"Might be," I said, then stepped across the line into the truth. "They need to know, it's time to come home."

"Well boy, that's just what Rawlins wants, and you'd be smart to let him handle it – it's his job. Best you tell him where they went, since you seem to have some idea. How you travelin'? You hitchin'?"

"Bus. And hitchin'."

"I'm obligated to tell Rawlins what he needs to know. He seems a good man, from what I can tell. Where *are* they, Woody? Only gonna get a slap on the wrist, for all the trouble they caused."

"But Jupe's scared now. Thinks he's going to prison. And he's not likely to call again anytime soon to find out the truth."

"He scared all right, so says his mama."

That's where we left it. I told Ty I needed time to think, which was extremely true at the time, and would call her or Nat or Rawlins sometime soon, which maybe wasn't. I ended with *tell Natalie I'm fine, don't worry, and I miss her,* all true except for the first part.

¤ ¤ ¤ ¤ ¤

Back to before the phone call:

Understand, I was a pretty sorry looking sight when I arrived at the Calders' house with Lacey and Cade. I had a bloody gauze bandage over my eye, a greasy salve on my purple face, an ice pack I was supposed to hold to my cheek, and nothing for my ailing ribs. To be fair, they allowed me to decide if I wanted to be wrapped up like a mummy or just let nature do its work – ribs do heal, in time, without much fuss. I chose nature over the mummy. I also had pain pills that they warned would stop me up a bit, and some pills for inflammation, and some antibiotics because of all the dirt that got into the wound. Also, my tee shirt was a little sketchy for presenting myself as a guest, with some blood and dirt smeared on it, but when I arrived they didn't seem to mind. All my clothes went with Vic in the Buick, so I was stuck with what I had on until I could get a chance to hit a thrift store or a Salvation Army place.

Judging by how their house looked, they had money. It was a big fancy log house with porches going everywhere and flowers on vines growing up trellises, and a big barn out back with cows grazing past the fences. Mrs. Calder, I never got her first name, oohed and aahed over me when I arrived at the door, but I tried to assure her it looked a lot worse than it was, which wasn't true.

When the oohing and aahing died down a bit and we were settled inside, Mrs. Calder cooked a terrific fried chicken supper with mashed potatoes and black-eyed peas with gravy on the side. The table was well laid out, with candles and silverware and flowers in the middle, as if it were a holiday. Though my face still hurt and I had to keep holding the ice pack against it, I managed to get everything down in short order, though my cheek hurt when I chewed and my broken ribs got irritated when I swallowed. I decided not to care about the pain, I was so hungry. Cade didn't say much except grunt with pleasure while he ate, but Lacey was a regular chatterbox and even as grease dripped down her chin, plop plop, right onto her shirt front, she kept asking me all kinds of questions about my home and family and school and such. It was hard to talk much while downing the chicken and dealing with the ice pack, but whatever I got out had them both half-hypnotized, as if they were starved for conversation in that house.

Of course, being known as Archie Wetherall, I had a chance to shovel it a bit, and make things up from scratch, so maybe that's why they were so attentive. I came from a small town south of Auburn, Alabama where my father, Morton, raised hogs and my mother was a romance novelist, both of them too busy to care for my younger brother Tack, who was born with only half a brain and four toes on each foot. He was twelve, but he could barely feed himself or use the bathroom, so that was mostly my job. He was clever in his own way, though.

"Which half of his brain is missing?" Lacey wanted to know.

"No half," I said. "It's just half the size it's s'posed to be. They did a scan, and that's what it showed on the film. So y'all can see he can be a burden."

"Why I should *say!*" cried Mrs. Calder. "The poor little fella. How's he clever? Must be interesting.

"Well, in the funniest ways," I started.

"Does your Mom sell a lot of books?" Lacey asked, sparing me the challenge of concocting how he was clever.

"Several hundred thousand. She uses a pen name, but she asks us not to mention it."

"What's she go by?" Lacey asked, as if I'd said nothing at all.

"I meant, it has to be secret. She values her privacy."

"Must be rich, I'd say."

"Lacey!"

"Well Mom, she must be, if she sells several hundred thousand books. If I were her husband, I'd quit hog farming for sure."

"It's not up to us to tell the Wetheralls how to live."

"Well, here's this beat-up boy half lyin' in a heap on the side of the county road that Cade and I found and rescued, nearly half dead from being beaten and choked, and he's *hitching* across the country or someplace, and Mom's back in Alabama endorsing huge checks and the younger brother Tack is soiling his pants because Archie isn't there to take care of him, because *Archie's* like running away from home or something, and either it makes me very sad or it strains my imagination to figure out why it don't make any sense at all."

Cade grunted. "Good chicken, Miz C."

"Thank you Cade. Well, I'm sure Archie can't explain *everything* –"

"Not running away. Forest Service," I partly blurted out, but my mouth was full of potatoes and peas.

"– and there's this huge Florence Nightingale part of me that wants to take care of him like a nurse till he's well, and another smaller part of me that's confused why his *parents* don't seem to care much about him, and his brother to boot, since they're so fat and happy with their hogs and romance books and big checks. Hitchhiking, in this day and age! Sweet boy like Archie takin' chances like that, and to look at him he's not much of a fighter."

I saw Cade arch an eyebrow at the word "sweet," but Lacey paid him no mind. Then Cade gave my stomach a small heave when he started licking chicken grease off his forearms, which were pretty thick with hair, like Trey Winkler's, only more blond than orange. He seemed nice enough in the truck, but pretty crude here at dinner in this nice house, licking grease from his arms.

"They can be," I said between mouthfuls, "a little distant sometimes." And then, "Like I hardly know them." And I added another, "Like they're not really there."

"Cade, sweetie, my appetite would improve if you stopped that," said Lacey.

"Well, Archie," said Mrs. Calder, "you're *here* now in a warm and loving house, so you can heal in all the ways you need to."

"In*deed*," Lacey tagged on, with a wink at me.

During all this, Mr. Calder, so they informed me earlier, was at his Elks meeting or whatnot, and was due back a bit later. I'd get the guest bed downstairs, and they'd put a towel over the area by my head so the bleeding, if there was any, wouldn't stain their nice knitted sheets. Also, there was a son, older than Lacey, in the army overseas. And three shepherd dogs, a tabby cat and a parakeet whose name was Whiskers. They had crosses and Jesus and Mary figurines here and there, so I assumed they were Catholic, though it's never easy to assume anything about religion. When it quieted down a bit, I asked Lacey,

"Might want to make a call home."

Which meant calling Ty back at Zee's place.

¤ ¤ ¤ ¤ ¤

When I finished the phone call and had a few minutes to mull it over, I was hooked on a new concept for my mission: *Jupiter can run all he wants, but I'm bringing my brother home.*

I planned to call Rawlins later, and tell him just that — without mentioning the details about Malibu and where I was at the moment.

If he objected, I'd tell him *it's a brother's job to bring his zoo-headed nonsensical thirteen year-old brother home, not the law's.*

When I popped out of the study, Lacey was waiting for me.

"I had a brilliant thought. You're just Alvin's size."

"Alvin?"

"My brother in the army. Five-ten and about one-fifty, right?"

Last time I checked, that's what I was, but I'd probably dropped a few pounds in the last couple of days.

"You take a shower or a bath and get that stink out of you. And that bandage might need changing."

She started shoveling clothes out of Alvin's dresser as I ducked into the bathroom for a shower. I had to agree, I might not be smelling my best. I tried all I could to wash my hair without drenching the bandage on my face, but it was no use and the bandage got soaked. After I toweled off and gave myself a nasty stare in the mirror, I put my dirty jeans on (with my wallet still safely in the back pocket) and returned to Alvin's room where Lacey had laid out different piles of clothing.

Well, I was standing there half naked, and boy did she give me the once over! I'd seen my bruises in the examining room, but this was her first look at me, and her eyes went wide. I was blotchy eggplant-purple on my left side where Vic had landed his foot a few times.

"Wow."

"They called it 'contusions.' Got a bunch of 'em."

"You poor kid! And you got no padding at all!"

Meaning, I gather, fat or muscle. I was pretty skinny, as I've told you before. I *do* have muscles, though; they're just not very big.

"Hey, Lace?" This was Cade's voice, calling from downstairs.

"I'm cleanin' him up! Down in a few minutes!"

That was quite a bark out of her; you'd think she couldn't stand this guy, who was her boyfriend and all.

"Where'd you say you were going? I missed that part."

"Volunteering for the Forest Service, kinda near Flagstaff." It used to be Albuquerque, but I had to keep moving the location farther west to give it some safe distance from where I was. Flagstaff was in northern Arizona, near the Interstate. "Just for a couple of weeks, clearing and bushhogging and stuff. Good exercise, I need to be stronger —"

"Have to change that bandage," she said. And she started pulling out gauze and adhesive tape from the bag the clinic gave me. I have to say, she was an outstanding nurse because of her gentleness in removing the old sopping bandage without making me shriek. She had the softest touch, and didn't seem disgusted by what she saw underneath, which was probably pretty oozy. "Stitches will dissolve in about a week or so," she said, examining them closely. Also, her hair smelled good in a musty kind of way. It was light brown and very pretty in the evening sunlight blasting through the window. She dabbed at me with a warm facecloth, and it stung a bit but not too much. Then she smoothed some antibiotic ointment gently into the cuts, without hurting me.

There was other stuff too, which I don't want to go into very much, but she was evidently a little clumsy or else accidentally affectionate because while she was bandaging me up again her hands would sometimes touch my shoulder or my arm. I was thinking, Lacey's very pretty, and quite friendly for a Texan, but I had my good friend Natalie back in Ogamesh and I didn't feel just right about some of her gentleness.

"When are you expected in Flagstaff?"

"Um, Sunday evening. Training starts –"

"Well, it's only Wednesday, you got plenty of time to stick around here and heal, I can't imagine you'd be much good to them the way you are, you think you should call them and tell 'em you're injured?"

"Maybe. Haven't thought it through yet."

"Bushhogging with busted ribs. But if you think you're up to it we can put you on a bus on Saturday, Amarillo to Flagstaff, we're not sending you out on the road again with just your *thumb* to get you in trouble. No sirree. The bus it is, our treat. When you called home, did you say what happened?"

"No. My aunt – I mean my *Mom*, she'd worry. I told her I was fine."

"Darn you, Archie, ain't you the martyr."

"Y'all been so kind, Lacey, I can't let you pay for the bus."

We both heard Cade's footsteps coming up the stairs.

"Put this on," she ordered, handing me one of Alvin's old tee shirts, which was black. I slipped it on pretty quickly and discovered it fit just right.

"Hi, honey," she said to him.

"Y'all better, Archie?" he said to me.

"Showered and bandaged. Good enough."

He turned back to Lacey. "Your Dad called your Mom, looks like he's gotta come home and grab his weapon."

"Oh, gee, *now* what?"

"Robbery up in Dumas, and they're lookin' for backup. Might be a hostage situation."

I was trying to imagine why Mr. Calder would want to tangle with such a thing. Lacey saw that I was confused.

"Daddy's the sheriff. Dumas is another county, but sometimes they ask for help. Try Alvin's jeans on – we'll give you some privacy."

They shuffled on downstairs leaving me alone with Alvin's jeans and an instant case of the jitters.

It was bad news that her dad was the sheriff. All sheriffs do is ask a lot of questions that make you jumpy.

But it was good news that he'd be distracted by the robbery up in Dumas.

So I thought.

I took my time getting dressed in Alvin's clothes and picking out a couple of extra tee shirts that looked halfway decent, and slowed down even more when I heard Sheriff Calder arrive downstairs, with doors banging and everyone's voice rising in excitement. I couldn't make out what all they were saying, so after I put my sneakers on I crept stealthily out of the room into the upstairs hallway and cocked my ear to the staircase. I bumped into a small table with an extension phone on it, but it didn't bang too loudly.

When I focused my ears, mostly what I heard was radio hissing and squawking, with urgent voices.

I moved down a couple of steps to get closer.

Sheez, they shot the car and now they got a fire!

I think that's what he said.

Then Lacey – *Daddy, they don't need you now.*

And then a lot of muttering and noises of frustration.

Well, I believed that the best time to be introduced and not noticed too much was during a hullabaloo like this one, so I moseyed down the steps into the downstairs hall and around the corner into the living room, pretending I'd heard nothing.

"Thanks, Lacey! Alvin's clothes fit great!"

"Oh, good." And she turned back to her father. "You can stay home now, Daddy."

"Reckon."

"This is our new friend Archie from Alabama. Had a bit of a dust-up."

The sheriff threw me a quick glance and then, seeing the gauze bandage, squinted at me.

"Run into a bull, son?"

I remembered Lacey saying that when she let me into the truck.

"No sir, I had a disagreement with a fellow. I'm fine."

Lacey gave me a smile for that, but soon the sheriff was back to his handheld radio, gabbing with someone up at the robbery scene, most of which I missed because Cade and Mrs. Calder emerged from the kitchen, after doing dinner dishes I guessed, with Cade tapping me on the shoulder and offering a jerk of his head to the back door.

So far Cade had seemed pleasant enough, and gentle, but I wasn't too keen on the look in his eye. I followed him outside onto their back porch where you could see the last glimmer of daylight on the horizon. The view was huge across the flat prairie, with the inky dark sky creeping down over it.

"Just to let you know," he said, "she's only sweet on you 'cause you're like a wounded bird. Never woulda stopped for you unless you were half dead, which you seemed to be."

I jabbered, "She's sweet on you, Cade, not me."

He shook his head. "I don't like you up there with her, half dressed."

"It was *me* that was half dressed, not her," I said, instantly seeing my mistake.

"S' what I meant."

"Well, not much to see, Cade. Just cuts and bruises."

"She's my girl. You need to be straight about that."

"Well, I am," I said. "And I'm glad she's yours 'cause she's a catch if there ever was one, as pretty as they come."

I might've said a word or two too many.

"I'll be the judge of that. You're just a kid anyway."

He gave his shoulders a heave, turned around, and went back into the house. I followed him in just before he closed the door.

Cade was asking the sheriff, "So they shoot him up there?"

The sheriff nodded glumly. He was seated at the head of the dining table with his sheriff's shirt half-buttoned, and fumbling with his radio.

"Was that bad?" Cade asked.

"Fella had a knife to the clerk's throat. They shot him through the glass. Very risky. Said the clerk wriggled loose for a second and that's when they fired, but it's still damn risky. Glad I missed it, helluva drive to Dumas anyhow."

"Who was he?"

The sheriff shook his head. "Drifter. Driving a Buick with a Georgia tag, they ran the number and it sure ain't his, but it's not reported stolen either. No matter if it's stolen or not, he's dead, and the car half exploded when the bullet hit the tank. Troubling, though, 'cause it's registered to a juvenile female, there's no sign of her, so they're gonna follow it up to see if she's missing or whatever."

To keep them from seeing my knees knocking I slowly moseyed out the back door to the porch again. I hoped they were so wrapped up in their own consternation they wouldn't notice I was gone.

I'd had other moments of everything crashing down, but this was the be-all end-all of brainhurt, if I can use a new word. I felt wretched and confused by it all, but I forced myself to puzzle it through. The sheriff in Dumas had probably already phoned Natalie or her parents and wrung the truth out of her, in which case they'd fear for my life, since the drifter might've killed me to steal the car. Worse, in a way, was that her car was now flaming wreckage, and dead or not I was mostly responsible for it.

Even worse, if I was alive, they'd get my name and description, and send out an all-points, probably starting right here in Texas. Charles Rawlins would be all over it, and just as likely Sheriff Calder, too. They'd want to know my connection to the drifter, like *he fell into bad company, he was an accomplice and he's wanted as an accessory.*

Dead, missing, or a criminal, Nat would be pretty upset, I figured. Not to mention Zee and Ty, and the Winklers, and others who knew me.

I didn't want Nat to start blubbering with grief or despair.

I had to call her.

And then I had to skedaddle out of the Calders' place, but in a non-suspicious way.

But for a few minutes I couldn't move, and it was mostly due to some phlegmy gook in my throat that made it hard to speak – which I'd need to do going back inside the house. The gook wasn't from my injuries, it was from my head strewn with sad feelings that I couldn't seem to shake loose. I wondered, if Milton Clayne were here, what would he tell his son to do? Though he'd run off from our Mom, did he have enough good judgment left in his head to do the right thing? If not, I could tell him a thing or two about what's right.

There are things that are right, and there are things that are *super right* that go over what's right.

It was *super right* to go after Tick and fetch him back, because he was in the clutches of Jupiter Strange, who was scared to death right now of the law and might do anything to stay free. That much I knew. It went against the lesser rightness of giving myself up to Charles Rawlins and Sheriff Calder.

Some of the phlegm was due to Vic. I don't know *what* all made him the way he was, damn near kicking and choking me lifeless and then holding a knife to some clerk's throat, but he didn't kill me or the clerk and now he was shot dead. It happens so fast, that little *snap* between life and death, it's scary in a way. He had me on the ground and I was out like a fish, and he could've kept squeezing for another couple of minutes till I was dead but at some point something in his miserable brain told him not to do it that long. He could have drawn the blade across the clerk's throat but he didn't. He chose to let both of us live. I always think, almost *anyone* can be rehabilitated. There are exceptions, but I didn't think Vic was one of them. He could go to jail instead of getting shot, and be one of those prisoner poets – he had the gift, for sure, and I was sure jail would've been better for him than death.

And it comes back to me while I'm on the porch, the *snap* of remembering Jake Culpepper before he died, maybe a month or so when he came over because Zee was making brownies and Jake was always here when she made brownies. We were twelve then, since this is four years ago, and Zee was smart and hearty enough to be a very good baker, which included shooing us out of the kitchen so we went upstairs to look at Tick's baseball cards or some such thing. We sat on the beds and Jake wanted me to find a comb, which I fetched from the bathroom (it was mine). I thought he was going to play it like a kazoo, but he didn't ask for waxed paper. Instead he sat next to Tick and started combing his hair. It was stupid, because Tick's hair is pretty short and goes in all different directions, but Jake was combing it anyway. I think

I said *you're wasting your time*, but Jake kept combing nice and easy while Tick sat there and purred like a cat. He said, does it feel better? and Tick would nod.

I think I asked him what in God's name he was doing, without sounding too harsh.

Tryin' to heal the damage inside.

I think I said *it's inside, not outside.*

And Tick was murmuring, *heal me.*

Jake put the comb on the bed and rubbed Tick's hair with his hands, as a head massager would do, but gentle. *I'm experimenting with my healing. Outside in.*

Well, I decided to leave them alone and got up to see how the brownies were coming when Zee turned the corner, almost bumping into me, and she stuck her head into our room and I saw her face freeze, while Jake kept up his massaging.

"That won't help him, Jake," she said. I remember it.

Maybe Jake said something, but then Zee added,

"Best not to do that. Brownies are ready." I remember that too.

So all this comes to me on the porch because of the tiny line between life and death, and me feeling so sad for people like Nat, and Lacey with her accidental touching, and these tender, gentle people scattered around that no one knows, and how they must hurt because they're different. It didn't matter to me at all if Jake liked playing with Tick's hair, or if he preferred boys over girls, it only mattered that he was my friend and he had to go off and hang himself.

I barely remembered the comb business. I can't figure why it was so easy to forget.

And I'd never thought to wonder, Did Zee call Jake's dad and tell him about what she saw? She might, she could be ornery enough, and suggest it was *improper.*

After a few minutes, I cleared the gook from my throat. Not to be crude, but usually I just swallow it instead of launching it.

⌗ ⌗ ⌗ ⌗ ⌗

In my absence, the Calder family and Cade had recovered enough from the crisis to settle in around the TV set. The police radio was off, and so was Sheriff Calder's uniform shirt. I caught Lacey's eye and easily enough begged another phone call in the study, back to Mom and Dad in Alabama, because I'd had second thoughts about bushhogging with my beat-up body, and might decide instead to return home.

Lacey smiled, as if this were a wise choice.

When I got inside the study and closed the door, I called Natalie's house. It was after eleven there, but I knew they'd be up after the call from the Dumas sheriff.

I got the professor. I'd always thought he was a decent sort, but he was so infested with snooty attitude I was forced to change my mind.

"Dr. Hawkins, it's Woody," I started.

"*Well.* Mr. Born to be Wild himself. I hope you have an excellent explanation for all this. But first, I suppose I'm compelled to ask if you're okay. Perhaps you're shot, or in jail."

"I'm fine, sir, and no I'm not shot and I'm not in jail – I got ambushed and he stole it. I'll pay it back, I promise, whatever the cost. Is Nat around, please?"

He half-covered the mouthpiece, calling out *he says he's okay,* and then I heard the receiver bang down on the table.

For sure, he was plenty sore.

"Woody." It was Nat's Mom. "Natalie will be on in a second, and please excuse Jordan's rudeness. He's quite upset about the car."

"Yes ma'am. I'm sorry for all the trouble I've caused, I promise to make it up.

"You put Natalie in a very bad position, forcing her to lie."

I heard her shout *Mom!*

"Did you have anything to do with that robbery? Please tell me no."

"No ma'am." Lordy, you spend sixteen years living a mostly clean and honest life, and as soon as you turn your back those sixteen years add up to nothing. "As I was saying to the professor, the drifter stole the car when I wasn't looking. I'm not a robber."

"We're all very upset, what with that sheriff calling us at such an hour. We *do* care for you, Woody, and we're quite worried."

"Please, can I speak with Nat?"

"Yes, in a second. We all know now what you're trying to do – with Tick and that other boy. We don't think it's so wise. Okay, I'm being told by my daughter to shut my trap. Here she is."

96

When Nat came on, she was all snuffly and low-voiced, and I felt my main job was to cheer her up.

"It's going to be okay, Nat. I'll get you another car, a better car."

"Thought you were *dead*."

"I'm not. I'm talking to you."

"Where *are* you? Can it be *Texas* already?"

"The greater Texas area," I said. "I've got a ways to go, but –"

"This is *such* a bad idea. Never shoulda happened. Everyone knows. Everything."

"Nat, things will be fine when Tick and I get back. But the thing is, they're scared now, Tick and Jupe. Jupe thinks he's an arson suspect, and I know him too well, he'll be desperate to stay away from the law. Who knows *what* all he'll do. So you gotta tell Rawlins to back off, it's *my* job to get my brother."

"You can tell him yourself."

"Nat, I don't have time for more calls, this place –"

"He's right here, Woody."

Oh *damn*, it's panic time! I didn't want to talk to Rawlins, but I didn't want to hang up either. It was the strangest feeling, wanting to stay connected to that phone in Natalie's living room and going completely jelly-kneed at the idea of talking with Rawlins.

"He's asking me if he has your *permission* to get on the line. Is that polite enough for you?"

"Okay. I'll talk."

"I miss you," she said. "I want you home soon."

"Yeah, soon."

Rawlins was on in an instant.

"Hello, Woody."

"Sir."

"You need to know that I'm off this case. I was assigned to the arson detail, and we've solved that problem, so the matter of Tick and Jupiter is in the hands of juvenile justice and technically they're both fugitives. But it's not my case."

I replied to him, "When Jupiter called his Mom, she blabbed he was wanted for arson. She scared him half to death. I'm afraid of what he might do, fugitive or not. That's why I have to keep going."

"Yes."

Oh *damn,* he was going quiet on me again. What's with this guy?

"You're his brother," he said. "Do what you have to do."

I just couldn't figure him.

"I'll try."

"I wish I could speak," he said. "I have – I have a stake in this. If you could tell me where you're going. Where you think they are. You're in a tough position, because you're obstructing justice. I can help, Woody. I have a responsibility."

"But – you're a lawman! How can you help – the idea is to get them both back without the law, don't you see?"

I could hear the loud whine in my voice and I worried a little it might carry through the door. But the Calders were all wrapped up in their TV.

"I do see. I wish I could say more. Will you call me at home tomorrow night? I have a day shift, I'm back at six."

"Yes sir, I will. Tomorrow after six."

"It's important. Please don't fail."

That was the end of it. We muttered good-bye, and as soon as it was silent my brain got all entangled with details of the law I didn't know, including the idea that Rawlins seemed to have some responsibility that went outside the sheriff's department in our county.

When I'd gotten myself more settled and popped out of the study, I met Lacey coming down the stairs to the hallway.

"Just straightening up Alvin's room," she said.

It seemed curious to me she didn't ask how my phone call went with "Mom and Dad," but I let it go.

I watched TV with all of them for awhile, took another pain pill and an antibiotic, and soon enough I started to get sleepy while they all sat staring at the tube in their peaceful, muttery way.

Next thing I knew, Lacey was patting me on the shoulder. "Hey, we gotta get you to bed, you've got a *big* day tomorrow, all that traveling."

I thought she had her days mixed up, since we'd talked about a bus trip on Saturday, not tomorrow, which was Thursday.

"Archie's leaving us?" cried Mrs. Calder. "With those injuries?"

"He's improving by the minute," said Lacey.

Sheriff Calder was grumbling at them, wanting to listen to his show.

"Where you headed, son?" Mrs. Calder asked me.

"Flagstaff, ma'am. Forest Service job. They'll probably stick me behind some desk instead of bushhogging. It'll be a nice bus ride though, I believe."

I was looking at Lacey trying to figure why she changed the plan, but she wouldn't put her eyes on me when she talked. You've got to look into someone's eyes to get deep into their real thoughts.

"He'll be fine, Mom. I've made up Alvin's bed for him, and I'll get him up at six for the morning bus."

She could hardly wait to scoot me out of there. I don't know why, but I was grateful. I stood up and gave a somewhat exaggerated yawn.

"'Night, Archie," said Cade.

"Good night," said Mrs. Calder, "it's been delightful to meet you. And *do* take care of your wounds, and take those pills by the *clock*. Lacey, make sure you pack plenty of extra gauze and such."

"I will."

"'Night, son," said Sheriff Calder, not turning away from the set. "Do what she says."

"Yes sir, I will."

"'Night then."

"'Night everybody."

✠ ✠ ✠ ✠ ✠

She got me up right on schedule, which was too bad in a way because I was deep in a dream about having supper with Milton Clayne, my father, in a diner somewhere, and the conversation was fascinating. But it was instantly lost in a fog with the sound of her voice.

"Let's go, sleepy head."

What she'd done the night before was pack Alvin's clothes, gobs of bandages and things in an old army duffel, and neatly laid out my wallet, knife, canteen, sunglasses, tube of ointment and bottles of pills next to my knapsack. While I rubbed the dream away from my eyes and got dressed, she was collecting toiletries from the bathroom and putting them into a paper sack. Everything from toothbrush and comb to razor and deodorant.

I rummaged through the sack feeling sorrowful and thankful at the same time, and suddenly she said,

"You got enough money, right?"

I remembered I had over two hundred and thirty dollars, and told her so.

"Good."

Before we left, she raided the kitchen and stuffed food into my knapsack – muffins and cheese, a banana and potato chips and who knows what all. At that hour, yanked from my dream as I was, I felt too groggy to be truly appreciative, so it was only later when we were in Cade's truck that I heaped a load of thanks on her. And then, as I woke up even more, I remembered what it was that was perplexing me.

I asked, "How'd you know, after I called Mom and Dad, I was going to stick to my plan with the forest service?"

She gave me a half-twisted grin. "You just don't have the look of somebody who wants to go home, Mr. Wetherall."

Well, *that* caught my attention.

"I don't?"

"*Some* day," she said, "I want to see you again. A year or two, maybe three. I want to see how you grow up. Are you gonna be a wandering puppy dog like now, or something else. I just don't know."

That also caught my attention, and it shut me up. In fact, we didn't say another word the rest of the trip down to Amarillo, as the ranchland and wheat fields gave way to little clusters of houses and trailers. In a while, we crossed over some railroad tracks and turned into a parking lot next to the bus station, and she stopped the truck.

"You're free," she said, as I opened the door to get out.

"Can't thank you enough. The medical attention, Alvin's clothes, dinner, all of it."

She turned the engine back on and was about to peel off, but she seemed to have one more thing to say, biting her lip as if to think what it was.

"I just hope," she said, "you find your brother and he's safe. I didn't hear everything, but I was a bit of a snoop on the upstairs phone and I think I heard enough."

I didn't know what else to say except, "Oh, Lacey."

"Bye, Woody."

ELEVEN

What do we remember from age three? Almost nothing. I was pretty sure my first memory was my fourth birthday, when I got a little wooden train set. My mother had secretly laid it out in a figure eight on the living room rug, and I remember she brought me in with her hands over my eyes until she shouted out "happy birthday!" and allowed me to see what she'd done. It was a freight train with a locomotive, a hopper car with coal, a cattle car with little cows in it, and a caboose with a man waving from the rear platform. The track had a bridge going over an underpass at the center of the figure eight. I loved that little set. I didn't seem to mind that the train was stuck forever in its figure eight and couldn't really go anywhere except back to where it started. It seemed okay for it to be stuck in its little world. I'd make *choo choo* and whistle noises, mimicking the sounds of freight trains that would run through Ogamesh.

But now I don't think that was my first memory, because I remember her taking my hand to pat her belly.

My Mom taking my hand, when Tick was inside her. She placed it on the big hard balloon of her belly.

And I remember a strong sense of a man in the kitchen, doing dishes. It was peculiar, because it was a man doing the dishes instead of my mom, and there usually wasn't any man in the house.

I remember looking up at him and thinking, *big*.

And I remember sandy hair, maybe even blond hair.

It came back to me in that fuzzy dream before Lacey woke me up, when I was eating with Milton Clayne in a diner. The short sandy-blond hair blazing in lamplight over his head, and a dark look of friendliness in his eyes.

Zoo-heady dream.

⌗ ⌗ ⌗ ⌗ ⌗

The clerk at the ticket window in the bus depot was one of those real old-timey western guys with a straw cowboy hat, a string tie, and a face so brown and creased and looked like he spent the whole summer lying on his back in the desert. I judged him to be retired cowboy, what with his face and the way he was partly stooped over.

Of course, I couldn't be critical of faces right now. There's nothing to start a conversation faster than to show up with a bunch of pulpy bruises and a big gauze bandage half-covering your eye. Fortunately, he was the only other person in the depot so I was plug ugly to just one set of eyes.

"Hit by a train, boy?"

"No sir, by a bad man. Rather not get into it."

"Well I won't then. Where you headed?"

"Los Angeles. One way please."

It's funny, back in Ogamesh I never got a good long look at a California map to learn just where Malibu was. But I knew movie stars lived there so I guessed it wasn't too far from Los Angeles and Hollywood, and I'd find out more when I got there.

I took my wallet out as he started getting my ticket ready.

"You'll have a lunch stop in Albuquerque, and a four-hour layover in Phoenix with a bus change, and an arrival about three tomorrow afternoon."

I wasn't paying very close attention because I was discovering a whole wad of fresh twenty dollar bills in my wallet. There were ten of them, to be precise, and easy to spot because all the rest of my money was raggedy and dirty from being counted so often. My grand total was over four hundred thirty dollars.

Lacey was such a sneak.

"Fifty-six dollars and twenty cents," he said.

I stood there frozen. I couldn't get on the bus with Lacey's money.

"Sir, you know Sheriff Calder?"

"As good as they get," he said.

"His daughter Lacey?"

"Fine girl."

"Well sir, she lent me some cash that I don't need and I forgot to return it. Have you got an envelope? And some note paper?"

He obliged me, and I started writing her. The important part was *this trip has changed me enough so I can't accept your gift. I owe too much to too many, thanks anyway.* The note and the money went into the envelope, and I wrote her name on the outside, but then got stymied.

"I don't know the address."

Well, I got half-beaten to death in Texas and then pampered so much it overtipped the scales in my favor. This old guy said he'd drive it up after work and stick it in their mailbox – he lived in the same direction and it wasn't much out of the way for him.

I thanked him has hard as I could.

♯ ♯ ♯ ♯ ♯

I was curled up on the very back seat of the bus where you can spread out, using Alvin's duffel bag as a pillow. There weren't more than eight or ten other people on the bus, so I wasn't hogging any seats. I went back to sleep, thinking maybe I'd get back into my dream in the diner with my father. The humming of the bus and the air conditioner helped put me out.

I don't remember dreaming, but I do recall that my legs jerked around a couple of times and once banged into the metal wall of the bathroom which was at the end of my seat. Lucky for me, nobody was inside. But the leg-jerking woke me up because it unsettled my ribs and they gave me a sharp jolt – like they'd just been kicked again.

My legs do that sometimes when I catch a nap. Usually it's because I'm grouchy or upset about something.

The next thing I knew I heard the bus's transmission grinding into a lower gear as we started going down a long hill. I righted myself, took a gander out the window and let out a gasp you could hear three seats away from me.

Down below were bumps of distant mountains, a wide desert, and a sprawling city with thousands and thousands of clay-colored buildings. It was an amazing sight, like I'd just stepped into a western movie. Even better, you could see a hundred miles or more to the west, as if space were cheap here and they couldn't make it fast enough. In fact, the gasp I uttered was a *holy shhh,* but I caught my tongue.

The driver came on radio and said this was Albuquerque and we'd be having a stop here for lunch. Soon enough we were down into the city where we left the highway and drove a few blocks before pulling into the parking lot of a Mueller's.

Now if you've *ever* been on the highway more than five miles from home you've seen Mueller's restaurants with their big red sign on top that has the happy kid's face. The kid looks so *stupid* with his big ugly tongue sticking out and licking his chops as if he actually choked the food down and enjoyed it. If you've eaten at Mueller's and actually liked it, then I have to apologize, but I've eaten there twice and it was two times too many – once with Zee when it was her idea, and once with the Culpeppers when we went bowling in Macon, Jake's birthday I think. My main problem with Mueller's is that the food doesn't *taste.* You think you're getting the world's best looking mac and cheese (which I ordered once) and you have a bite and there's no *flavor* of any kind. You have more bites searching for flavor, and it never comes. The other problem I have is the bright fluorescent lights hanging overhead that turn everything green, including your skin. It makes you look like you're diseased.

Mueller's, like any other chain restaurant, has the same lousy food no matter where you are, Georgia or Michigan or New Mexico. They don't discriminate – they make sure all their crap gets spread equally all over the country.

We were all off the bus with our hand luggage and the driver said we'd have an hour here. I was near starving, but I wasn't going to eat at Mueller's.

I stood outside with my duffel and knapsack watching all the passengers waddle into the restaurant like lemmings to their death, except for this one guy, a man about forty, I guessed, who stopped on the steps and looked back at me. He kind of cocked his head and squinted.

"Gonna eat?" he said.

I said back to him, "Not at Mueller's."

Well, he must have had the same idea 'cause he came down the steps and walked right toward me. He had a nice enough roundish face with kind of puffy eyes, and a bad hairpiece on his head where you could see the stitching in the part. I've got nothing against hairpieces – Harmon Crews wears one – but it seems to me if you're going to go to the trouble of pretending you're not bald you should spend enough money to make it look halfway decent so you can actually fool people.

"I don't like Mueller's either." He stuck out his hand for a shake. "My name's Marv."

"I'm Woody."

"There's a good Mexican place about two blocks from here. I'll buy you lunch."

I protested the offer, but he was firm about it so I had no choice. Mexican food sounded great, and I was willing to bet that here in New Mexico it would be pretty authentic.

Well, we traipsed along the hot street for maybe five blocks and just shot the breeze. He said he'd noticed me getting on the bus in Amarillo and thought I looked like a "nice person," in spite of my war injuries. I said I hadn't noticed anybody on the bus, I was so sleepy. He said he had a son about my age, named Andrew. Well, five blocks is a pretty long way considering we had only an hour for lunch, and I was concerned about getting back to the bus on time, but sure enough, here was a genuine Mexican place called *Vern's Vittles* with plastic red chili peppers hanging in the dark windows. Marv was happy about it, because it wasn't too fancy looking and it also had a bar.

We went in and sat in a booth next to a window looking out on the street.

It was natural he'd ask me about my wounds, and for the first time I felt safe in telling the truth, that an evil-tempered drifter damn near killed me so he could steal my car. Luckily, I was cared for by a very kind family in Amarillo.

Marv wanted to know the details about my trip, but this is where I had to abbreviate things on account of their complexity. I just said,

"My brother's in California and I need to bring him back to Georgia."

I had a chicken enchilada with a Coke and he had a beef burrito along with two giant margaritas which he ordered both at once. I remembered it was time for my pills, but I only took my antibiotic and anti-inflammatory pills, not the pain killers. The ribs still hurt, of course, but my face felt better and I didn't want to get all plugged up, as they'd warned me might happen with the codeine.

Marv would eat his burrito and drink his huge margarita and basically stare at me. It wasn't a hard stare, as if he were inspecting me, it was gentler and friendly enough, with his puffy eyes crinkling around the edges. When he got into his second margarita his face started to flush pink and his eyes seemed to well up as he kept staring at me, and it was then that it crossed my mind, *oh, maybe he's one of those.* I decided to get him talking so he wouldn't exhaust himself looking at me, but he beat me to it.

"My son's about your age."

"That's Andrew, right?"

He nodded, and then said this while he chewed. "He'd be fifteen now. He's with his mother. Somewhere. It's been ten years. I live here. I sell signs. My house is a tomb."

I got the main idea, and it was sad, and the sadness just swept over his face.

"That's too bad," I said.

"He was five. I got drunk and hit my wife. They left that night. Gone. Handsome boy. A boy needs his father. Maybe he has a new one."

"I'm sorry, Marv."

"You have a father," he said, guessing wrong. "Your house is not a tomb."

"Well," I started.

"Another margarita," he said to the waiter, who just showed up. "Por favor."

"Another Coke, please."

"I'll buy you a margarita, son."

"No thanks, Coke is fine."

"You sure?"

"Sure as I'm born, liquor doesn't agree with me."

The waiter left.

"Tell me about your home, your family. Mr. Woody."

I didn't see much reason to lie so I told him the truth. If he wanted to feel envious about how cozy and loving my family was, he'd be disappointed. As I laid out the basic facts about my parents, about Aunt Zee and her failing state, his face actually seemed to brighten.

"You're an orphan," he said. "No mother. No father. An aunt who needs your care."

"I don't *feel* like an orphan, though."

"On the bus. You reminded me of Andrew. Same dark brown hair. Blue eyes."

"Well sir, I've always been Woody, just myself."

The third margarita came and he drained half of it before putting the glass down. He was going to be in miserable shape for the long walk back to the bus. I reckoned I needed to adjust my words to suit a man who was getting a buzz so fast. It was the same tactic I used with Natalie.

"I was a loving father," he said, and I could see the tears start to well up again. "Never hit him. Only his mother. Shouldn't have. But I'm reformed. I'm at peace."

"That's good, Marv."

"I was a decent father."

"Good."

"If you needed a father —"

"Well, if I did I'd like to find him someday," I said quickly. "I'm sure he has his reasons for leaving, but darned if he might enjoy knowing me now, how I've grown and changed. But I'm not sure I need it. Remember, he walked out on my mother, before my brother was born, and it made her very depressed and in a way it killed her, on account of her suicide, so I wonder if this is the kind of father I need, and maybe it isn't."

He finished his drink during my oration and immediately started looking for the waiter, who was helping another couple at the other end of the room.

"One more of these, I could say it," he said. He was getting all mooshy and it distressed me a bit, so I launched into another oration.

"The thing is, having a father can be a big risk. Sometimes you're lucky, you get a good one, but other times you get a father who walks out on you or else he wants you to play football instead of the violin or being an artist, and he's so damn *stubborn* about you being a *man* that it ties your stomach in knots and it makes you so lonely, if you're just twelve, that you can't stand it, and you're not sure *what* you are, but it's not what your father wants, so the only way out of it is to go swing from a rafter in your barn and leave everybody else behind, and they *are* left behind, and they'll hurt till their dying day because they didn't know how to love the kid in the right way."

I believed I outspoke his ability to keep up with me.

"Woody. I sell signs. Short words. Simple thoughts."

"Well, I *know* you sell signs, you said that, but signs don't always tell the truth, like the Mueller's sign with the goofy kid licking his lips because the food actually *sucks*, Marv, we both know that, so it's a lie. I'm not saying *your* signs lie, I'm just saying just 'cause a thought is simple doesn't make it true. You're sad about Andrew, and I understand that, but I'm on a journey to California to meet my brother and so I'm not much help to you. I mean, I've seen it with my girlfriend, liquor makes people mooshy and even the shortest words and ideas may not be so honest."

He was pretty gassed but now I think he was following me.

"I live here," he said.

The tears welled up, and how he was sputtering and grabbing the napkin to hold to his face.

"Get off the bus to go home, but instead I'm gonna *eat* with the other passengers because one of them is a nice kid. Mueller's or this place, who gives a shit? I just wanna have lunch with this *nice kid.*"

"Well, we're doing that," I said, a little more gently.

"Not go home. It's a tomb."

He was really sobbing now, and it got the waiter's attention but I sneaked a signal at him with my hand that it was okay, it wouldn't be right to interrupt.

"Be like a – *father,* for an *hour!*"

"It's okay, Marv."

"Just an *hour.*"

With his hands to his face I could read his watch upside down. I had ten minutes to get to the bus, so there wasn't much time for good-byes. I started to wriggle out of the booth.

"You're *going?*"

"Well sir, the bus won't wait. I can pay for my meal, I got money –"

"It was a *treat!*" This came out as part laugh, part snarl, and the way it put a stopper on his slobbering caught me by surprise. "Don't you remember? I say something, I mean it." He was struggling to stand up, then thought better of it and fell back down.

"Well, I was being polite."

"Just say thank you and go."

"Yes sir. Thanks, Marv. Appreciate it."

He wouldn't look at me.

"Don't be an ass. Just get out of here."

I grabbed my bags and obeyed him as quickly as I was able, busting out of the dark little restaurant into the blinding glare of the sun. It was extra bright out here, and hot, with the clear summer sky and the sandy-colored buildings.

I hoofed it double-time two blocks and briefly turned the corner to hide from view, in case old Marv decided to have second thoughts about his behavior. Whether it was all about fathering or he had something else in mind, it didn't matter, I didn't need either one, especially from a guy who hit his wife and might have hit his kid, too, for all I know. I didn't trust him for a second.

I had three blocks between me and Mueller's parking lot, and in just a few seconds those three blocks might as well have been three hundred miles of twisting mazes, as things turned out. First off, I nearly got run off the sidewalk by a big convertible, all painted with flames, loaded with crazy Mexican teenagers, that was careening down the street and took a sharp corner going *over* the sidewalk. Next, it was being chased by a big coupe, also loaded with Mexicans, that was so low slung to the ground its rear bumper hit the pavement and shot off sparks as it raced around the corner. Third, when I caught my breath, I saw two kids trotting across the street a block away, a tall black kid and a shorter scruffy blond kid tailing behind him and there was no doubt in my mind, not a shred, that I'd just had a sighting of Tick and Jupe.

TWELVE

I took after them. If I missed the bus, it was no big deal – I could always get another one if I had to, and if these kids really were Tick and Jupe then I wouldn't have to. Of course I had to haul my bags with me, the knapsack on my back and the duffel slung over my shoulder, and it slowed me down some, along with my aching ribs and the hot sun. But my heart was hammering at me – *go get them.*

I got to the corner where they'd trotted across and I saw them now about two blocks away, loping away from me. *Damn,* it sure looked like Tick's lope, but I wish I'd been close enough to make sure. And I thought, what's the chance, I mean, *what is the possible chance* we'd meet here in the middle of New Mexico instead of Malibu, since they had a two-day jump on me out of Georgia and could've taken any route they wanted? Go figure the chance.

Must've been *some* chance, because I was ninety-nine per cent sure it was them, even if the view was blocked by other people on the street, and my excitement helped me turn on the gas and start sprinting after them, weighed down as I was with too many of Alvin's clothes and all the toiletries Lacey had stuffed into the duffel. But the faster I ran, the faster *they* ran, which made no sense at all since they hadn't seen me. No sense at all except when I started to hear the police sirens.

Damn, this ain't right.

The two kids (I could've sworn it was them) blasted across the street into what looked like an alleyway just as a police cruiser roared by me, all lights flashing and sirens screaming, and then it hit the brakes hard when they must've seen the guys cutting into the alley. I was almost there, had a clean opening in the traffic, and I spurted across the street to go after them down the alley. In a situation like this, when your heart's pounding and your mouth feels like cotton, you're in animal mode and you don't think. If I'd thought a little, I'd remember that the police are usually right in what they do. In my life, that's been my experience, though some people might argue it. When the police are after somebody, chances are pretty good they've got good reason for it. But being in animal mode as I was with my veins all rowdy with adrenaline, I saw the police as a terrible danger to my little brother and I had to catch up to him and protect him somehow.

The alley was one of those surprise dead-enders, though it was hard to see with the sun so bright in my face. It looked like it had a chain-link fence at the end because the two kids – just dark shapes because they were in shadow – were climbing up on it.

The siren noise behind me ground to a stop and I heard the shouts of men.

I dropped the duffel and ran close enough to yell it out –

"*Tick!*"

Damn it *was* him, with Jupe grabbing his hand and pulling him up the fence, and my brother spun his head around and saw me.

"Woody!"

In that one second of time, I saw Tick's face open up into a plea for help, an expression that said *save me,* but at the same time Jupe was yanking him to the top of the fence even as one of the cops banged me against the wall and I heard Jupe bellow it out, as if to the whole planet – "*Surfing or death!!*" – at the same time that the cops were hollering *stop, hold it right there* and such things, but they were about ten yards too short and Tick and Jupiter were down on the other side of the fence and running for their lives into a complete mishmash of broken-down sheds and old junk cars.

I wanted to get it out – *they found the arsonists, you're innocent!* – but with the cops on the scene it would've made a mess of things for all of us.

One of the cops was trying to climb the fence, but he was pretty fat and the effort was too much for him so he gave up. The other one was blabbing on his radio right next to me, and just when I lost sight of the fugitives in the junkyard this cop grabbed me and held me by the shirt.

"Don't go away," he said.

"Let go my shirt and I'll stay."

Well, these must have been Wild West cops instead of the more gentlemanly types we have in Ogamesh, because he seemed to take exception to my tone and he gave a hard jolt with his elbow to the midsection which, as you know, is where my ribs are, and I doubled over with a gasp and fell right on top of my duffel bag. He either broke another rib or collapsed my lung, one, because I couldn't seem to draw a breath and when I finally did it felt like a blade was stuck right in my chest.

Half on the pavement as I was, I saw two pairs of cops' legs a foot from my face, but it was the fatter one who did the talking, in a higher-pitched voice.

"Who the hell are you?"

I managed to squeak out, "I was chasin' 'em!"

"You some kinda hero, is that it?"

"Tryin' to stop them." I might've been crying at this point, which would have been from the pain more than anything.

"You witness the mugging?"

I had to hold off for a second till my breath slowed and my brain cleared a bit.

"Saw them – run from the scene," I said.

"Can you get up?"

"Ribs. Busted. Yesterday."

Well, the fat one took my arm anyway and hauled me to my feet and it half-blinded me with pain and I couldn't stand straight up. But this is when they saw my face with the bandage and bruising, and it seemed to have a calming effect on both of them.

"Didn't mean to hurt him," said the cop who did. "Hardly touched him."

"Did you know the kids you were chasing?"

"No sir," I said, bent over and staring at the pavement. "I heard a shout, I saw them run, I gave chase."

"One against *two*? You are a hero type, aren't you?"

"Just instinct," I said. "Never saw their faces, just saw 'em running."

"Any description at all?"

"Just – one bigger one, colored, and a smaller one, white."

I was trying to weasel out of the case as fast as I'd gotten into it, and I wondered if using the word "colored" was the right strategy with these two. Even if their behavior was improving, the less time spent with them the better, and if I was one of those kids raised to be a bigot they might not want my company for too long.

The guy who hit me said, "They knocked a lady to the street. Took over two hundred dollars. She hardly saw them either. Vermin."

"She hurt?"

"Knee abrasion. Not serious."

"Son," said the fat one, "the black boy shouted out something on top of the fence. Just when we got to the alley. Did you hear it? You were right there."

"Somethin' about surfing," said his partner.

"I'm asking the *boy*."

I chewed on it a second. "It's a book character I heard of," I said. "Sir Finger Death. A villain type that lots of kids know about."

"Whaddyaknow. Sir Finger Death."

"Yes sir."

I managed to pull myself more upright and could see their faces better. Like a lot of people I'd seen in Albuquerque so far, they were Hispanic and didn't look as mean as they'd acted. Figuring I was on their side, they asked a few questions about who I was and where I was from and how I got beat up. I risked the truth, mostly, offering up my real first name, and admitting I was coming from Georgia, heading on the bus to Los Angeles to meet my Dad, who was divorced. I got beat up hitchhiking, near Amarillo, and was rescued by the county sheriff's family, name of Calder.

But, I went on, by instinctively choosing to chase the muggers, I'd missed my bus ride to Phoenix, curse the luck. Still, with my ribs all smashed up again would I dare get on a bus when I might need emergency treatment? At the least, I'd have to take my pain killers again, which I didn't want to do because of their constipating effect.

I ended my blithering by saying, "I tried to be a hero and look what it got me."

That's when Fat Man and Elbow Boy left me and went back to their cruiser.

¤ ¤ ¤ ¤ ¤

The junkyard led to a scrap metal yard and then to a junkyard of old cars. Eventually, after dealing with some fences and vacant sandy lots where I was sure I'd confront a rattlesnake, I caught up with some railroad tracks heading west toward a bridge across the river. If I were Tick and Jupe, this is where I might travel with my stolen two hundred dollars, because there weren't any roads here and the brush on either side of the tracks was tall enough to hide in if you had to.

It was as plain as the nose on my face: Tick wanted no more part of this crazy adventure with Jupe. I saw it in his eyes, heard it when he called out my name.

I'd never heard such hope and happiness in his voice.

I said to Jupe in my head, *add kidnapping to mugging and truancy.*
You and your moral instructions.
If I have to, I'll shoot you.

I walked the tracks like any kid, on a single rail with one foot after another and trying to balance myself without killing my ribs. I got Jupe out of my mind and figured I was due for some good luck with people the next time I came across them, because of how they'd laid themselves out in a kind of sequence across the country.

Irv and Lindy at the campsite in Mississippi: bad. Not that they were bad to me, just bad to each other.

The woman and two chubby kids in Oklahoma the second night: good folks.

Vic the drifter: so bad they shot him.

The Calders: good and generous.

Marv: started good, became a jerk.

Albuquerque cops: both jerks.

For sure there was no telling that Tick and Jupe had come this way, but based on how kids like them think – more Jupe than Tick, of course, since Tick doesn't think like anyone else I know – the railroad seemed a decent bet, a whole lot better than leaping fences through private property, no matter how raggedy or abandoned.

Carrying the duffel over my right shoulder eased the strain on my left side, where all the rib damage was. But the strap was chafing my shoulder. I had to put up with it because carrying the load on my left side hurt too much.

Damn that cop for jabbing me.

114

I hated Jupe for crying out *surfing or death* like some battle-cry because if he was that indifferent to death he probably wouldn't think twice about dragging Tick into the bargain. Tick would do his bidding till the last second when he'd realize he was about to meet his maker, and then it would be too late.

I'd shoot him if I had to, to keep my brother safe.

Of course, I'd never held a pistol. Rifles yes, with Dave and Trey Winkler when we went boar hunting one fall, but never a handgun.

Down below, the tracks were being met with other tracks and I could see a small rail yard with old boxcars and sheds, and past all that was a bridge across the river, which I learned later was the Rio Grande.

¤ ¤ ¤ ¤ ¤

There wasn't anybody around the yard or in the sheds that I could see. In fact, I'd wager the yard hadn't seen a train come through it in some months, based on the disrepaired look of everything around me. Typically, you might find a bum or two living in a place like this, but the air smelled so strong of dirty oil and spilled diesel fuel I didn't think it habitable even for a hobo. Diesel's one of my least favorite smells; it just churns my stomach, and I know other people who agree with me. The desert-y heat didn't help, either; you could almost see the fumes wafting up from the ground.

Man, it's hot in New Mexico in June!

Off on a spur of track was a train of boxcars hitched together, a couple of them with their doors slid partway open. They looked tempting as hideaways, so I decided to investigate. I figured, if Tick and Jupe weren't in them, I'd give up on Albuquerque and continue on to Malibu, California, since they were staking their lives on surfing.

I decided right there and then: Jupe was much crazier than Tick, if that's possible.

So I ambled through the diesel stink and across some tracks to a boxcar with its door open. The deck of the car was a little too high to jump into, maimed as I was, but fortunately the car had a step just below it. I hoisted myself up on the step and peered inside.

THIRTEEN

When Tick was about eight, as I recall, he announced to me one night in our bedroom that he'd figured out what dreams were. It was important for him to know what dreams were, because he'd been having a whole string of them lately that were none too pleasant, and pretty vivid at that, and he wanted to get to the bottom of it.

Dreams happen, he said, *when your mind takes a vacation from your head.*

He saw the mind as a physical thing that physically vacated your head and traveled to real places that were hidden from us at nighttime, places where the rules of time, space, common sense, and normal emotion were all twisted up in different ways to become completely dreamlike. Not that he said it like this, but that's how I fathomed it from him.

"Well," I challenged him, "you also dream during daytime, like when you take a nap. So it's not just nighttime places."

He said yes it *is,* your mind just has to travel a little farther to get to the nighttime places.

Better to argue with a post than with Tick.

What we never got around to discussing was what happened to your mind when you were unconscious, as opposed to sleeping. You can remember bits of dreams when you wake up from sleeping, but I can tell you from firsthand experience you don't remember a *thing* if you've been unconscious, at least I didn't. When you come to, it might be a minute or an hour or day later, you just can't tell.

My first thought wasn't a thought, it was a craving. *Water.*

Man, I was thirsty! My mouth felt like a dust storm had blown through it.

Then nausea. I despise nausea, and I always work pretty hard not to throw up. I almost always succeed, and I managed to succeed again in this hot, rumbling dark place, wherever it was. But not by much.

For some reason, my head hurt. Not the side of my face that Vic had rearranged, but the top of my skull where the blood was pounding inside my scalp.

For another some reason, I had a memory of wearing my knapsack, but now it was off. I also had a sense that the canteen was stored in it and was mostly full. I didn't feel like moving much, but I could move my arm across the rough floor, whatever it was, and grope for the knapsack. But the groping turned up nothing.

I muttered, *damn!*

I heard a gurgly-sounding chuckle from another person not far away.

I thought, I'm on a train. I'm in a freight car. We're rumbling along the track. And there's someone else here.

"Guess you din't kill him, Cletus."

"Thought I did."

"Good that you din't."

I still hadn't opened my eyes but I called out to the voices, "I need water." The words were weak and throaty, but I heard some shuffling about and a clang of metal, like my canteen.

"Might be a few drops." This was the first voice I heard, a black man's voice.

That made me angry, dazed and pained as I was. "Used to be *full.*"

"Used to be is used to be," said the other voice, white-sounding, who I gathered was the fellow named Cletus.

I managed to get my eyes open. There wasn't much to see except a small crack of light on the floor, just grazing my duffel bag. I couldn't remember where I'd gotten that bag, but it sure looked like mine.

How'd I get in here with these dolts, and what had they done to me?

I rolled enough on to my right side to see large black shoes stepping into the crack of light.

"Teaspoon, maybe." The black man. "We had a few sips while you was nappin'."

I told him, "Give it here."

When he crouched down to hand me the canteen I got a dim look at his huge face, I swear the size of a basketball or maybe a soccer ball, and a great gash of a scar across a cheek, with bumpy stitchmark scars and all. It unsettled me a bit.

And Cletus said, "Careful of Jorlane, Archie. He been eyein' you, like he likes the young fellers."

"Pay him no mind."

It baffled me why they called me Archie, but I was too thirsty to address the issue just then. I slurped the water down. It was a fair amount more than a teaspoon, and it tasted fine and wet, though warm.

"Take it all, we'll be in Winslow soon," said Jorlane.

I asked, "Where's that at?"

"Desert," said Cletus. "Like most of Arizona."

"Arizona..."

"Boy, you been out fer a few hours, *shiii*, we thought you'd die on us."

I muttered out, "We're going west."

"Hope to shout," said Cletus. "I *want* some of that. Surfer girls."

"How's that head, Archie?" Jorlane asked me.

I told him it hurt like hell.

"Goose egg on it. Cletus din't mean it. He thought you was law or something'."

"Put a crack in the bottle!" And Cletus seemed to find it gleeful, for he shrieked out a laugh. "Hard head, boy!"

I said *fuck both of you* and I swear it wasn't my own voice talking – it didn't sound like the person I was supposed to know inside of me.

They didn't care about it. Jorlane patted me on the shoulder.

"Best to stay calm. Rile up the blood, it'll pound in your head."

"What's left of it," said Cletus with a snort. "You been in some scrap, looks like. Mr. Wetherall."

I didn't have a clue why they had these names for me.

"Why you call me that?"

"Archie Wetherall ain't you?" Cletus came back. "You forget who you are, or you pilfer these pills? Ain't you from Amarillo?"

At the moment, I wasn't so sure. Things were coming back to me slowly. I said back to them, "He's a friend of mine."

Jorlane asked me, "What you go by, son?"

You can be dazed and half dead from thirst and still manage a joke. It popped out without a thought –

"Car, usually. Sometimes bus."

You might expect a whimper of a chuckle at that, but I guessed they were too serious for my humor.

"I meant your real name."

That's when it struck me I should have a wallet on me, in my hip pocket. I did a half-roll on the floor to feel its pressure on my butt, and sure enough it was still in there, nice and plump.

"You do have a name," Jorlane went on.

The part of my brain that had this information must have been slightly damaged. I searched for it, and then recalled someone shouting it to me while he climbed a fence. How long ago did that happen?

"I'm called Woody."

It's good that people call out your name from time to time; it helps cement who you are.

"Woody," said Jorlane.

"Got anything else that's wet?"

Well, suddenly Cletus turned generous and offered me a tin cupful of what he called his finest Shablee, which tasted a lot like wine as I drank it. When he scuttled over to me, I got a look at his scraggly white beard and ravaged face, a white guy who might not yet have been forty but who could pass for sixty, easy. He said it was only fair to be generous, since he'd sampled some of Archie's codeine pills while I was out, and they'd helped improve his disposition considerably.

(It's so odd, recalling this now. I remembered some things perfectly, like my knapsack, the beating from Vic, coming into the rail yard, how much water I had in the canteen, and other things. But I'd forgotten the Calders, Archie Wetherall, my brother, and almost who I was. This can happen when you have a bad concussion, which is what I was ailing from).

I barely remembered having the pills that Cletus had sampled, but it slowly came to me.

"I'd like one of those," I said. "I got damaged ribs and now a bonked head."

Since there were still a few left in the bottle, he obliged me, and it was then that my eyes adjusted enough in the darkness to see that Cletus had a pile of my stuff strewn around him — my knapsack and clothes and toilet items in a heap.

I didn't argue it just yet, I was too weary and pained and feeling drowsy as the train rumbled along. Instead, we all settled in and calmed down, and as idiotic as these two men were I didn't feel they intended to hurt me. I tasted a little more of the Shablee and got to feeling pleasantly tired and less painful. We had some bits of talk here and there about getting to Winslow, which they said wasn't more than another half hour, based on their experience. They expected a change of trains there, since they'd taken this route a couple times before, so they planned to linger a bit in Winslow with some friends. I looked forward to the stop. I was thirsty again, and missed the sunshine and a view of the outdoors, and believed getting out and about would help clear my head some more and straighten out all the facts of this trip.

¤ ¤ ¤ ¤ ¤

I've gathered up my stuff that Cletus and Jorlane had rifled through. They haven't taken anything, though Cletus showed he was overly fond of my hunting knife since it was so similar to the one he used when he attacked Jorlane last year and cut his face open. They were both drunk at the time of the scrap, so they managed to get over it, and Jorlane forgave him.

There's a cold water tap outside in this train yard, and I've had plenty to drink. I've filled my canteen. I have my medicine, and I remember who Archie is and why, and how kind Lacey Calder was to me. It's late afternoon now, so I take another round of pills to keep my swelling down and stave off infection in my face.

I'm sitting on a stack of railroad ties close to the water tap. The sun burns my face and my arms, and I don't mind. I need a little sting of pain to distract me from the ache in my head and my sore ribs.

I study the backs of my hands, as I've done before in my life, and I know they belong to Woody. A couple of moles, the tiny hairs, the way the veins poke out are familiar to me. If I'd had a little more sense at the time, I would've viewed my face in a window pane somewhere, but maybe I was jumpy about seeing how banged up I was.

It also comes back into focus that I'm on a mission to retrieve my brother, Tick Elmont, from the sands of Malibu Beach, and ferry him back to Ogamesh. He and Jupe came within a fingersnap of being snagged by the law in a blind alley in Albuquerque, and now I know Tick wants no more part of Jupe's crazy adventures, but he's probably too scared by Jupe's zoo-brain to voice his opinion.

Something about Charles Rawlins is playing around in my head, but it's dreamlike and I can't get a good fix on it. I have a sense that he's not going to chase us anymore. I have a very *flimsy* sense that he's still tied up with us in some way that he hasn't explained.

(You may remember that I promised to call him back this particular evening. But at the time, I have forgotten it.)

¤ ¤ ¤ ¤ ¤

While I sat on the railroad ties in the burning sun examining the backs of my hands, I was off by myself, away from the others. They were sitting around a makeshift table, playing cards or rolling dice or something similar.

Except for Jorlane, who was standing behind them with his arms folded. Man, he looked like a giant! He must've been about six-seven or six-eight, and had the biggest chest I've ever seen on a man.

I don't know if they kept him out of the game because he was too dumb, or black, or both. I got the idea he wanted to play, and was disappointed they couldn't fit him in.

Cletus was the noisiest with his sharp laugh and loud whines, but a close second was a chunky woman with snarly gray hair who had a cackle that made my skin goosefleshy. I'd find out later her name was Pixie, and she used to be a roller derby skater, which caused her to lose several of her teeth when they threw her to the floor and whatnot. Now she was a hobo, like the rest of them.

There were two other men that I didn't get a good look at, one pretty old, the other maybe twenty. I was the last one off the box car and on account of my thirst I headed straight for the cold water tap, away from their reunion, so we never had proper introductions.

The next train out, Cletus told me, would be later at night. This yard had four or five strings of cars on different spurs of track, and it was his belief the farthest one away would be the one moving out to California. It looked like it had thirty cars or more, most of them empty hoppers, with a grouping of blue and yellow box cars at the rear. No caboose, though. Jorlane wasn't sure if he wanted to ride any more tonight. I wished he would, because I felt more secure in his company than alone, even if he had less of a brain than Tick.

I must have passed an hour or more sitting there in the sun and drinking cold water when I got dusty. It was a mostly pleasant and thoughtful time, getting my memory back, and I think my body needed the rest – just to sit still for a spell and recover from my beatings.

It might seem odd to you that they showed no interest in me. But it's been my experience that kids are more easily ignored than adults, and typically don't get noticed unless they become a nuisance or speak up. So it was fine with me to be invisible to them, for the time I had. My privacy also allowed me to check the contents of my wallet, not that I didn't trust them. It was gratifying to find all my money safe, down to the last dollar.

But I was more cautious now than a few days earlier, and I believed I should be extra protective of my cash when in the company of people who appeared to have such uncertain values. I carefully plucked out four twenty dollar bills and after I put my wallet back in my hip pocket I snuck them under my butt. Then I took off my sneakers and made a show of dumping dirt and sand out of them. I folded the bills so they got down to matchbook size, and tucked two of them under the foamy insole of each sneaker.

When I'd laced my sneakers back up, they felt a little lumpy but much better than before, in a way.

I must've dozed off because I quickly snapped to attention when I heard a commotion from the group playing their game. I perked up and took a few steps in their direction to see what their fussing was all about, but that was a fool's errand because with a bunch like this there's no rhyme nor reason to their dissatisfactions. The one doing most of the caterwauling was Cletus, who stood up all red-faced with anger and brandishing some kind of stick or rod, I couldn't tell.

She was not! is what I heard Cletus shout, over and over, to the younger of the two strangers.

What I heard is what the younger guy replied.

The younger guy, he couldn't've been more than a couple of years older than me, was lean but muscly, and even as he sat at the table I could tell he would easily outmatch Cletus, who looked like a half-starved weasel.

Was not.

Was too.

Just like a playground. Except on a playground kids normally don't hit you on the side of the head with an iron pipe (that's what it was, not a stick, I could tell from the *clang*) because kids know *instinctively* you could kill somebody that way and they tend to hold back. But Cletus was an adult and had lost such instinct, and he gave a pretty good whaling to the kid's head and sent him sprawling into the greasy dust.

Things moved pretty fast. Pixie and the older guy scooted away from the scene, around the corner of a shed where they poked their heads out to watch. Jorlane didn't move a muscle – which says a lot, considering the muscle he had.

Take that back, Lyle! Cletus stood over him, raised the pipe which was as long as a broomstick, and whaled it down on his back. So Lyle was the kid's name, and the closer I got to him the younger he looked, as well as more likely to suffer severe damage from the drubbing. He was conscious but staggery as he tried to get to his feet, then crumpled down again just as Cletus whacked him a third time around the hips.

A whore is what I heard Lyle croak out, and wouldn't you know it but Cletus went half nuts hearing that, and swung a mighty blow aiming for his head again but missing and getting him on the shoulders. Lyle was face down in the dirt now and not moving much.

I have to tell you, I wouldn't have let a fight like this go on this long if it were up to me, and I kept looking at Jorlane, who could've subdued Cletus with just his pinky. When Jorlane looked back at me, his face said, *leave it be.* This struck me as nonsensical, since a few more whacks would surely end Lyle's life, so I hoofed it over and called to Jorlane –

"You stop this!"

"Nope."

That's when I made a lunge for Cletus and caught one end of the pipe in mid-swing and held on for dear life.

"Not your business, you runt!"

"You're gonna kill him!"

"*Can't* kill 'im! I've tried, but Hell keeps spittin' him back out! Leggo my pipe, and we'll still be friends!"

Well, during our brief conversation, Lyle found some life in him and started to wriggle away. Cletus was wrestling mightily to free up his pipe from my grip, and I have to say he twisted me around in such a way my ribs screamed in pain and I couldn't hang on. I ended up in a stumble near Jorlane's feet.

"Jorlane," I said, "please!"

"Boy should be kilt. He's all devil."

I heard, but didn't see, another *clang* of impact.

I take it back!

The kid was tough and good at reviving, that's for sure, getting out a coherent sentence like that. I managed to scramble around to get another look, and Cletus was acting like he hadn't heard him. He had Lyle face down in the dirt, with a fair amount of blood coming out of him, and now the pipe was wedged under his neck.

Take it back again!

Well, he couldn't take it back again because he was being choked by Cletus pulling up on the pipe, and all you could hear was Lyle's gagging noises. Lyle tried to wrench himself free, but Cletus was kneeling on his back so it wasn't much use. Cletus didn't let up - the more the kid hacked and gagged, the harder he pulled the pipe into his neck. I thought, I've got to break this up, but I also knew with my ribs the way they were I might not be effective at it.

Behind me, Jorlane started to intone a chant of some sort, maybe an old Negro spiritual. I looked up and saw his face bent down as if in prayer and his eyes closed.

The sound from Lyle's throat was awful, and in time it died down to little bits of wheezing that half-turned my stomach. That, plus how the veins stuck out of his neck like ropes, made me feel miserable being part of a human race that could treat people this way.

Cletus was commanding him, *die!*

Pixie and the older man, who had been observing from the corner of a shed, had flown the coop. I don't know where they went and I never saw them again.

Having been on the receiving end of similar kind of hurt from Vic, I had sympathy for what Lyle was going through, and, devil or not, he didn't deserve to die in such a way. I got to my feet and started toward them but Jorlane's huge hand grabbed at my shirt and held me back.

"Let 'im finish it."

"*Hell* I will."

"Boy needs chokin'."

"What that kid ever do to you?"

"Stabbed a baby, that's what he done."

"You *see* it? You see him do that?"

"Din't have to."

I got stuck there for a few seconds, mostly because Jorlane had my shirt in a grip but partly for other reasons. I could see the effort in Cletus's arms and face as he tugged hard on that pipe, and now Lyle's legs were jerking in a kind of spasmodic way. If he was truly a baby-killer, then Jorlane's reasoning had a shred of sense to it, but maybe only in the law of hobos and train yards. In American law, you're not allowed to kill for *any* reason, unless of course you're a jury or the act is in self-defense.

I swear it had been a couple of minutes of Cletus trying to kill Lyle, and the boy was good and unconscious now, but Cletus wasn't taking any chances the way he pulled on that pipe and kept ordering Lyle to *die*. Another minute and he might get his wish.

I told Jorlane, "Okay. You win."

He relaxed his grip on my shirt just enough for me tear loose, leaving half my shirt in his hand, and I made a dash for Cletus and piled right on top of him grabbing him by his hair and beard and ripping as hard as I could. *Man,* did he howl!, but my ripping and tearing didn't immediately have the desired effect of him dropping the pipe. I swear I became like an animal trying to save the devil-kid's life, and you wouldn't believe the cursing that I poured forth at Cletus, and him responding in a similar way. Well, darned if he didn't let go of the pipe long enough to send his elbows back into my ribs, such as they were, with the result that I rolled off him and couldn't catch my breath. All I could do was writhe in pain and watch him go back to work with his weapon.

I told myself, I'm not going to witness a murder. Cletus choked him so hard that Lyle was twitching in a kind of convulsive way and his mouth was getting foamy. I guessed he didn't have much time left.

With everything I had, and it hurt me so much I yelped, I went after Cletus again, going for his head and finding myself on top of him again. I tried pulling his head back and clawing at his face and eyes, and it's as if he'd rather die than let Lyle live, and my hands were now dripping with his blood. It wasn't working the way it should have because the more I clawed at him the harder he seemed to pull on the pipe – as if he got confused that maybe *I* was Lyle magically on top of him – and the only way to end it was to stun him in some fashion. Lacking a rock, I pounded at Cletus' head with my fist as hard as I could, several times over right in the temple, and the final blow did the trick. He went limp on top of Lyle and rolled off to one side, and just to make sure he stayed limp for a bit I jumped on top of him and pounded him twice more on the side of the head.

I'll tell you, I was made *different* by that whole scene. Something important inside me was lost, and I wondered if I'd ever get it back.

I ended up sprawled between two bodies. Catching my breath, stifling the urge to cry. I was spent.

Jorlane's feet went by my eyes. He grabbed Cletus by the hand and dragged him like a sack of laundry across the dirt away from both of us.

I looked over at Lyle's face. It was bloody, but I managed to ascertain that his eyes were closed. I thought this was a good sign, since you see so many dead people in the movies with their eyes wide open. The light was such that I could clearly see the skin at the base of his neck and although it was rubbed raw from the pipe it was flickering with a pulse.

Jorlane shouted out to me –

Shouldna done that

I saw you

Let 'im stay dead.

I ignored him. I thought, if either of them wants revenge on me, I'd be ready to do all the damage I could.

I said to Lyle, "Wake up," but he just lay there in a heap, out cold.

I stood up, feeling kind of dizzy. Jorlane and Cletus were safely far off; Cletus had come to and was rubbing his bloody face, with Jorlane sort of cradling him in his arms. It was more peculiar than I could reckon for those two to be such friends considering how Cletus had attacked him with a knife. Nothing made sense here.

126

I fetched my canteen from the stack of railroad ties where I'd been sitting, went back to Lyle and splashed some water on his head and face. That didn't do it, so I knelt by him and kind of swatted him on the back to see if that would get his lungs working again, and sure enough, after a minute or so, he started to rouse himself up.

He coughed and retched for a bit, but I couldn't blame him.

I was glad he didn't die in front of my eyes.

FOURTEEN

When you save somebody's life who's a complete stranger, it's best to avoid expectations because you're likely to be surprised.

You might end up with a lifelong friendship, or a heap of gifts, or a big check. Or you might get a simple word of thanks and then he goes his separate way. In such a case, you can't predict anything so it's best to forget that the lifesaving ever happened.

When Lyle got steady on his feet he barely noticed me. He rubbed blood from his face and neck, wiped his hands on his jeans, and then massaged his sore throat.

Jorlane was still cradling Cletus and keeping a close eye on both of us.

Lyle took a few steps toward them, stopped, and managed to croak out, "Guess you didn't kill me."

"I *tried!*" Cletus yelped back. "That boy got in the way!"

"Saved you," Jorlane piped in. "You was all but dead, and he stopped it."

Lyle turned back for a second and saw me. I swear, except that he was more muscly than me and had blood on him, it was like seeing my reflection. But he didn't seem so interested in me and he turned back to Cletus.

"Second time you done that to me, Cletus. And the last."

"First time shoulda worked! But Hell didn't want you, it spit you back out!"

"Two's enough. My neck hurts too much."

He took very slow steps over to the table where they'd been gaming. He picked up a gunnysack of stuff, probably his belongings, and went through it.

"Don't care about your *shit*, you devil boy," Cletus yapped at him. "Jus' wanted you *dead!*"

He flung his gunnysack over his shoulder and headed back in my direction with his face lowered to the ground. He hacked and spat a couple of times, then came up right next to me and stopped in his tracks, without so much as a glance at me.

"Don't care if I died. It was no favor to me."

And he kept on walking.

Along the tracks, headed east.

I was buffaloed. I'd saved his life and it was no favor to him – he was that disrespectful of living and breathing. Curiosity almost took hold of me and sent me running after him to find out why life seemed so worthless to him, but I had to snap the temptation out my head.

Instead, I watched him shrink to the size of a dot on the horizon.

You hurt me! Cletus cried.

I went back to my stuff sitting on the stack of railroad ties. I took a long drink of water at the tap, and splashed water on my face to get rid of the dirt and other people's blood. Then I ripped the gauze bandage off my face and threw it in the dust.

My eye's half-clawed out! shouted Cletus.

I threw my knapsack on my back, hoisted up the duffel over my right shoulder, and without laying my eyes on either of those two crazy sons of bitches I moseyed around the corner of the shed and away from the yard and headed for a hillside dotted with trailers, which must have been part of the town of Winslow.

☒ ☒ ☒ ☒ ☒

I'd have a story or two to tell Tick and Jupe, that's for sure. If I ever found them. And I judged they'd have one or two of their own to tell me.

Yeah, I guess I grew up a bit, I guess you did too.

It might start like that, and then we'd have to explain how.

Hit a man with my fist till I knocked him out.

Jupe and I robbed this rich lady...

Met two hobos who coulda passed for you and Jupe, thirty years from now, if you'd stayed on the road.

I had to shake out those voices, since neither of them was on the mark about growing up, more like growing *down,* like how people in the Dark Ages treated each other.

Ogamesh was just four days in my past and it seemed like a month or more.

I was sitting in the bed of a Ford pickup cruising along the interstate having these thoughts, watching the eastern horizon drift away from me. When the guy stopped to pick me up, he took one look at me and asked, very polite, if I'd mind riding in the bed since he had an abnormal fear of infections *just like Howard Hughes,* he confessed, though I didn't know much about Howard Hughes. It was probably my nasty looking face that scared him off, or maybe my smell, but either way I was glad for the ride and I didn't mind having solitude in back. It was more pleasant than just solitude; there was the warm wind, the fragrance of the desert plains, and a great view of northern Arizona. I felt calmed by the ride, and sighed relief to be putting miles between me and those crazy railriding bums back in Winslow.

The guy dumped me off at his exit near Flagstaff. I knew as well as him that it's illegal to hitchhike on interstates, but I didn't care and hoofed it back up the ramp to the edge of the pavement. Sundown or not, I imagined I looked pathetic enough to get fetched up by a girl like Lacey, riding in her boyfriend's truck.

I got a ride pretty fast. It was a woman in her forties with dyed blonde hair and sparkly blue lipstick, driving a fancy Mercedes with California plates, and I thought, *man, I'm in luck!* but we hadn't gone more than two miles before I started to have my doubts.

"Oh, you poor kid! Look at you!"

"Yes, ma'am, I believe I tried too hard to defend my property, he was too much for me, and —"

"You should have that attended to."

She was referring to my face, which you probably guessed.

"Well, it *has* been attended to, at a clinic, and it's healing up as it should, it just takes time."

"I own a motel now, but I used to be a nurse and I can tell you, my young friend, that cut needs to be restitched."

Well, the car had those sun visors with a mirror on the other side, and I flipped it open to get a better look at myself. She had a point; during the various tussles back in the train yard the cut had torn open a bit and was starting to ooze.

"Yes, ma'am, so it looks. Where's your motel at?"

I was still thinking, I can't believe my luck, I'd get some free nursing and maybe a free bed for the night.

"Right over the line, in Needles."

She added that Needles was a small desert town, but world-renowned as a waystation for truckers and travelers coming into California, or leaving it, and her motel was one of the more popular ones, called the E-Z Rest.

She patted my leg and with a rubbery-lipped smile told me, "I'll fix you up."

"Well, I'm grateful."

She patted my leg again and gave it a squeeze.

"My names' Sadie."

"I'm Woody."

"I can tell you have a healthy body and you'll heal up good."

And she squeezed me again, a little longer this time, and that's when I started to have my doubts about her, because of her flirting.

"Well, it's *been* healthy, though I confess it's been tested –"

"And a bath, too. You got kind of a locker room aroma to you, no offense."

Another squeeze, and I wriggled my left leg away from her.

"Oh, sorry! Is that tender there?"

"Everything's tender, ma'am."

"Sadie."

"Sadie, I meant."

"Give you a bath and clean you up. I can tell, you're a fine boy, and not from here."

"No ma'am, Georgia. On my way to Los Angeles. Meet my brother." Well, these and other pleasantries continued as we drove, but her flirting kept up in a kind of sneaky way with questions about my girlfriend or girlfriends and inquiries into how she or they showed their affection, and it wasn't more than a half hour or so before I entered a quandary if it would be best to part company and take my chances with another ride.

"When you're my age," she said, "you learn all kinds of ways to express your tenderness. Every last one of my husbands will attest to it."

I'd be giving up free nursing, a free bed, and probably a free dinner to boot, and I was sorely challenged to make the right decision.

I said something safe, like, "I'm glad they each had an opportunity to know you."

"You'd benefit from a massage," she said. "I'm very good at it."

"No, Sadie, I'm grateful, but I don't want a massage, I'm too sore for it."

"It would be very gentle."

Everybody wants something that they hide. I hated being pressured like this and wrestling with the quandary of it. I'd compromised myself *plenty* in the last week or so, and felt I'd run out of room for more of it. Hasn't that happened to you, when you say okay, that's enough, that's all? I know I'm not the only one.

"Ma'am, you may have some thoughts." It was stuttery getting it out. "About me. Maybe not the right kind of thoughts. For me. I'm from Georgia, and I'm more traditional than some."

That pretty much ended it. She offered up a squinty grimace and a bit of her advice.

"You're just a pup. You'll have your day, but you're not ready."

I didn't reply but mentioned, "The next exit will be fine."

In a few minutes I was standing at the side of the highway again with the sun just a sliver of red over some distant brown hills.

☒ ☒ ☒ ☒ ☒

Go figure late June in Arizona. When the sun disappears it starts feeling downright wintery in the desert and even the sunburn you got during the day turns cold on your skin. I threw off the duffel to see if by any dumb luck Lacey had slipped in a sweater or long sleeve shirt in the bag, and while I was rummaging through it I heard someone slow down and pull over about a hundred feet past me. It was another pickup and I thought, *damn*, it's too cold to ride in the bed, if that's where he wants me.

I couldn't see who it was through the back window, because it was darkly tinted, but whoever it was acted with patience while I reassembled the duffel bag, gathered up my stuff, and trotted down the breakdown lane.

When I got to the door I looked in and couldn't believe it.

"Hey Lyle."

He gave a little nod of his head at me. "Hop in."

As little as I knew him, he struck me as one of the strangest and darkest-minded kids I'd ever meet, not caring if he lived or died and maybe a baby murderer to boot, so I stood there giving his offer a few seconds of thought.

"C'mon – hop *in*."

"Don't want to travel alone? 'Cause I can get another ride if you want."

"*Damn*, I need the company, and I know you're an okay sort, so get *in*."

I got in. Of all the choices I've made in my life, this was the riskiest, and it would lead to the kind of adventure I hoped never to repeat, or wish on anyone else. I'll do my best to tell it the way it happened, though little bits of it may have been crushed by forgetfulness, the sort of forgetfulness your mind forces on you when it's needed.

First, as we drove off, I got a good look at the right side of his face which Cletus had whacked with the pipe. It was pretty swollen and purply, and his hair, which was black like mine, was matted with dried blood. I also believed his ear had been flattened by the blow, the way it looked.

Also, when he talked, his voice was thick and raspy, as if his vocal chords had taken a beating (which of course they had, and pretty bruised, too). From time to time he sipped some pop from a can, as if this might help.

"How far you going?" he asked.

I didn't hesitate. "The Pacific."

He kind of wagged his head. "I could do that."

"Where *were* you going?"

"Desert. Somewhere. Ocean might be better."

I had my bags at my feet. There wasn't much on the seat except some cigarettes, matches, and a screwdriver. I was wondering why a kid would socialize with railriding hobos if he owned a fairly new truck like this; it didn't make sense to me. So I asked him,

"*Dang*, you got a ride like this and you hang out with hobos."

"Not my truck, exactly."

I held onto my thoughts.

"Hippie and his girlfriend left it for me back in Winslow. They went into the movies. So we got maybe another hour before the movie ends and they come out and see it's gone. You got money?"

I was thinking, *he's a truck thief* and maybe desperate because of it.

"A little," I said.

"Enough for gas?"

"Plenty for gas," I said, wishing I hadn't.

"Enough for food?"

"Might be."

"Good."

"What happens when they see it missing?"

"Not much. We'll be in California, or close. We're good, so long as I don't get stopped."

True enough, he was driving pretty close to the speed limit, with cars and trucks and semis passing him by.

"If we do get stopped," he said, "you'll have to be my hostage."

He wasn't kidding. I just stared straight ahead at the orange glow above the hills of Arizona, cursing myself for getting in the truck.

"Sorry about that," he added.

I just shook my head. I wasn't *scared,* as such, but I was plenty unsettled in spite of my calmness, and quite angry about it.

"How old are you?" he said. "Maybe fifteen."

"Sixteen."

"Well, that's one thing we got in common. Not much else, though."

"You don't know me."

"Bet I do."

"Can't be your hostage, Lyle. I got important stuff to do, and a tight schedule."

"Well, I'll be! You think you got a choice? You know how fast, with *one* hand, because the other's on the steering wheel – you know how fast – what's your name, anyway?"

"Woody."

He picked up the screwdriver and waved it at my face.

"Okay, you know how fast I could render you lifeless? *Woody?* I don't even have to look at you to know where your carotid artery is, and my right hand would flash out so fast to your neck you wouldn't see it coming, and maybe I also have considerable experience at it, which makes it even more deadly. You'd spurt blood and die, unless I put direct pressure on it."

I thought, maybe right now I could pop him with my fist right in his temple where it's bruised and swollen, and we'd career off the road and be killed unless I could wrestle the steering wheel away from him. But it felt far too much like a scene from a movie, and too risky to work.

"Just letting you know. You don't have a choice about being a hostage."

He calmed a bit, and put the screwdriver back on the seat right next to him. Then he looked over at me, as if to check how scared I was.

"Shit, look at you, you're already banged up. What happened?"

"Hit by a bull."

"Fuck you. What happened."

"Got ambushed by a drifter. He got shot and killed, sometime later."

He processed it for a second. "I been shot at. Never hit."

This didn't surprise me, but I didn't say anything.

"Hurts quite a bit," he said after some silence while he drove. True, he was wincing often when he spoke.

"Which part?"

"Head, neck, shoulder, you name it. Cletus had no business. 'Cause I called his old lady friend a whore."

I told him, "I got pills for pain."

"Gimme the pills."

I opened up my knapsack and pulled out the pain pills. I took out two and handed them over. There were just a few left, but I didn't care to take them any more, the way they made me feel.

"That's it?"

"That's it unless you want to start driving drunk and get everybody's attention, like the law."

He popped them down with a swig of pop.

"If I do have to kill you, I'm gonna apologize right now for doing it. But I don't think I'll have to."

I had just an ounce of belief that his talk was worse than his bite, so I ventured at him,

"I'm relieved to hear that, Lyle."

"I'll try not to. All I can say."

"Not often," I replied, "someone who saves your life gets killed by the same guy, on purpose."

135

"Well, I told you, you did me no favor."

"Fine. Next time Cletus chokes you, I'll walk away and have a cheese sandwich and he can finish it."

"You do that."

"You're the devil anyway. Stabbed a baby. Deserve to die. Jorlane said it."

"Jorlane."

"That's what he said. I don't care if it's true or not at this point."

"Jorlane said that about me."

"He did."

Well, darned if Lyle didn't turn thoughtful for quite a while and consider these words in silence. In a way, I was impressed. In time, he said,

"If I ever killed a baby, I don't recall it."

Well, slowly you learn. As long as you're not being held hostage and wrapped up in fear, you're still able to be educated.

"Most people would remember it," I suggested.

It seemed a struggle for him, digging into his memory.

"You recall *telling* them you were a baby stabber?"

"Not exactly. Knowing me, it could be true."

"Well, Lyle," I said, "I believe your brain's popped a few vessels and might be ailing."

He slammed the steering wheel with his fist. "Don't *give* me that shit!"

I let him gather himself together after his outburst before venturing any more conversation, witty or not. Anger is best when it's in a single short burst, and the best way to keep it short, I learned in my dealings with Zee, is not to feed it.

I wondered if his memory problems were lifelong, or more recent, as a result of being choked – didn't he say it happened twice? I imagine you could injure your brain that way. Still, Lyle's angry outburst sounded like it came from further back in time and from longer experience.

We said almost nothing for several miles, and then it was time to exit the highway and get some gas. The gas stop went smoothly. Without showing him the contents of my wallet, I gave him a twenty for about twelve dollars worth of gas. After he paid, I saw him pocket the change. We drove across parking lots to a convenience store. He parked, went inside, bought a bag of sandwiches and two cans of Coke, and came back.

"Half is for you."

Go figure: I have lunch with a mental case, and now I'm having supper with a mental case. In between, I get knocked unconscious by a bottle, save a kid's case's life, get flirted with by a bleached-blonde middle-aged woman, and then threatened with death by the same kid whose life I saved.

When he went into the gas station to pay, I could have made a break for it. I could have made a break for it when he went into the convenience store. I *should* have, in retrospect – there was tons of room to run into the desert in the dark and be safe from him for an hour or so. He'd drive off in frustration, and I'd be free to hitch a ride into the nearest town and find a bed for the night and never see him again. It's so odd, looking back on this now, that I chose to stay with him, based on the things he said about using me as a hostage. My best guess is that I was too darn *curious* about why he was the way he was, and I needed to probe a little to find out. The second reason was that he looked so much like me – except he was more wiry and strong – that I couldn't quite convince myself to walk away from the mirror. I needed to stick around and understand why I felt that way, that we were almost like kin when, of course, we weren't.

Sometimes I just can't figure myself.

FIFTEEN

We drove on through the dark toward California. Now and then I'd see him jerk his head around or even slap himself on the chin to stay alert. The pain pills do make you tired, no question.

It turns out the cigarettes on the seat belonged to the hippie, not Lyle, but I suggested he have one as a way of staying awake. He said he almost never smoked but he'd try it this time, just to humor me. Inhaling, he coughed a bit, but then got used to it.

For sure the truck had been reported stolen by now, and we'd have to be extra careful.

Off and on over the next few hours I gave him a good accounting of my journey and the reasons for it. I tried to make it as interesting as I could, and varied the tone in my voice as a way to keep him from dozing off.

In return, he told me little things about his life so far. But they were just bits of things, and scrambled, so I had to fit them together like puzzle pieces.

He said, for instance,

"Stupid guy – the hippie – had one of those magnetized key cases, right under the rocker panel by his door. You know, extra key, in case you get locked out. Never ever do that. Always put it in somewhere in back. At one of my foster homes I learned that. Stole one of the older kids' car, got as far as Idaho."

And later,

"Couldn't keep me in the kid joint."

And,

"Worked in a gravel pit, shoveling, got strong from it. They fired me when I hit a guy with a shovel, he kept calling me names."

Later,

"He knocked me cold. Spent a week in the hospital, couldn't remember my name."

And,

"Railriding's free. Don't have to keep robbing people to get someplace. But you meet crazies like Cletus. Twice was enough, my neck won't take it. My last name's McLean, I should have family somewhere but I don't think about it. I make up stories sometimes."

His brain might have been damaged, but it kept firing off rounds from different places, so I suspected it was agile, in its own way.

"You write stories?" I asked.

"No, I tell them. Can't write them. Stories – I mean like *lies.* Maybe stabbing the baby was one of those stories. I don't know any babies. How much money you got?"

He asked that before.

"Enough for gas and some food."

"No, I mean, how much do you have in your wallet? The *amount.*"

"I need to keep it, Lyle, to save my brother and get him home."

"I'm not asking what you need."

"You gonna rob me?"

"*Look,* I'd rather not, but if I know what you got in your wallet I can anticipate whether I need to rob you. I'm trying to say it simple. How much?"

I wasn't going to win this one, partly because of his peculiar logic. "Fair amount over a hundred."

It's so odd, because I only had about seventy in my wallet, and eighty tucked into my sneakers. Why did my mind put all the money back in my wallet?

"How much over?"

"Closer to one fifty. I'll share some of it –"

"No, don't make any offers about sharing. One fifty, that's good, we might get a motel. Did you ever think about finding your father?"

Jumpy brain! "Oh, sometimes. Not sure I'd like him, if he gave us up so easy."

"What's his name?"

"Milton Clayne. No idea –"

"Spell it."

I spelled it for him.

"If I find him, and I just *might,* you got any messages?"

"You can just tell him we still live in Ogamesh and we're okay."

"Okay, Woody, I'll pass that on. Still in Ogamesh, still okay. Genius off a leash, I'll say."

I'd never heard that phrase before, but it sounded sarcastic enough to ignore.

Sweeping into our headlights now were signs for Needles, the first town in California, just a few miles ahead. Of course that's where Sadie had her motel, the E-Z Rest, but my hope was we'd find some other place where I wasn't known.

When we got to Needles we drove through town looking for the cheapest place. He saw the E-Z Rest sign with its prices and said,

"Cheap."

"Bet there's cheaper," I offered.

"You got money, you can afford it."

"Let's keep looking."

Well, darned if he didn't take my advice, which was a first! I chalked it up as a small success and hoped for more of the same.

"I was here once before but I can't recall it," he said.

"It might come back."

"It was unpleasant, that's my feeling."

Down the road a few blocks we found a raggedy looking motel called Rancho 66, with a Vacancy sign, and it advertised free coffee and TV, which didn't seem very special, but the rates were the best yet for a single room. It had already crossed my mind that we would need a room with two beds, which would cost a little more but be worth it.

It was almost ten o'clock, according to the clock I saw through the window of the motel office. An old bald guy was fiddling with something behind the counter.

Lyle turned the engine off and said, "You go in, you got the wallet."

"Okay."

"And you're not as ugly as I am right now."

True, but I was ugly enough with the lump on my head and my face wound, where some of the skin had torn through the stitches. I hadn't rebandaged it since the fight in the train yard, and I probably should have.

I dabbed at it with a corner of my shirt. It looked to be dry, no more oozing.

Lyle was nearly asleep where he sat at the wheel. Just like that.

I got out, straightened out my clothes, and went into the office. The door set off a jingling bell, and when the old guy looked up at me he seemed mostly disgusted by what he saw.

"Yes?"

"Yes sir, I apologize for my appearance, but we'd like a room with two beds for the night, if they're available."

Before answering, he paused to light a cigarette while he looked me over. The first match went out, so he tried again and eventually got it going.

"One room left, and it's a single." He had a scratchy voice, probably from the smoking. "Eighteen plus tax. It's out behind the laundry room."

The sign said twelve dollars for a single, so I was surprised.

"There are no twelve dollar rooms?"

"It's high season now, with tourists. Who's with you?"

"My friend."

He seemed to like me less and less with every word. "Is she female?"

"No sir, a boy. And we were hoping for two beds, or a very wide single bed."

He puffed hard on the cigarette.

"Son, it's a double bed, so if you're good friends you won't mind, and it's all we got so you can try some other place, or you can take it for eighteen dollars."

"Yes sir, we'll take it."

"And I'd appreciate if you washed up before going to bed, because of the clean sheets."

Now I have to confess that at my age I'd never rented a motel room before, and actually had only been in one once, a weekend where Zee took Tick and me to Tybee Island near Savannah when we were smaller. So I didn't know how the rules worked.

I got my wallet out and took out a twenty. "Yes sir, we will."

"Son, if it's cash, I need a fifty dollar deposit for the room and the phone."

This also surprised me, and I had to think it through. He didn't let me hesitate very long, and explained it was for damages if we caused any, and for long distance phone calls if we made any. The rules came from experience, he said, because of truckers and others who skipped out first thing in the morning without tallying up their phone calls and damages.

I gave him all the money he asked for, which left two dollars in my wallet because of the eighty dollars folded up in my sneakers.

He asked me to fill out a little form for my name and address. I became Archie Wetherall once again, from Alabama, with a fake phone number. There was a place for "vehicle" and "license plate."

"I forget the tag number," I said.

"Don't need it. I see your truck, I know it's you."

As I left with the room key, his last words to me were a strong encouragement to wash.

✕ ✕ ✕ ✕ ✕

The room behind the laundry room was a dump, and when Lyle woke up enough to make sense of it he vowed some sort of revenge against the thieving motel clerk. I tried to calm him, saying I didn't care so much for its appearance as long as we had a bed for the night.

Which was a problem, because it wasn't a double, it was a *single* – what they call a twin (which never made sense to me) – and too small for the both of us.

"I don't sleep with guys," he said, and I fully agreed with him. The one exception was Tick. He would sometimes crawl over to my bed and get in, but he was my brother and he helped warm it up nicely. That was years ago when he was small and didn't know better.

"Flip you for it," Lyle said, taking a coin from his pocket. He flipped, I called tails, and when he looked at the coin on the back of his hand he said, "you get the bed."

I never saw whether it was heads or tails; I had to take his word for it.

He found an extra blanket and cover in the closet, and laid them out next to the bed. I offered clothes from Alvin's duffel for a makeshift pillow, and he took several and tied them into a lump. From his gunnysack he pulled out a pint bottle of whiskey, brand new, uncapped it, and took a long swig. With his head thrown back, I had a good look at his throat and the purple bruising of it, and I couldn't help but shudder.

"Booze and pain pills don't mix," I told him.

He said nothing but handed the bottle to me.

"Just a sip," I replied. I had one, and passed it back.

"Pint won't hurt," he said.

"Well, I believe you're wrong about that. You'll be out like a light and I don't want to revive you again, twice in a day."

He drank about half the bottle and set it down.

I grabbed it and had two more sips.

"I *am* tired," he said, starting to lie down and get comfortable.

"Before you sleep, you should wash that wound on your head."

"*Damn*, you're like a nanny."

"If you want it to heal. I gotta wash mine, you should do the same. I got ointment for it, too."

"Gimme the bottle."

"No." I had a couple of good slugs so it was almost gone. Yes it stung, but it was worth it.

"Damn you, anyway."

"Go wash yourself, Lyle."

I felt I was talking to Tick. He wrangled about it for a bit because he'd gotten so comfortable curled up on the floor. I felt I had to lay it on a little thicker to make a stronger impression.

"Of course, you don't care about dying, the way you live. Or so you *said*. Sure, shoot me or choke me, it'll be over soon enough. But with that wound, the infection will slowly spread and you'll be delirious with fever, and someone will discover you and haul you over his shoulder into the emergency room, and they *will* revive you *but*. And here's the 'but.' They will have to cut off the infected flesh from your face because it will be *necrotic*. That means, essentially like gangrene. They will save your life, but they'll kick you out on the street too ugly even for the circus, and you'll never have a girlfriend. So suicide will be your only hope."

He hoisted himself up and went into the bathroom. In a few seconds I heard the shower running.

It *was* like talking to Tick, and it did bring the nanny out in me, if that's what it was. He was so tough he was immortal – unless someone killed him. A lot of kids my age act like that, and it shows what kind of sense they have.

I took out my pills from my knapsack, the ointment, and some bandaging. I took just one antibiotic pill, skipping the one for inflammation. *By the clock*, Lacey's Mom had ordered me last night, and so far I'd been pretty much on schedule, every four hours. I tried to swallow it without liquid, but it wasn't working, so I downed it with the last inch of whiskey.

When Lyle was done, he came out with just his jeans on and I could see a lot of bruising on his upper arm and shoulder, but his face looked much better. He sat down on the bed and pulled the hair away from the skin above the ear to show me.

"That's the cut."

It was nasty enough, and mangled, so even in a hospital it would have been hard to stitch.

I said, "I got antibiotic ointment for it. It's not infected, from what I can see, but this'll help."

"Put it on then."

It was tricky, because the wound was mostly open, but I did it as gently as I could. In the bag of bandaging stuff I found a couple of butterfly bandages that actually help pull the wound together and keep it closed. Lyle could have one of these, and I could use the other for my own cut.

"You should shave the hair away," I said.

"I'm not shaving my hair away."

"It should attach to skin, not hair."

"I said no."

"Well you should, but I'm not going to argue it."

I took the plastic backing off the butterfly bandage and stuck one half of it to as much skin as I could get to above the wound. Then I had to try to squeeze the wound closed before attaching the other half.

"This might hurt a bit," I said.

"Just put it on."

I pressed the skin above his ear gently upward, readied the other flap of the bandage, then squeezed it up more forcefully as I stuck it to his skin and rubbed it in to make it stay. He winced, but didn't yelp. My only concern was that the ointment had greased his skin a bit, and the

144

bandage might not stick as it should. But for the moment it was holding fine.

"How is it?" he asked.

"Good enough. That bandage should be changed once a day so we should get more tomorrow."

I went into the bathroom to attend to myself, starting with a long hot shower. When I was done, I washed out the cut, dabbed on some ointment, and bandaged myself the same way. I felt happy, in an odd kind of way that could have been whiskey-related, and said to myself in the mirror –

"Yep. Maybe a doctor. Or a male nurse."

I tell you all this in some detail because I've never forgotten it, in spite of what happened later. It felt good to take care of Lyle's wound, which he never would have done for himself. And it felt especially good that his personality seemed to be moderating from its homicidal, hostage-taking self into someone much more human, who felt pain and loneliness and doubt as much as anyone else on this earth.

When I came out he was sitting on the bed with his back toward me, and with the bathroom light shining on him I could see the skin very clearly.

His back was scarred up with old wounds, and peppered with a dozen or more brown circles, like buckshot wounds. But I knew they weren't from buckshot, they were something else.

"*Boy*, you've had a time, I guess."

"What."

"Marks on your back. Looks like cigarette burns or something."

"As a kid, yeah."

He said nothing more for awhile and soon got into his bedding. I stripped off one blanket from the bed and gave it to him, turned off the bathroom light, and then crawled into the sheets.

"My mom," he said.

I lay there for a minute considering it. If I were a doctor or a nurse, I would need to confront such things, and I wondered if I could handle it properly. In time, I turned off the bedside lamp. I felt a little guilty getting the bed, but I doubted I could argue it with him since he was the one who called the coin toss.

"She told me, my name meant 'island.' Guess it fits, all right."

This came from nowhere, and I wasn't sure how to pursue it.

"Maybe it does," I said, and then added, "Have a good night," which is exactly how I addressed Tick before turning the lamp off in our bedroom.

And, wouldn't you know, that's when Lyle started to jabber like a dam bursting, and it must have gone on for about an hour in the dark until sleep overtook me. I cannot relate everything he said because it was just as jumpy and scrambled as when he talked to me in the truck, but there were several highlights that I can't forget. One was his recollection of the baby.

He was with a *good* foster family when he was about six or seven, and was becoming attached to the parents when a baby arrived at the house and it was determined that Lyle would have to be the one to move on. Alone in the room with the baby while it slept, he stood over it for awhile with a knife and gave considerable thought to stabbing it through the back, not caring if he went to jail for the rest of his life. It wasn't sensible, in that either way he'd be forced out of the family's home, but it was vengeful, which felt right to him.

But he never stabbed it. He decided in the most simple way it would not be fair to the baby.

And yet, as the years rolled on and he went from one place to the next, he became confused about whether he had stabbed it or not. If he was drunk enough, he would admit to it and gussy the story up so much it could only be the truth. Days later, he'd realize it wasn't true. On many other days, like today, he'd have no remembrance of any baby, anywhere.

He thinks his memory problems started when he was in the hospital after getting knocked out by the guy in the gravel pit, which was two years ago when he was fourteen. But it might also have kicked in from the cigarette burns from his mother, or possibly the time with the flying saucer.

Well, since I've never seen one I don't have much attitude about flying saucers, for or against, but my ears perked up anyway and I paid close attention.

He was ten, he figured, and living with a family who were not too harsh and had taken the whole foster gang camping at a lake. Before going to bed, the foster father had told them a campfire story about a

146

small, very gentle grizzly bear that lived in the area, and loved to tease children by sneaking up behind them and licking them on their napes. The bear was so kind he glowed with a bright warm light in the woods, like a full halo around his body. The children would try to chase him, and he'd lead them deeper into the woods, playing hide and seek behind trees, and throwing hard candy at them while he laughed. If the bear's father showed up, who was a full-sized and usually mean grizzly, the little bear would safely herd the children back to their camps or their homes and stand guard over them until the mean father went away. Lyle said it was a fairly dumb story, because it seemed to have no point, but if you're just ten you get caught up in it, especially the candy part.

This is where he paused and asked for another pain pill. I turned the light on and fetched him one, and an inflammation one too, and he swallowed them down without water. It was almost four hours later, so I figured it was safe, in spite of the whiskey.

He continued with the story. He slept in his bag but woke up awhile later because of a glowing in the woods. *Oh,* it's the gentle grizzly, he thought, and he decided to go have a look. Well, he moved through the woods barefoot toward the light figuring he'd be completely doused with hard candy, but he came to a big clearing and instead of the bear saw a large round ball of bright light, about the size of a house. Not exactly round, more blimp shaped, and gently glowing. It was confusing to see this instead of the little bear, but it was intriguing, too, so he stayed and watched it for awhile, and the next thing he knows it's day-light and his foster father is standing over him in the clearing cursing him to beat the band. The next day, he had nosebleeds over and over, and he read somewhere that nosebleeds can come from an experience like this.

When he stopped the story, I asked, "Sure it wasn't a dream?"

"I have other dreams. Not like that one."

Sure enough, he had plenty of dreams through the night, after the medicine wore off. Shouting, groaning, crying, over and over, so much so that I thought several times of rousting him out. But it's better to let sleeping dogs lie, as they say, so I left him alone.

SIXTEEN

I can sleep through noise and trains rumbling through and all other kinds of commotion, but I can't sleep through light. And darned if we hadn't left about a two inch crack in the window curtains for the rising sun to blast me square in the face where I slept. The sun in the desert does a lot more than shine – it *stings*, it's so bright.

I rolled over to get out of the shaft of light, and cracked my eyes open just enough to see him all dressed and sitting at the little table with two plastic cups of coffee.

"I forgot to back the truck in last night," he said.

I wasn't sure what his meaning was but I started to wake up fast.

"There's no tag on the front, just the back."

I was beginning to understand.

"Only if they're looking for it, but why take the chance. Have some coffee."

Both my tongue and my brain felt furry, most likely from the whiskey and being partly dehydrated. I went into the bathroom to pee and splash water all over my face, then drank a couple of glassfuls of water which, even after I ran the tap for awhile, was warm and chemical-tasting. When I came out, he said,

"I make mistakes like that and I pay for them. Back the truck in, people don't see the plate."

"No one's bangin' on the door."

"Yeah, but we gotta move. Get your fifty dollars back. Coffee. Sugar if you want it."

I stirred in a couple of sugar packets and had a few sips. It was disgusting coffee, more like tea. I took my pill with it, then had a pretty long look at his face as my eyes started to clear up.

"You're better," I said. He was still plenty purple, but the swelling had died down a bit and the bandage was holding on.

"I needed the sleep."

"Want a pain pill?"

He shook his head. "Drink up."

I pretty much drained the coffee, and then told him what was just occurring to me.

"I think we should ditch the truck. Then hitch."

He frowned at this. "Sure, we look like a couple of sweet kids, we'd get a ride fast."

"Safer, though."

"Two hundred fifty miles to L.A. Worth the risk."

I really needed more coffee to get my brain working right, but I was reluctant to go back to the motel office and deal with that clerk again, if that's where they had the coffee. I decided to let my brain wake up at its own speed, but it was challenging.

"You're coming, right?" he asked.

"Look," I started. "This is kind of nuts. We don't *have* to have the law after us, with me becoming a hostage. I'm thinking —" and I was, "— it's so easy to do things right and start over, do you see?"

From his cocked head and squint, I don't think he did.

"More coffee," he said, getting up.

"Yes, more coffee would be good."

He headed out the door and closed it behind him, giving me time to think. *You're coming, right?* was an offer of freedom, taking me aback enough so I had no good answer for it. If I said no, he'd probably take all the deposit money and hightail it in the truck and for sure get caught somewhere and expect to die from the police, rather than go to jail. If I said yes, we'd have a better chance because I had a clearer brain than him and could act as his hostage, if it came to that. With me along, our decisions would likely be more intelligent.

What it came down to was something altogether different. And when he returned with two more cups of so-called coffee, I laid it on him.

"I want you to consider something, a new idea."

"What."

"Come live in Ogamesh. Start new. It's a good small town. Good people. We've got a spare room in the house — Aunt Zee's old room. The weather is great, there's plenty of jobs, a good school if you want it. We'd be good company for you, my brother and I."

He was chewing on it while he had his coffee, and I started to picture all of us together in the same house. There would be some rowdy moments, for sure, but I had a decent understanding of him now and could be a help to him during his bad moments.

"Where is it?"

"South of Macon, south of Atlanta. It's cotton and peanuts, pine trees, pecan groves, gardenias everywhere, a great river for swimming. It's beautiful, smells great, and has great thunderstorms."

Boy, he actually smiled! I'd never seen it before.

Thunderstorms, he muttered, and wagged his head.

"If you lived there," I went on, "you could ante up a little money for rent and food, but it wouldn't be too much. There's farm work, lumber mills, auto mechanic work, all kinds of stuff."

His eyes were just boring right into me. "You *know* me. I don't get it."

"It's like –" and damned if I didn't choke up a little on it – "I could use a second brother." I coughed away the phlegm. "Tick – he's a lot of work and I guess I love him but sometimes he's more than I can handle. Of course he'd be at St. Anselm's mostly, for a few months to come."

He kept staring at me, and he had those kind of eyes that seem to see everything.

"Maybe your nightmares would ease, if you had a home like that."

Again, I got phlegmy and needed to cough it away.

"You had a noisy night," I added.

"Woody Clayne," he said from nowhere. "A brother who knows a word like 'necrotic.'"

"No, it's not Clayne, it's Elmont, my mother's name."

"Woody Elmont."

"Right."

"Okay, then, let's ditch the truck."

"Yes."

I just felt enormously light, a helium balloon in my body.

"You need to fetch your brother."

"Yes, I have to keep going."

"So I'll head east," he said.

Wow, he was agreeing to it, outlandish as it was.

"Good. And I've got more money – the deposit, but also eighty in my sneakers, and we can split it down the middle."

"In your sneakers."

"With Cletus and Jorlane, I didn't trust them."

I felt lighter and lighter. I wanted to hug him, or anybody else that was around. I got one sneaker and took out the forty dollars under the insole. "Yes. You take Interstate 40 to Little Rock, then angle southeast. It may take me a few days to find Tick, and a few days to get back. You need to give me a couple of weeks at the most." I told him about Natalie's family, where they'd most likely take him in, and Trey Winkler, who would *certainly* take him in, but held off about Charles Rawlins because he was a lawman and had done nothing lately but confuse me. I gave him these names because I wasn't sure Tychander and Zee would understand enough to be hospitable, even if I called them and laid it out for them.

I gave him the forty bucks and he stuck it in his pocket. I never saw if he had a wallet somewhere, or a driver's license, or anything like that.

For all of the wonderful things I said about Ogamesh and its people, he said he would definitely head east *towards* it but would keep giving it thought along the way. He'd spent so much of his last few years running off from one place to the next it would be a new experience for him to settle in somewhere.

Fine. At least the invitation had been extended.

We started packing up. We'd get the deposit money back, split it two ways, then drive the truck to a busy parking lot somewhere and head out to the highway to hitch in opposite directions.

What I didn't consider right away was Lyle's chances of making it to Ogamesh in one piece. There were many miles between here and there, and the way his brain was ailing he could pop off at any time.

✡ ✡ ✡ ✡ ✡

I wonder, looking back, how much he indulged himself in storytelling with me. A really good liar can fool you almost all the time. In the truck he called himself a liar, but then those who lie most of the time can lie when they confess to being liars. Psychologists might make sense of it – I can't. Maybe there's a need to beat yourself over the head when there's not the usual crowd around you to do it for you. From cigarette burns to iron pipes, it seemed people were waiting in line.

I judged he was being straight with me, possibly even with the flying saucer story. He might lie to get money or food, but not about a walk in the woods to find a glowing grizzly cub strewing hard candy.

Cigarette burns and other scars don't lie, either. And my heart wasn't lying to me when I understood the kinship I felt with him, a McLean and a Clayne.

When we packed up the room, we were brothers.

We left it nice and clean, even neatening up the bed and taking out the trash, most of which was from the people before us. I gave him my remaining pain pills, anti-inflammatory pills, ointment, and some bandaging; I also threw in some of Alvin's tee shirts.

From what I'd seen of his gunnysack, Lyle didn't have a knife. With just two hundred and fifty miles between Needles and the Pacific, I was optimistic I would get to Malibu today, and therefore wouldn't need mine. He had much farther to go, and might need to camp a few nights, so I laid it on the bed for him and said, "You take this."

"You don't want it."

"Only when you get back to Ogamesh."

I always kept the knife in my knapsack, but it was in a cowhide sheath designed to hang from your belt, and so Lyle strapped it right on and looked pleased.

Now it makes sense to ask *fine,* you get to Malibu today to fetch Tick, but what about the return trip? It would be a fair question and I had no ready answer for it. But in my mind I saw Tick and myself returning by bus. Somehow we would get money for tickets, even if it meant borrowing from Aunt Zee (through Tychander, of course) or Natalie, or even Dave Winkler, through a Western Union moneygram of some sort. It needed to be a safe and civilized trip home, unlike the trip out.

You can see: Jupiter wasn't part of my thinking. I wanted nothing more to do with him.

We hauled our bags out to the truck and threw them in the cab. It couldn't have been past eight in the morning, but it was already hot from the morning sun. Amazing! Then we traipsed around the corner of the laundry room to go to the motel office to check out and pick up the deposit money.

I led the way in, with the bells jingling, and found a woman behind the counter instead of the bald man. She was sixty, maybe, with a big pile of dyed blonde hair and she wore those horn-rimmed glasses that have glitter on the frames.

"You boys checking out?"

"Yes, ma'am," I said. "Room three."

I put the key on the counter.

She was rummaging through a box of receipts or something, and found what she was looking for.

"We had a good sleep," I threw in.

"Oh, it's cash, so there's a deposit. No phone charges, but I need to check the room."

"Okay. We left it clean."

Lyle was poking through Needles postcards on a rack. The woman left the office, and I realized she'd barely noticed us because she hadn't yet looked up at us. Some people do that, like store clerks and such – they don't look at you when they speak – and I always find it rude.

Lyle said from nowhere, "You've been good company. And a help."

"No sweat."

"K-Mart across the street. We'll leave the truck there."

"Okay."

"Keys on the seat, windows down. Maybe it'll get stolen again."

I looked out the window toward the street and saw a police cruiser crawl by. Maybe he looked toward us in the office, maybe he didn't, but it gave me the heebie-jeebies either way.

Lyle found a roadmap of the area and was studying it while we waited. I chanced a third cup of "coffee" from the table in the corner, adding a little milk this time to kill the taste.

The woman was sure taking her time, and it made me just a bit nervous.

I wondered if she'd find damage that we didn't cause. I never took inventory of the dumpy room, but I remember one picture on the wall had a frame that was pulling apart, and there were cigarette burns on the edge of the bathroom sink, and a few other things, like a couple of missing hooks in the window curtain. Raunch-O 66 was a better name for this place. But she'd have to know the room was like that before we arrived, making it their fault, not ours.

153

I looked at Lyle, and he rolled his eyes at me. He said, "This is dumb."

Just then, the woman trundled back and came in the office.

"It's okay," she said, without looking at us.

"Yes, ma'am. We tried to spiff it up."

She went behind the counter and opened the cash register. She slapped a ten dollar bill in front of me. "You boys have a good day, stay out of trouble."

Lyle had his map in his hand and was headed for the door but stopped when I said, "Well, ma'am, thanks, but we left fifty last night."

That's when she looked up at me.

"*Fifty?*"

"Yes, ma'am, the gentleman asked for fifty and I gave it to him."

"For heaven' sake," she said, "that would be a first for this motel. It's always ten. But if Sonny decided to charge you fifty, that's his business. Just show me the receipt."

Lyle had come up next to me.

"You boys – were you in a fight or something? What happened to your neck?"

"Accident," I said. "We're okay. Ma'am, I didn't get a receipt, I'm sorry."

She took quite a long look at me over the rims of her glasses. "It's policy, for a cash deposit. Sonny's good about that."

"Well, ma'am, he didn't offer me a receipt. I'm sorry, maybe I should have asked for one."

"He should've given you one," Lyle said to me.

"Well, you boys have me in a pickle, I'd say. Sonny worked late last night, I hate to wake him up. Don't understand why he didn't give you a receipt."

"We left fifty dollars, plus the room fee," said Lyle.

"You keep *sayin'* that –"

"It needs repeating," he rejoindered, and I gave him the slightest nudge of my arm.

"Ma'am, we could sure use the forty dollars we're missing. We're not rich, and we're traveling."

She took a deep inhale and shook her head. She turned from us and left the office through a door, down a back hallway.

Lyle was getting steamed, I could tell. His eyes were on the cash register and the drawer that was still open.

"No," I said. "Let's do it fair and square, it'll work out." I didn't tell him about the cop cruiser that went by, fearing it would crank him up even more.

"Done it before," he said, and I believed him.

"Yeah, but we got a truck that doesn't belong to us."

"What was I shouting about last night?"

Jumpy brain.

"Couldn't get the words. You were pained, though."

"Don't remember."

"I almost rousted you, but sleeping dogs should lie."

"Wish I could remember."

"If Sonny can't remember about the deposit, I say we just walk away from it."

He scowled. "That wouldn't be fair and square."

"No, but it would be safe. We can't have trouble, the way things are."

The ten was still on the glass counter. I took it and gave it to him.

"You got fifteen more coming," I said.

He pocketed it and patted me on the back. I will say, Lyle wasn't much for niceties like please and thank you, but then you need to consider where he came from.

"Pay you back in Ogamesh," he said.

We could hear both their voices raised as they came along the hall toward the office, but I couldn't make out the words.

Sonny popped through the door in his bathrobe, with the woman trailing.

"Yes sir," I said, "good morning."

"What's this about? Georgia says you've got a beef."

That made me bristle a bit.

"Boys say they left a fifty dollar deposit last night.," said Georgia. "But no receipt."

"Fifty?" he asked, looking at me.

"Yes sir. You don't recall?"

He was at the cash register and lifted up the till box to poke around underneath. "Son, this is where the deposits go, and it's always ten."

"You don't recall?" I repeated.

"Sonny," said Georgia, "they say they never got a receipt."

"Well, pumpkin, there was another couple waiting and it could've slipped my mind."

Damn liar, there was no other couple waiting.

"Woody was the only one in here," said Lyle. "You're not being straight."

"It was ten," he repeated. "Never charge fifty." He looked at Georgia. "How was the room? I was concerned."

"Neat enough," she said.

Lyle grabbed my arm. "You gave him fifty."

"I did."

"We need forty more," Lyle said to Sonny. "You lied about another couple in here, you're lying about the deposit."

Georgia took Sonny's arm. "Should I call?"

"No, wait."

Call, I gather, as in the police.

"Don't like being called a liar by a little piece of shit like you. Now you get out with your ten bucks, both of you."

I put my arm around Lyle's shoulders and could feel his whole body trembling. "Let's go. Ogamesh is calling."

He kept shaking, and it scared me.

"Lyle, it's not worth it."

"Go on, *git*. You've stunk up my office long enough."

"Sonny!" Georgia protested at him, but it was too late, he'd uttered an offense too vile for Lyle's stomach, and Lyle leapt at him across the counter and grabbed his bathrobe and was trying to bang his head down on the glass.

This is where things get hazy.

I do remember lunging for the phone that Georgia had grabbed to call the cops, and jerking it so hard the wire popped out of the wall and sending her staggering against the postcard display. I also remember Lyle trying to bang Sonny's head on the counter with one hand while the other was trying to reach in the cash register. Georgia was screaming, Sonny hollering, and Lyle cursing up a storm. I tried to grab Lyle from behind to fetch him off Sonny, but the kid was so *strong* I had no chance with him, and I resorted to reason, like "Let's go, leave it be, come on," and other such things, and finally he pulled free of Sonny and sprung back with me in a heap on the floor, nearly crushing my ribs, just as I heard a large bang that shook the room, which I knew to be a gunshot.

I thought, *who shot that? What happened?* and looked up to see Georgia with both arms outstretched and a pistol aimed at us, some kind of big semi-automatic.

"What are you *doing?*" I said nonsensically. "Don't shoot us, we'll leave."

The gun was quivering in her hands as Sonny recovered from his head-banging.

"Please," I said, and to Lyle, who was basically in my lap on the floor, "let's go."

Lyle was still trembling with his anger.

I thought.

"Let's go, man."

I smelled the blood before I felt it warming my hands wrapped around his chest. Sickly sweet.

He was hit, and dying.

I called out his name. *Lyle! No!*

I laid him out on the floor and saw how the bullet had gone straight through his neck, one side to the other, and torn up the muscle of his neck so much his head became all floppy. I hugged him close and tried hard to stop the bleeding with my hands but I knew it wasn't going to work, the way the blood was pumping out of his neck. He gurgled as I held him. He closed his eyes, and shook and gurgled a bit more.

Lyle! I was screaming for an ambulance and moaning and sobbing all at the same time and trying to find words to damn those two people to Hell forever. They hadn't moved, except the woman had lowered the gun and wasn't going to shoot me, since I was made all but paralyzed. I held Lyle's head and rocked it gently and rubbed his face until he died, my brother, my friend, the one who could be so easily me, with just a small adjustment in past events.

I've thought since then: where was he born? Was his father really McLean, or could it have been Clayne?

I kept hanging on to Lyle, even though he was stone still. I could hardly see through my sobbing eyes. But I thought the woman had gone. Sonny muttered *self-defense. Police are coming.*

I eased Lyle off of me to lie flat on the floor. I was raging as I got up and wanted to attack this man Sonny, but I just cursed instead and finally did say something coherent, which was about the knife Lyle had on his belt and how easy he could have used it, but didn't, and Sonny was lucky to be alive right now *fucking thief, fifty bucks,* and other things I can't remember as I walked out of the office and into the desert heat toward the truck.

All the sense I had right then was focused on getting my bags from the truck and walking away to save myself from the evil of those people, the evil of a small town where the police would *of course* believe them and not me, and probably lock me up. Away from them, and the death of my friend. Not walking away, but running, through parking lots and in back of buildings, alleyways, into where it was cooler, the shadows, rushing as if grief was a kind of fuel for my flight.

SEVENTEEN

For the rides I got between Needles and Los Angeles, for the people I met and for the way I talked to them, you'd have to get them all together in one room to compare notes on how my craziness progressed, one mile to the next, across the immense oven of sand known as the Mojave Desert into the raggedy suburbs of the city. You'd also have to bring them all together to dig into the truth, since I could no longer perceive it or store it. They would surprise each other with their stories of the wacky kid they picked up on the highway, and they'd surprise me as well. I have a sense that it began in a small park in Needles, where children ran through sprinklers to cool off – or maybe it was a fountain. I stood under the water until Lyle's blood had washed from my skin and clothes and seeped into the grass, with one little girl in a bathing suit watching me while she sucked her thumb. She was old enough to understand when I told her, "red paint."

I must have changed somewhere because I felt dry soon thereafter. My load was lightened – half my stuff was in Lyle's gunnysack in the truck – and I was down to a couple of Alvin's black tee shirts, which heat up fast in the desert sun. I didn't care, of course. In the sprinkler (or fountain) no one can tell you've been crying.

Life ends with a *snap*. Jake Culpepper. Lyle McLean.

He might tell me later, if we ever met in Heaven or wherever we're meant to go, *he did me a favor. It wouldn't work – not on the road, not in Ogamesh.* I would argue with him that his life was turning a corner. History is full of people who gave up too soon on what could have been.

I remember tuning my ear to the whine of semis roaring by on the interstate and following the sound. Walking through dust, staying away from other people, and ignoring the sirens that were sweeping down the street where the motel was. I'm not sure where the strength came from to move my feet, one after the other.

I was wearing shorts, and I don't remember changing into them. Maybe the blood wouldn't wash out of the jeans.

I remember seeing the highway in front of me through a windshield and hearing the squawking of a CB radio. A coffee can on the seat next to me half full of tobacco juice. The truck driver would chew tobacco from a pouch and spit into the can. He wanted to know if I had a sister.

Somewhere I'd lost my butterfly bandage. It didn't matter. But the left side of my face was the damaged side, and it got his attention. What happened? And I hear the words *fuck all if I can remember*. He was kind enough to share his cold water with me; the canteen water was hot.

Later, I was in an old Jeep or a Bronco, with a young woman driving. Every now and again I would start to cry, and I couldn't tell her why because I was back in the motel office on the floor holding onto Lyle and trying to calm the shaking of his body. The blood on my hands and arms was hot, and the heat came back to my skin as we drove.

The desert seemed to go forever, hundreds of miles.

She pulled off the road at one point and stopped.

I had to get out. She was driving deep into the desert to meet a friend and shoot rattlesnakes. I could come if I wanted to, they had an extra gun. If I shot rattlesnakes, she noted, I might stop my crying.

No, I had to find water and wash the blood off me. It's a terrible mess and I don't like the smell.

She looked at me as if I was crazy, which I was.

The Jeep disappeared into the desert spewing up dust and I sat in the sand a hundred feet or so from the highway cradling Alvin's duffel in my lap and talking to it.

I must be insensible, I'm watching an ant going in circles and I want to be that small. I look at myself to stop envying the ant. The skin on my arms is brown and my legs are white because I never wear shorts. I consider that I am made up of other people's bodies, that I can't really be me anymore. My face pounds with my heartbeat, almost drowning out the hard music of the trucks going by. Am I sick again?

I walk around the desert for awhile with the canteen slung over my shoulder trying to remember life back in Ogamesh and the people I once knew. The girl with dark hair and thick eyebrows – Natalie. A friend. When did I last talk to her? Rawlins, the deputy. Didn't he ask me to call him? When did we talk? I can't remember his face, but pieces of his voice come back to me.

I'm supposed to call him.

He's an adult and has power. Does he have the power to make all of this right?

I couldn't tell how long I wandered in the desert, but soon enough the canteen was empty and my white legs were turning pink, then red, from the sun.

Later, I'm with a Mexican man in another pickup truck with gallon jugs of cool water on the floor of the cab. He knows very little English but we manage to get by. *Agua*, yes, *mucho*. There's enough for me to drink and wash with, and refill my canteen. Most of the blood is off me, I believe, but I still smell it.

It comes back to me that I need to call Rawlins. Yes, I could use his help now, my brother's being kidnapped. My friend's been killed. I am low on money. I need to save my brother.

I tell the Mexican, *phone*. I hold an invisible receiver to my face.

"Barstow," he says. "Phone in Barstow."

¤ ¤ ¤ ¤ ¤

I made change from my second to last twenty dollar bill and called the sheriff's department back home. It was evening in Georgia, I guessed, since it was late afternoon here, but I couldn't find Rawlins' home phone anywhere, just the work number.

For some reason, the Mexican guy stayed in his truck at curbside, with the engine running, while I used the pay phone. He seemed interested in my situation and eager to help me, but the truck noise made it difficult to hear.

I didn't get Rawlins but some secretary instead. She told me he was off today for a week's vacation, but she had to say it twice for all the racket from the truck.

I was angry and shaking, hearing about his vacation.

"Where?" I asked.

"Charles goes fishing, that's all I know. Way up in the woods somewhere."

They call him Charles. I told her I was a friend on the road and was sorry to miss him. She replied that when Charles went fishing, he really went *fishing*, and wasn't likely to check in for messages.

I got more change and called Natalie's house, but nobody picked up. I had the same problem with Zee's number – there wasn't anybody home, which was very peculiar, considering she was all but bedridden and had a full time helper.

It was almost as if Ogamesh had fallen off the map.

I felt faint from the stink of the truck's dirty exhaust in the dry heat, mixing with the smell of Lyle's blood. I grabbed at the phone booth to keep from falling over, and that's when the Mexican turned off his engine, hopped out, and rushed over to help me. *Teng cuidado, que pasa?*

I said, *his blood's all over me, my friend. Muerto, mi amigo.*

And my brain delivered me flashes of images that didn't make sense together, but still come back to me today. Vic slamming down the cola can on the table while a woman stubs out cigarettes on a little boy's back. Zee scolding Jake for playing with Tick's hair while the giant Jorlane, eyes closed, hums some prayer. Cletus trying to choke Lyle to death as the motel woman raises the gun to shoot him. The thumb-sucking girl observing my bloody baptism under a sprinkler while Tick climbs a chain link fence to escape the police.

The pictures and sounds and smells all swam together in a spin, the way the world looks to a kid on a merry-go-round out of control.

¤ ¤ ¤ ¤ ¤

"*Hola,* Archie?"

I *think* that's what I'd heard. If so, I'd been named once again by my bottle of pills.

"Mama, he's awake!"

I was caught under a blanket in someone's sagging bed. I smelled cooking oil. Spices. Frying meat.

I opened my eyes and saw a boy about Tick's age, I judged, a brown-skinned Mexican, standing over me.

162

"Where's my wallet?" I asked. My throat was raspy. "*Dinero*." Rubbing my thumb and fingers together, the money sign. I knew about ten words in Spanish, and that was one of them.

"I speak English okay. It's here on your table. We haven't looked in it."

"Hope not."

His name was Mike. Last name Vigil, pronounced Vee-hill. He was twelve. He would translate for the family, though he said his mother knew a little English.

"You are sick," he said. "A high fever."

"I'm in your house?"

"Yes."

"Where."

"This is Barstow."

In the doorway the mother and father appeared. She was fat. He was the man who gave me a ride in his truck. They both smiled.

"They're happy you're awake."

Showing up behind them were three girls, younger than Mike, with white dresses and wide eyes. The mother stepped forward and laid her hand on my forehead.

"Better," she said. "You were *muy caliente*."

"She means very hot," said Mike.

"What day is it?" I asked. The light through the window was too bright for evening.

"Saturday."

Piecing it together, I soon found out that I'd passed out on the street and then been brought here by the truck driver, Carlos Vigil, and laid into a bed and tended to by Mrs. Concha Vigil. I'd taken water and my medicine, but couldn't remember it, then I'd slept right through Friday night till noon today. I had a wet teabag taped over my wound, which (they said) was healing fine. It wasn't infected; my fever was from a virus that had been inside me all along and had seized the opportunity, in my weakened state, to make me sick.

I wanted to get up, but Concha would have none of it. When I tried to hoist myself up, she pushed my shoulders back down on the bed – gently, but with considerable force behind it because of her heft. I inquired about using their phone to call home, but unfortunately they didn't have one right now because they were so poor.

The room was impressively humble, not much more than a wooden shack attached to the house with wood siding that had dried out and shrunk, allowing light to peep through the cracks. From the sounds and the smells, I guessed it was right off the kitchen. This was Mike's room, and Mike's bed, but they'd thrown together some extra sheets and blankets for him to sleep on the floor next to me, which was generous of them. Mike seemed pleased to be making the sacrifice. The walls were full of posters of kids on dirt bikes.

I soon corrected them on my name, explaining that there had been a peculiar mix-up at the clinic in Texas, but that the pills really were meant for me because of the gash on my face.

For the next two days, I said *gracias* more times than I can count, sometimes throwing in a *muchas* before it. *De nada, de nada, de nada,* it was nothing to them, since they had almost nothing to give except their time, attention, and food. I swear, poor people are like that. They're unusual that way, giving you almost everything they have.

Concha kept taking my temperature. It seemed every time I woke up she'd be sticking the thermometer in my mouth, tisking at the results.

When it got down to ninety-nine (she wrote "99" on a piece of paper), I could go. Mostly, it was a hundred and three or so, but slowly dropping.

Sunday morning they'd usually all pack off to church, but on this day Carlos' friends were picking him up by truck to go north to pick artichokes and garlic. This happened through the summer and fall, where he'd need to go off for a few weeks at a time to work in the fields. With the kids hanging behind him, he came in to say good-bye and to thank me for providing some extra entertainment for the family.

Mike thought the word was "entertainment," but it may have been closer to "diversion" or "interest." I was baffled that someone like me, white and sleeping most of the time, could be of any interest to them. Perhaps he was being polite. I thanked him several times for rescuing me from the street, and for their kindness, and hoped I could repay him in some way. *De nada, de nada.*

Sometimes it was peaceful, other times not. The girls played in the yard outside my window and bickered, teased, and cried. With Carlos gone off to the fields, Mike was the boss and tried to break things up, but he wasn't patient with them and sometimes made it worse. Whenever they spoke Spanish, he harangued them in a kind of old-maidish way that they should shout and cry in English.

The only complaint I had, aside from not being allowed to leave, was the heat. It was dry, deserty heat, so I didn't sweat very much, but I often felt it was hard to breathe and I was thirsty all the time.

I forget the day – it may have been Saturday or Sunday – that Concha came in with Mike and asked if I was strong enough to explain what had happened to me, with my face, the bump on my head, and my sore ribs. I kept it as short as I could, telling her I was in search of my brother and had met some bad people along the way. The trip had started out okay but had become more painful the farther I went west. No offense to the west, since I'd run into good people like *them,* but I'd had a nasty string of luck generally starting in Texas, then Albuquerque, and couldn't figure it.

Mike had problems with my Georgia accent, so sometimes I'd have to repeat myself nice and slow.

First thing Monday morning, Mike raised a fuss with his mother in the kitchen and I heard her belt him, raising a howl of indignation. As she was cursing at him, he trundled into our room holding his hand to his mouth and tears pouring down his cheeks.

"Let me see," I said. He sat on the edge of the bed and leaned his face toward me, taking his hand away and wiping the blood on his leg. His lip was cut, but it wasn't too bad.

"Get some cold water on it."

Here I was nursing again.

"She hits me."

"I can see that. Soon you'll be too big to hit, because you can fight back."

Concha was in the doorway watching us, and I guess she understood what I'd said because boy, did I get a scowl out of her! She turned away and instantly reappeared with the thermometer.

"I pray for ninety-nine," she said, jamming it under my tongue.

Three minutes later, I was pronounced healed. *Graciases* and hugs all around, even with the girls. I gave Mike an especially good hug, rubbed his hair, and told him he, too, was *mi amigo.*

EIGHTEEN

The rich people, the movie stars and the famous producers, the joggers on the beach – they can't see you when you're underwater. Swimming is a risk because the Pacific is damn cold, even in June in southern California, which is sunshiny and warm all year long. The water's so nippy that the surfers wear wetsuits, for the most part. Little kids just splash along the edge of the waves. I'm the only one actually swimming underwater and I keep my eye out for surfboards on top of me, or sharks in any direction, since they occasionally cruise in close to the beach.

Because of my ribs and not being able to stretch my arms out too far, it's slow, relaxed swimming. It's good, though, because the cold eases the pain.

I'm risking hypothermia for two reasons. One is, I'm tired of being noticed. The other is, my body is hot. I'm sick again from something, but I don't know what it is – maybe the virus coming back, or maybe from my facial wound becoming infected, since I lost my pills my first day here. I didn't actually lose them, they were swiped right out from under me when I slept on the beach, along with my canteen and some toiletries and of course my wallet, too. I have a couple of changes of clothes, a toothbrush and two bucks, and that's about it. I feel more small and lost and disconnected than ever before in my life.

I think swimming in cold water will also keep my head from going totally nutso from the fever. My head keeps screaming *food*, since I haven't eaten much in a few days, and it drowns out almost everything else.

No sign of the Mutt-n-Jeff vagabond muggers, nowhere along this endless beach that goes for twenty miles or more and is all known as "Malibu." I've given up asking, "Seen a big black kid about my age with a shorter white kid with sandy hair?" Or sometimes, "Seen a scruffy freckled white kid tagging along behind a muscly-looking older black kid?" Whatever the combination, I come up zero. The beach goes for-ever, and it's crawling with surfers and kids and jogging movie stars and dogs, and sometimes families, but I swear I've seen maybe *two* black folks here, and they weren't Jupiter.

It's annoying that they're not here, because with the extra time I spent in Barstow at the Vigils' house those two had plenty of time to get here, even if they'd run into a snag. And here it is, Day Four in Malibu.

My God, I'm swimming underwater off the coast of *California* and I'm freezing to death! Dave Winkler would say something crude like *chilly biscuits,* and I'd know what he meant. Crazy, to come so far to be this cold.

This evening, I decide, I'll start my trip home.

¤ ¤ ¤ ¤ ¤

I just told you I was tired of being noticed, and it was true. I swear, I can travel through all those states and hardly draw a glance – unless somebody was after something – but as soon as I hit the beach at Malibu I got stared at so much it made my skin crawl. Possibly it was the bandage and bruises on my face, but more likely (I believed) it was my raggedy tee shirt and shorts with my pink legs and tanned arms. People out here seemed to care more about their looks than in other places; they dressed pretty well and looked fit, for the most part. So it made sense they'd care about how you looked, too, and spend some time examining you to come to the right decision. The attention made me self-conscious, because of the damage my journey had done to my appearance. Also, for lack of food, I was getting too thin.

A few times, I met some nice people. The day after my stuff was stolen while I slept on the beach, I met a blonde-haired girl about my age, named Roxy, who seemed to take an interest in my plight. She was a surfer, and was quitting for the day because the wind had kicked up and was churning up the waves so they weren't useful for surfing any-more. In any event, she was sociable enough to come sit next to me after she spotted me.

I figured out pretty fast she was a bit of a tease. She got me talking about my adventures, and I told her I'd just arrived here last night and had already been robbed.

"Oh, bummer," she said. "That means you can't take me out."

"Right. It also means I can't buy any food, which I wouldn't mind right now."

"*I* could take you out and buy you lunch, but I always believe the boy should treat first. In your case, it won't work."

"Right."

"What's your name?"

"Woody."

"I'm Roxy. So we won't go out."

"Right."

You get the idea. She might have enjoyed her own humor, but it was useless to me, and irritating.

However, she was very pretty with bright green eyes, she wore a nice bikini, and she had an appealing physique that got my interest enough to tolerate being around her. In time, she took enough pity on me to fetch a hunk of cheddar cheese and an apple from a cooler in her car, adding her personal philosophy that she never gives to beggars or other people in need because *it's not necessary to be in need.*

Including this –

"It's not necessary to sleep on the beach. In fact, it's not legal either."

"I don't have much choice."

"Well, you *do,* you just don't know it yet. Go ahead, ask me."

"What choice do I have?" I said.

"You can sleep on the beach and be arrested, or stay somewhere else."

"There's nowhere else I can think of."

"*I* can think of somewhere else."

"Where?"

You see how she liked to talk – in tiny mysteries that eventually get solved, thanks to her advanced knowledge of things.

"A guy I know."

So without loading you up with any more of Roxy's conversational skills, I'll explain that she knew of a beach house about a mile away where the *guy* came only on weekends, but he was in Hawaii for a couple of weeks so it was empty. The house itself was locked up tight, but he had a shed underneath where he kept a couple of kayaks and his surfboards and whatnot.

"But the shed's locked," she added.

168

"Then we can't get in."

"But I know the combination. He's a *friend,* I told you."

"Then we can get in."

"*You* can get in, I don't need to."

Instead of telling me the combination, she wrote it in the sand. If I could visualize it, she said, it would be easier to remember.

And instead of taking me there, which was quite a long hike if you have to carry a surfboard, she told me there were two big iron pots containing red geraniums on either side of the shed door, and as far as she knew it was the only house along that stretch that had geraniums.

In time, she asked me why I'd come out here, and I told her about needing to retrieve my brother back to Ogamesh. He was with an older black kid (she hadn't seen a black kid here in some time, she said), and they'd had some trouble. Well, she completely fixated on Tick, wanting to know everything about him, including every detail she could think of about his appearance. Did he wear braces? Were his eyebrows blond? Did he have freckles on his nose? The more I responded, the more questions she asked about him till I thought she was just yanking my chain, and I stopped talking to her.

After some silence she admitted, "Haven't seen him."

She stood up to leave, grabbing her surfboard and tucking it under her arm.

"Nice meeting you, Southern boy."

"I'm Woody."

"Some day, you should write about your trip."

"Might do that."

"Bye, Woody."

That was the end of Roxy and her loop-de-loop conversing.

I put what was left of my apple and cheese in the knapsack and hustled my way down the beach toward the house and shed with geraniums. It was more or less a mile, I guess, and a welcome sight. I worked the combination lock, and sure enough the door opened, and I got a good look at the place that would be my home for the next three nights.

Because it was a beach shed, it had a soft sand floor with plenty of room to sprawl and sleep. Aside from the kayaks and surfboards, it offered me a sink with cold water, various tools hanging on the wall, and a big old canvas sail that would make a useful bed for me. Also, the door locked from the inside, so I'd be safe from any robbers.

¤ ¤ ¤ ¤ ¤

Looking back on this now – the days following Lyle's death at the motel – I have only some understanding of why I behaved the way I did. I could have solved a lot of problems by making one collect phone call back to Ogamesh, explaining everything, begging forgiveness, conceding defeat and asking for help. Natalie could send me a moneygram so I could go to a doctor and get medicine, have a square meal, get my strength back and make better sense of things. I could even walk into a Malibu police station, tell them the whole story, and plead with them to use extreme caution because Jupiter Strange believed he was wanted for arson and would do anything not to be captured, which could be a great danger to my younger brother.

But at the time, I wasn't thinking like that. I had it in my head that telephones were futile instruments. Back in Barstow, when I passed out in the phone booth, there was nobody home at Natalie's or Zee's. *Odd.* Rawlins was off fishing in the hills, impossible to reach. Earlier, phoning Natalie from Lacey's house while she was secretly eavesdropping on me upstairs, I got no help from anybody – it just made me feel miserable to talk to them.

The police weren't much better. I'd come to think, you can't ask the law to be *gentle* when approaching someone like Jupe. I'd seen them in action enough to figure they saved all their gentleness for their wife and kids, and couldn't use it on the job. I just didn't trust them.

Another factor in my behavior was that I was sixteen and bullheaded. I was somewhat bullheaded when I started my trip, and much more so after knowing Lyle. I'd never met a kid my age who was so single-minded and free of doubt, and I know that Lyle's mind and his strength rubbed off on me. I believed I could be as strong as he was in my purpose. Nothing will stop me from finding my brother, and I don't need anyone's help. If I'm as strong as Lyle, I will succeed.

But I must confess that at the bus station in Barstow, and later in Los Angeles, I took a few minutes to stare at the banks of pay phones and wonder about it. One call could make things so much *easier.*

I guess, being sixteen, I didn't want it easy.

Back to my life on the beach. A couple of times when I was so hungry I couldn't stand it, I'd stroll past the houses at night and sometimes find bits of decent food in trash cans. My luck was spotty. I found an artichoke, which as you know is scarcely a "food," but I ate what I could of it. I found a half-eaten cheeseburger, which was pretty fresh and tasty. And I managed to eat a few other things that weren't moldy – they went down okay and stayed down.

I have to say, I missed southern cooking – all the things Zee would make for us and then later on, Tychander and myself in the kitchen. Beans and rice, jambalaya, good chicken gumbo, Brunswick stew, eggs and grits, biscuits and gravy, and Ty's fried chicken which to this day cannot be beat. And sweet tea, too. They don't have such a thing outside the deep south; iced tea with sugar is not the same thing, I can tell you, and if you want the recipe, I can give it to you.

So, I ate enough not to go crazy.

But the fever was another matter. I woke up the last day after a miserable night of trembling with the cold sweats, wrapped in the canvas sail, feeling like my skin was going to burst into flames from the heat. It felt kind of like flu, but I wasn't so much achy as just *hot*, with the heat doing a particularly good number on my brain.

I had to remember where I was, why I was here, and *who* I was.

I spent some of the day in the shed drinking lots of water and trying to rest, but when I dozed off I had crazy dreams that I had to snap out of. Natalie slipped into the dreams. So did Lyle. So did I, *becoming* Lyle. Cletus, swinging that pipe at me, turned into Charles Rawlins and I begged him for mercy. Jorlane transformed into Jupiter and Cletus became Tick. Aunt Zee's face floated overhead, scowling at me with disdain.

When I was awake, I found a pane of windowglass so I could study my face. The last time I'd changed the bandage was back at the Vigils' house in Barstow, four days ago, and it was no longer fresh by a long shot. In fact, it was soaked with a mustard-y, infected ooze. I tore it off and did my best to wash the ooze away.

Salt water helps wounds. I went out in my shorts to swim underwater, clean my wound, and cool off.

I gathered up what was left of my stuff, neatened up the shed, walked out and snapped the combination lock shut. I said *thanks, guy* to the unknown guy who owned it, and headed up through his driveway past the house to the highway. The highway is Route 1, but locally it's called the Pacific Coast Highway, or the "PCH," if you're cool.

Where I'd been staying was about eight miles from the Malibu Pier, which sticks out about a thousand feet into the ocean. Right next to the pier was a state park set aside for surfers, and you can bet I spent a fair amount of time there the first couple of days looking out for the vagabond muggers and asking around. I thought, on my way back toward Los Angeles, I'd give it one more try.

I wished I'd hung on to my pills, not just for infection but for pain. Two bottles of pills stayed with Lyle.

I got to the road and hitched.

Maybe Roxy would drive past... but then she'd see I was needy and dump me out of the car.

Two bottles of pills were in Lyle's gunnysack in the stolen truck.

The sun was hot, and I was in my filthy shorts and stinking tee shirt, not to mention my last pair of *socks* (I won't discuss them) and of course no one's going to pick me up.

My name is Woody. I am not Lyle; I am not Archie.

I pat my butt, imagining that my wallet's been returned to my pocket, but it hasn't. *Man*, you feel naked without a wallet. How did Lyle manage himself, with no wallet?

How would the police back in Needles identify him? I did shout out his name when he died, didn't I?

Do *not* lick dried salt from your skin, if you're thirsty. I did anyway.

A Mexican guy picked me up in an old super-powered coupe. I said *Malibu Pier*, and then claimed to know no Spanish so I could focus on my thoughts and try to remember things.

The pill bottles said *Archie Wetherall* on them. Also printed on them were the name and phone number of the clinic in Amarillo.

I'd stayed at Sheriff Calder's house; the clinic knew I was the Calders' charity case.

Also in Lyle's gunnysack were some of Alvin's clothes and my hunting knife.

Nutso as I felt, all these bits of things were flashing around in my head. Oh, and then nosy old Lacey had eavesdropped on my call to Natalie's house.

When did Lyle die? Friday morning, a week ago. Forever ago.

The Needles police call the clinic, then Sheriff Calder, Lacey gets into the act – *he's not Archie, his real name is Woody!* – and they track me down through Natalie's phone number and spread the word all over Ogamesh.

Describe the body, officer.

Hair, height, eye color, all the same. He was a little heavier than me, because of his muscles, but would they wrangle over that? We look so much alike.

I'm him, and he's me.

I cursed out loud, and the Mexican gave me a stern stare.

"Sorry."

The Needles police would confab with Calder and the sheriff in Ogamesh, and they'd nail my identity right down to the bruises on my body and the bandage over my facial wound. We'd taken similar beatings, hadn't we?

Would they bother with the scars and cigarette burns on my back?

In the morgue, bodies are face up.

I'd taken an alias, stolen a truck, attacked a motel clerk, tried to rob the till, and been shot through the throat. After all the work Zee Morton did to raise him, that's what Woody Elmont has come to. That's the boy who set off on a hero's journey to save his brother – he lost his moral reckoning and when things got tough, he turned to crime.

I said aloud, *I'm dead.*

The Mexican ignored me.

I must be dead, because I haven't called Ogamesh since – *wait!* In Barstow, I got through to the sheriff's department looking for Rawlins, several hours after I died. She said he was fishing. Did I mention my name?

No, I held onto my name and said I was a friend.

I got let out at the beach next to the Malibu Pier and staggered down into the sand and sat. Not far away was a small state park hut with a phone booth outside.

If only they'd flip the body over to see the burns on the back. Could a woman like Zee Morton ever do such terrible things to a child? Or my own mother, or Milton Clayne when he was around?

Nonsense. I was the same Woody who'd been to doctors and gone skinny-dipping with friends and been barebacked hundreds of times with witnesses, including Nat. Just a few moles here and there, that's it.

Who from Ogamesh would take the trouble to fly out to the pissant desert town of Needles, California, to identify me? Who would ask to flip me over?

I didn't go to the pay phone at the hut.

Being dead when you're really not dead is the most amazing sensation, though I have to admit between my raging fever and near-starvation my opinion of it couldn't have been very accurate.

The surfers taking the last waves of the day might know the feeling, when you paddle way out and see only the edge of the world, blue meeting blue.

I felt so light, almost like mist.

But it was a selfish good feeling, because of people like Nat and Ty, and others in town like the Winklers and how they must be taking it. And Lacey, too, the way she cared for me.

Still, I didn't go to the phone. My legs felt like they couldn't handle the trip, struggling through the sand.

Someone was clapping at the shore, standing at the water's edge.

People were whistling.

I saw a sawed-off sandy-haired kid crouching on a little surfboard with his arms outstretched, sliding across a wave. He wasn't wearing a wetsuit, like everyone else.

It wasn't possible. I'd scoured this beach the last few days.

I looked as hard as I could, though my vision was a little blurry. For sure it was his body with the wide shoulders and arm muscles, though not quite as chunky as I remembered. He looked a bit sunburned.

The kids at the shore called out his name. They were all white kids.

The wave broke over him and he landed in a heap. I sat and watched as they gathered around and plucked him up from the water. They gave him slaps on the back and mussed his hair, and one kid all but hugged him.

The zoo-headed little thieving pain-in-the-ass had surfed Malibu. He'd not only surfed it, he'd wowed the pants off the crowd.

He grabbed the surfboard from the waves and handed it over to a taller kid. I sat and watched as the little scamp borrowed a towel and dried off. Then he started up the beach toward me. My legs were like jelly; I wasn't going anywhere. I managed to lean myself forward so I was kneeling in the sand to try to get his attention. Oddly, I couldn't seem to find the breath to call out to him, but I got one arm up for a little wave.

He stopped about fifty feet away from me, I guessed, and gave me a hard squinty look. Then he waved back, smiled, and started running up to me.

"Woody!"

"Help me up."

He grabbed me under the arms and hoisted me to my feet and I threw an arm around his shoulder.

"You hurt?"

"No. Sick."

"What kinda sick? Throw up?"

"No. Fever. Get my knapsack."

He reached down to grab my knapsack and said, "Did you see me?"

"Yeah. You were good. You did it."

"Yesterday, too, but not as good."

"Where's Jupe?"

"Dunno. You're heavy. Where we going?"

It's so frustrating having a brother who doesn't see how obvious some things are. I was crying a little bit then, so happy he'd seen me and found me, but so sad about so many other things. I barely got the word out.

"Home."

He screwed up his face for a second, then said,

"Okay."

"Back to Zee and Ty."

"Okay."

"Do you have stuff somewhere, 'cause we gotta hitch."

"No. No stuff. Jupe has it."

"You don't have a *shirt*?"

I felt him shake his head. We were up now to the edge of the highway. I added, "A toothbrush? Nothing?"

He got poetic on me. "Just the sea and the sun. Malibu!"

"Well, your breath stinks," I said. It did, too.

We sat down on some rocks at the edge of the highway. I ordered him to take out the last tee shirt in the knapsack and put it on, which he did, though it was too big for him. He fingered his upper lip.

"Jupe says I'm growing a mustache."

Blond fluff.

"Yeah, a bit. Do you have money?"

He reached into the front pocket of his soggy shorts (which I'd never seen before) and pulled out a limp ten dollar bill.

"Ten."

"Good. We can eat."

"Jupe's getting more money."

That didn't sound very positive, knowing Jupe and how he'd been acting lately.

"Well, he can keep it. We're not going to see him anymore."

"We're not?"

"Tick, I don't think Jupe wants to go back to Ogamesh."

"No, he doesn't. He wants to go to Hawaii. We're s'posed to meet at the Gas-N-Go."

"We can't see him. We need to get food."

Tick needed a moment to work through this, and I could tell it bothered him.

"If I don't meet him, he'll shit."

"Hey, watch your mouth."

"He *will*."

"Can't talk like that. I need to eat."

We set off down the road back toward town where I'd seen some stores. I was so woozy I had to lean on Tick to make the trip, but the closer we got to food the stronger I seemed to get. I was motivated by hunger, no question.

Along the way Tick rattled off enough of the highlights of the last few days, in his own scrambled way, that it started to make sense why

I hadn't located him. I'd always asked if people had seen an older black kid with a younger white kid, and no one ever did because Jupe was never here. He'd drop Tick off in the morning with ten dollars in his pocket, go off and do his business, and then come fetch him around suppertime. He didn't care about hanging around to watch Tick surf; he had other more important things to attend to.

Like, stealing another car or mugging somebody to get cash. Tick couldn't keep track of the number of crimes that had happened along the way, but he believed it was "more than a few."

When we got to the store I snagged a quart of orange juice, some dinner rolls, two celery stalks and a jar of Skippy. That was fine with Tick; he'd been eating a lot of garlic beef jerky lately (which explains the bad breath), plus Swiss cheese, and needed a good dose of peanut butter and a crunchy vegetable. At the last minute I grabbed a bottle of aspirin, too. All the while, I managed to keep an eye on my brother to make sure he kept his hands to himself, which he did.

We hung out in the parking lot sitting on old tires behind a dumpster. I popped down two aspirin with the juice, and we ate. The money that bought the food was probably tainted, but if you're hungry enough your morals tend to adapt to the situation.

In time, Tick let on that he considered it odd to find me here, and so raised the question.

"How'd you get here, Woody?"

I told him: every means of transportation but airplanes and camels, and then added, "You knew I'd come after you."

He nodded. "Jupe and me put a clue in the mailbox. I said, that's not how you spell it, and he said, Woody can figure it out. And you did!"

"He never could spell."

"No."

"Has he been good to you?"

Another nod. "He's been teaching me stuff."

"I bet he has."

He didn't catch my tone, so I had to elaborate for him.

"Were you with him when he did his stealing and mugging?"

I saw him wince and squint, as if trying to remember. "Coupla times."

"Did you *help* him do it?"

He thought again and said, "I was s'posed to distract them. I ask a lady directions, or what time it is, and he sneaks up behind and grabs her bag and we run. Like when I was climbing the fence and I saw you."

That's how they worked it when they ran out of bus money, which he thought was in Oklahoma but he couldn't remember all the states they went through.

The aspirin was taking enough effect so I could make a little sense of it all, and I couldn't help but scold him a little. "Tick, what you and Jupe did, starting at St. Anselm's and ending here, is about the most dumbass thing a couple of kids could do, brains or not. It's just plain nonsensical, start to finish, and you broke all kinds of laws, too, and it's only because you're thirteen and a little off your nut that you won't go to jail. Most likely. God *damn* it all, anyway. What I've been through to get here."

"Well, me too, Woody. *I* been through stuff, too."

"Malibu. Surfing. Can it get any dumber than that? I swear it can't. And I bet whenever Jupe says 'jump!', you say 'how high?', like you'd do anything he wants. You've been kidnapped and brainwashed and you don't even know it."

He looked good and scolded, as he usually did when I reprimanded him for his thieving.

"It's past time," I added, "you started thinking for yourself."

"Okay."

"We're *not* going to the Gas-N-Go. Whether he shits or not, we're not going to see him because we're going home."

During this, he'd been giving me the once over.

"What happened to your face?"

"My face, my ribs, my skull – I met some bad people."

"Well, *I* made a friend this morning."

"I can see, at the beach, you made lots of friends."

He shook his head. "Not a kid, a man."

"A man."

He nodded and ate. "He wants to help me."

Well, I was naturally suspicious, because we were no longer in the deep South where it was not uncommon for a grown man to show interest in helping a boy. Ever since leaving the South, I'd seen a change in how adults behaved toward kids.

"How old was he?" I asked.

He chewed on it for a second. "Maybe as old as Trey."

"Kind of like, forty or so."

"Yeah, forty."

"A nice man?"

He nodded. "He said he'd find me later."

I was suspicious of that, too.

"Does he have a name?"

"Well, I *guess* he's got a name, but I don't know it."

"Well, he could be a pervert, we need to be careful."

"He's not a pervert."

"All the same, we should be careful."

Tick persisted in objecting to my doubts, which was a skill in him I hadn't noticed before. He'd talked with the man for some time this morning, with the man being curious and asking all about his family: where he went to school and such, and, in learning about me, when I was due to show up.

More and more, he sounded suspicious.

"He has a bright red Oldsmobile," Tick told me. "It's a rental car, he said."

"I'm glad he wants to help," I said. "But that's why *I'm* here. *I* came to help. I came out here to bring you back home."

"Do you have enough money?"

I finished off the juice and said, "We'll manage."

"Well, *he* has money. He said he'd share it."

"I don't know if I trust this guy, Tick."

"Well, *I* do."

Nineteen

After finishing nearly the whole jar of peanut butter, we ambled out of the parking lot toward the Pacific Coast Highway to start hitching back toward Los Angeles. I had no idea where we were going to sleep tonight, or how I was going to get medicine for my infection, but my fevered brain told me it made more sense to get back into the big city than hang out here with the surfers and movie stars. I'd heard it said, if you were sick enough, you could walk into a hospital and they couldn't turn you away just because you had no money. That was the case in Georgia, anyway. I didn't know how it worked in California.

As we chatted back and forth while waiting for a ride, Tick told me once I wasn't making sense, and I had just enough sense to realize he was right. Sometimes crazy ideas or images popped into my head, from the fever, and it took a fair amount of effort to shoo them away.

We'd been out there for about fifteen minutes with no luck when I heard a police siren fast approaching, and then the cruiser itself screaming toward us at a good eighty miles an hour, with full lights flashing.

"Sheez," said Tick.

It zoomed past us, headed west, chasing who-knows-what.

Just a few seconds later, another car came racing toward us from the same direction, a convertible with its top down and Jupiter Strange at the wheel.

Tick, like a fool, jumped up and down, waved his arms, and shouted out *Jupe!* Well, sure enough, Jupe caught a glimpse of us and hit the brakes, pulling a tire-squealing one-eighty in the middle of the highway and nearly clobbering a station wagon loaded with surfboards. The convertible roared toward us and shrieked to a halt right next to us.

"They're chasin' me! I'm goin' up the canyon road – I'll wait for you!"

I had the sense to be holding Tick by the arm, and I could feel him trying to pull free to hop in the car. But Jupe wasn't waiting – he hit the gas and spun across the highway toward a road that snaked up into the hills on the other side.

He'd hardly seen me. I wondered, battered up as I was, if he recognized me.

I couldn't hold on to my brother in that situation. After all the brainwashing and training he'd received, he got it in his head that he had to be with Jupe no matter what I said. Plus, though he was small, he was muscle head-to-toe and too much for me to restrain in my weakened state. Without hardly a look either way, he dashed across the highway to the canyon road, running his little heart out.

I knew one thing for pretty sure. If I lost him now, I'd probably never see him again.

He hesitated for a second on the other side and gave me a big wave of his arm – *C'mon!* – then kept hustling up the road.

Damn it all anyway! My legs were all like Jell-o, I could scarcely walk, let alone run.

And, as luck would have it, the traffic got way too thick for me to cross over. I edged out a bit on the highway and got honked at, and so I could only watch my brother's bobbing head disappear into the distance up that road. And now a caravan of Harleys was coming up from the east with their pipes open and you could hardly hear yourself think. There must've been forty or fifty of them, some with girls on the back.

Damn, there was a helicopter circling over the canyon road, high up in the hills, just like a hawk.

My heart went wild in my chest and somehow I got across the highway, weaving through cars and motorcycles and getting screamed at for being crazy. You can figure the language – I don't have to repeat it.

The canyon road was twisty and you couldn't see very far, but I did my best to hoof it around each bend, hoping for a glimpse of them. But Tick was a speedy runner and I guessed he could be half a mile up into the hills already, way ahead of me. And Jupe in the convertible – he could be *anywhere* by now, up over the hills and down the other side, forgetting about Tick altogether, what with the police helicopter trying to track him down. If I were a car thief and mugger like Jupe, being chased by the cops, I wouldn't be waiting around for anyone else.

I trotted upward past a bunch of fancy houses and in time there were no houses at all – just lumpy hills with dead brown grass and sometimes a tree or two. I had to slow down to a walk, I was so tuckered, and soon enough I couldn't take one more step without falling. I sat down in the prickly grass and laid my head on my knees to keep the earth from spinning out of control.

A cop car flashed on by me, running lights but no sirens. I got just a glimpse of it, disappearing around a bend.

It was hot up in the hills, and I cursed myself for polishing off the orange juice. I was gushing sweat now, all over my body, and I was so thirsty that my mouth felt swollen and cotton-like.

One more time I tried to stand up, and I just crumpled back down into the prickly grass.

The next thing I knew was just a sound. A big *whumpf*, like a car door closing.

I was lying on my side in the grass – I could feel the prickliness under my cheek. How long have I been like this? I need to wake up.

I managed to open my left eye just enough to get a sense of a car's tire just a few feet away.

And a pair of boots stepping in front of them.

I croaked out, "Don't hurt me. Please."

I could see the person lowering into a crouch, a man with tan trousers.

"I won't," he said.

The car behind him – it was bright red.

The man laid a hand on my forehead, and I could hear him suck in a long breath.

My eyelid kept fluttering, not wanting to stay open. I was so *tired* and achy it was as if my whole body wanted to shut down for a long rest. But I had the sense the man went away for a minute, and then came back.

"Want some water?"

I guess I nodded, because he wrapped an arm around me to try to straighten me up so I was sitting. I felt the rim of a plastic bottle on my lips and I started taking it in. It was good and cold.

My eyes started to open but they couldn't focus very well. Still, just the size and shape of this man seemed familiar to me, and the hair color too.

"Woody. How you've made me *work*."

Now I recalled the voice, too. I managed to get the words out, "I thought you went fishing."

"I thought you were dead."

⌗ ⌗ ⌗ ⌗ ⌗

We hardly said a word driving up to the top of the ridge. I sat with the seat tilted back a bit, and felt refreshed from the water but still half insensible in my head as bits of grass and trees flashed by through the window.

I heard squawking from some police radio but didn't process what I heard.

The car slowed down, and I asked, "What's happening?"

Charles Rawlins said, "We have to get him before they do. I see him."

I pulled my seat up as the car stopped.

Rawlins nudged my arm. "Woody. Can you call out to him? Are you strong enough?"

"He can't go to jail."

"He won't, if you call to him. He knows you better than me."

He got out of the car, came around to my side to open the door, and half-lifted me from the car, then pulled my arm around his shoulder to prop me up.

"Can you see? Down there."

We were on top of the ridge and I could make out three cop cars down below on the road, five or six cops scattered about with their guns in hand, and Jupe's convertible in a ravine, upside-down and billowing brown smoke. Halfway between us and them was Tick, crawling on his hands and knees toward the ravine.

None of this made sense, the way my brain wasn't working.

"Please," said Rawlins. "Try."

I sucked in a deep breath and hollered out his name as loud as I could.

Rawlins grabbed my hand and made it wave.

Tick stood up and saw us.

The cops saw him too, and let out a shout.

We kept waving, and darned if the dopey little squirt didn't start clambering back up the hill toward us.

"Hurry!" Rawlins shouted at him, and I tried to echo him as best I could. Tick seemed to put on a burst of speed to climb up to us, while two of the cops made a dash for their car.

My vision caught a great burst of hot yellow light and a second later the *whoom!* of the fire exploding around the convertible.

Tick glanced back but kept scrabbling up to us and soon enough Rawlins had him by the hand and all but threw him bodily into the back seat of the car.

We were all in, and racing down the windy road. *Man,* could this guy drive!

And I thought, of *course* he can drive, he's a cop.

Deputy sheriff, close enough.

"Jupe was under the car," Tick moaned.

"I'm sorry, son. Belt up and hang on."

We made it. The sirens got fainter and fainter, and soon enough we'd vanished into the traffic on the Pacific Coast Highway, headed east for Los Angeles.

TWENTY

I t took seven days in the hospital for me to get well enough to fly home. I had a tube going into the back of my hand loaded with antibiotics to fight the infection on my face. I also had three *terrific* meals every day, a great nurse who reminded me of Lacey, and frequent visits from both Charles and Tick. He was "Charles" now, at his request, and I got used to it fast.

By the time we all got on the airplane to Atlanta, I had most of the story straightened out.

It goes back to that day when I arrived in Barstow, in Carlos Vigil's truck, and found a phone booth to call people in Ogamesh – Nat's house, Zee's house, and finally the sheriff's department (which said he'd gone fishing). Before fainting in a heap on the street, I'd called and gotten no answer at Natalie's, and then at Zee's, which seemed very strange to me.

It happened there was a darned good reason nobody was home that night.

Zee had suffered a pretty bad stroke that afternoon, and everybody I knew was up in Macon at her hospital – Ty, John Dandridge, the home nurse, Natalie and her parents, and a bunch of others, too. In their absence, Charles had volunteered to delay his fishing trip for a day and keep an eye on the houses.

He kept an eye on them all right, especially our house. On it, and *inside* it, top to bottom, poking around here and there until he ferreted out all the Malibu posters I'd torn from the walls and folded up in our bedroom closet. A little more sleuthing about and he unearthed the "Mal Boo" postcard from a bunch of junk on my desk, plus other things in the house I'll get to later. The odd thing is, I'd sworn I'd brought the postcard with me in Natalie's Buick, in my duffel full of clothes, but I'd missed it altogether and left it in our room.

Lucky for Tick and me, I'd been momentarily lamebrained.

Charles sleuthed out the mystery enough to risk changing his vacation plans without telling anyone.

Zee died the next day. The couldn't do anything to stop the bleeding in her head, and then her heart gave out.

I died the same day as Zee. From the cops in Needles to the Calders in Amarillo to Natalie and to Charles the word spread fast – Archie Wetherall *was* Woody Elmont, and I'd been shot through the neck during a knife-wielding assault at a motel, and I'd bled to death.

Of course the question lingered that it *could* be someone else who wasn't me. The problem was, I had no family or guardian at that moment to fly out and identify me in the morgue, and so Charles took it on himself to get some papers together that made him temporary guardian of both me and Tick, and requested they transmit police photos of the boy's face and body, lying on the floor of the motel office.

That sealed it for them – Charles, Tychander, Natalie and her parents. The photos weren't all that clear, but no question it was my dead face looking up from the motel office floor. And Natalie added the clincher: that's Woody's hunting knife, for sure, gripped in his bloody hand.

(You know that Lyle never took the knife from its sheath during that miserable incident. I guess the man and his wife figured it would help their cause if they monkeyed with the evidence a bit to adjust the truth in their favor.)

Arrangements were made to fly the body to Atlanta, and then transferred by Hearse to Zane's Funeral Home in Ogamesh. Now there were *two* deaths from the same household, barely a day apart, and that left only Tick Elmont stalking the beaches around Malibu, the sole survivor of the Morton-Elmont family.

As Tick's temporary guardian and someone who'd developed a strong caring for both of us, Charles was compelled to do what must be done and fly out to Los Angeles to resume the job I had tragically failed to finish.

⌗ ⌗ ⌗ ⌗ ⌗

On the plane ride home there were several empty rows, and so the three of us snagged two rows front to back. Tick raised all the armrests in the row behind, and sprawled out to sleep. In my row, I got the window and Charles took the aisle so he could stretch out his long legs. I'd forgotten what a sizeable man he was, and also how gentle in his speech and manner.

In fact, he was so gentle and reserved I sometimes had to labor a bit to get him talking. A good example is all the times in the hospital I'd thanked him for his generosity and efforts to track us down, and usually he'd just nod back at me. Sometimes, since he was an emotional man, I'd see his eyes redden up while he nodded, and he'd have to leave the room. I still couldn't figure him.

On the plane, he leapt into conversation on his own, while I was staring out the window, consumed with thoughts of Zee. I can explain more of those thoughts in a short while, but for now it's more important to tell this part of the story.

"Tick's sleeping," he started off.

"Like a baby," I added.

"I can't get over it," he said, shaking his head. "How proud I am. That first night at the hospital, after they got tubes in you. And I called Natalie and her mother and Mr. Hawkins and told them you were both safe and alive. How they reacted. All of us, weeping. First them, then me."

I looked at him and saw him clearing his throat and dabbing at his eye. He was an emotional man, for certain.

"Proud that you have such friends."

"They're nice people," I said.

"People do love you."

That embarrassed me and I sort of winced.

"I need to show you something, Woody. It's quite important."

He managed to pull something out of his pants pocket. A letter of some sort, in a blue envelope, all battered with age.

"I've been a good cop, ever since I was twenty-three. I always went by the book."

"Yes sir, I believe it."

"I cheated a little when Zee got taken to the hospital. I told myself, there has to be something here in her house that has the truth in it, and I do believe I've found it."

"The truth?"

He was flattening out the letter on his knee.

"It should be in here," he said. "It's yours to know. You can use it in any way you see fit."

Well, I suddenly felt jumpy and uncomfortable. As he handed it to me, my hands were as trembly as bird's wings.

"Its yours to know," he repeated.

The letter was addressed to my mother, Martha Elmont.

"You knew her enough to write her?" It was a bit of a jolt to me – I always thought my mother was a stay-at-home, and in any case I couldn't imagine Charles being friendly with her.

"Yes."

"Well, it's never been opened," I said.

"I know. But that's my handwriting, and I remember the day I sent it."

The postmark was thirteen years ago.

"It came from a shoebox in Zee's downstairs closet. It was full of stuff belonging to your mother, mostly old Christmas cards and bank statements and all kinds of things. She never threw it out."

"But she never opened it," I said numbly.

"I wish she had, but she never did. Go ahead, you need to read it."

I opened the envelope, pulled out the letter and unfolded it in my lap. The handwriting was good clean public school script, and it was easy to read.

"My dearest Martha," it started.

> *My thoughts are always full of you, little Woody, and the tender new child Aubrey. I wish for you to be strong and healthy through the time ahead of mothering and, if you can't care for me as I do for you, then I pray you care for the children and be patient with them.*
>
> *Judging by your silence in recent weeks, I assume you don't care for my letters, or else have tossed them aside. It fills me with hurt, after such a hopeful and loving time together in the summertime, though we worked so hard to keep it secret. I do*

hope you read this one, because it may be my last chance to appeal to you.

I stopped for a second and looked up to him. For a brief second I thought I recognized the large, sandy-haired man from my first memory – the time I patted my mother's swollen belly in our old house. He was there with us, in the kitchen.

"This is kind of personal."

He nodded solemnly. "It's a letter of heartbreak. I don't mind sharing it with you."

As I've written before, I love you completely and wish nothing in life but to be with you and help raise the boys. At the same time, your heart keeps turning to Milton. It pains me deeply, but I need to be respectful of your true desires, and will understand if you continue to ignore me. I, too, can walk away from you to carry on with my life, though it will be with a heavier heart than that of the man you loved before me.

At my work in the department, I was able to gather information that others would not be able to learn, and it is sad information indeed. I ask you to be strong at this moment, but if you are not feeling strong, you should stop reading here.

That's when the letter continued on the other side.

Milton Clayne sadly died over a year ago in a lumbering accident in Maine. The county has the death certificate attesting to this fact. He left a widow, and a baby.

If you can recover from the difficulty of this news, I stand ready to join you and build our lives together in happiness and grace, challenge and sorrow, sickness and health. My love extends to delightful young Woody, and to the sweet new child we made together, young Aubrey.

We can live the truth, together.

Else, we live a lie.

If you choose the lie, I'll regret it but honor it with my silence.

All my love dear lady,
Charles.

Well, I didn't burst into tears right then, though if I looked at Charles long enough I surely would, since tears were flowing down his cheeks while he watched me read. I didn't cry at the time because my head was full of the news from the letter, and I felt a kind of confused tingling all over my skin. My father died when I was two. Tick's father was alive and sitting next to me.

"She should've read it," I managed to squeak out.

"Her son has read it." His chest was heaving a little and he mopped his eyes with the little airline napkin. "Maybe that's enough."

"She didn't want you back. She kept hanging on to Milton and he ran off to Maine and got married."

I handed the letter over to him, and he started reading it for the first time since he wrote it.

I cried later when we were back at Zee's house around midnight, Tick and I in our beds and Charles downstairs curled up on the couch. It was just us three, the familiar smells of mildew and old furniture, and the gardenias in full bloom in the neighbor's back yard wafting their sweetness through the window. Some of the tears were for Zee not being here, but mostly they were tears of gladness that we'd gotten home safe, and that my brother, though he didn't know it, had inherited such a good and gentle man for a father.

I almost never pray, but that night I sent up silent prayers for Zee, for Jupiter and Lyle, a prayer of thanks to Charles, and prayers of safety and hope for my baby brother, and for myself too.

¤ ¤ ¤ ¤ ¤

In the morning he fixed up bacon and eggs and biscuits with grits, and set the old oak dining table for the three of us with placemats and neatly folded cloth napkins. It seemed to alarm Tick, who after rubbing his eyes asked what company was coming.

"Just us," said Charles. "You might recall, this is your first home-cooked meal in some time."

He'd also laid out two mugs of hot coffee, knowing I'd developed a taste for it on my travels, and some hot chocolate for Tick. Plus, butter, jam, and honey. It seemed like a lot of work just for breakfast, which traditionally in this house was fairly sparse and just as likely to be eaten standing up as seated at a table.

Tick threw off the bonds of Zee's old house rules by appearing in just his underwear and a filthy tee shirt, but he didn't fuss when I put his napkin in his lap while he spooned up some grits. He and Charles sat facing each other, with me at the end of the table, and while we all plowed through the food I'd look up at them and see their same straight noses with the same small bump at the end, same blond eyebrows, same sandy hair, and the same kind of squinting doubtful look in their eyes. It was uncanny, once you knew the truth of it.

"Sorry about the eggs," Charles noted.

"Hard," said Tick.

"Well, we might use 'em for coasters," I quipped, and this seemed to strike Charles as so funny he almost launched his mouthful across the table, but managed to hold on till he swallowed.

"Warn me," he said, wagging a fork in my direction, "when you're going to be humorous."

The biscuits were worse, like blackened stones.

"I could take these to geology class," I quipped again, but it wasn't as funny as the first one, and Charles let me know it.

"Doin' my best, Woody. I can't cook too well. Also, it's a brand new kitchen to me and hard to find things."

"But you'll *stay*," Tick said. "And the eggs'll get better."

"Only if y'all want me to."

"I want," said Tick.

Charles looked over to me.

"Fine with me," I said.

He nodded and seemed pleased. But then he kind of wagged his fork in Tick's direction and said, "Son, do me a favor and get some clean clothes on, would you? Pants especially."

"Okay," Tick replied, and got up to go change.

⊠ ⊠ ⊠ ⊠ ⊠

With no car to drive, Natalie had taken to long-distance running. She admitted it was partly to get from one place to the next, but it was also a form of powerful therapy to help her stop worrying about me on my travels, and, soon enough, to help ease the heavy weight of her grief over my death. Learning a few days later that I *wasn't* dead, she ran because she had too much energy not to. Whatever my circumstances, she had plenty of reason to race all over Ogamesh at top speed. When I saw her that morning after the overcooked breakfast, she'd run all the way from her house to mine and was pouring sweat from the summer morning heat.

Ogamesh gets very sultry in the summer, no question. Those who can't handle it hunker down in their air-conditioned houses day and night. The rest of us – and you'll sweat through your shirt standing stock still in the shade – just grin and bear it.

Well, I was so glad to see her I gave her a big hug, regardless of all the sweat. She took my head and we had quite a kiss, right there on the sidewalk in front of the house with cars going by. It was a good long kiss, and it felt wonderful.

We both agreed the other had lost some weight, which wasn't necessarily flattering for either of us, but it didn't matter. We really were like best friends – you discover that when you've been apart for awhile – and I had no misgivings that she wasn't as magazine-pretty as Lacey or as curvy as Roxy. Natalie was beautiful in her own way, and her friendship was a comfort to me.

Naturally she wanted to hear what really happened on the trip, instead of all my half-truths and confabulations on the telephone *plus* the rumors that had been flying around, and how on earth I figured I could go all the way to *California* on such a small budget and not run into trouble. But there wasn't time right away to unload all the details on her, and certainly no time to picnic at the river, as she wanted. Too much was going on, we had three funerals to prepare for, and strangely enough I was fixated on her Buick.

"I have to pay you back."

"No you don't. It was stolen."

"I *do* have to pay you back, and that's the end of it, though it might take awhile."

"It's *not* the end of it. I don't want your money. It wasn't your fault."

"It *was* my fault. I shouldn't have tangled with that guy."

"Rawlins said the police shot at him and hit the gas tank and it exploded. Is that your fault?"

192

"Nat, I want to pay you *back.*"

"No. I won't take it."

She could bicker with the best of them, which I'd neglected to remember. We let the subject drop, and I promised, in time, I would tell her the whole story of my trip start to finish, but for now I had to see people like Tychander and the Winkler brothers, and when I had the strength for it, Viola and Saturna Strange. Also, Charles and I had to put our heads together to work on Tick's case, *plus* dealing with Zee's affairs and estate, not to mention getting a jump on the three funerals which were scheduled to unfold one day after another, three in a row.

It was enough to make your head spin.

¤ ¤ ¤ ¤ ¤

Which is reason enough for me not to untangle it for you in the way you might expect. It's enough to know that now, in late summer, Tick is under our roof again after a short stint at St. Anselm's, thanks to Charles' long efforts as guardian to assure the state he was much better off at home with a deputy sheriff in residence. We both labored on it for some weeks, twisting through the maze of our juvenile justice system, until the judge threw up his hands and agreed the "legally correct" way of adjudicating the case of "A.E." (they only use initials for kids these days) was pure nonsense, and it was much better to do the "right" thing and remand the little scamp to the custody of Deputy Rawlins in the boy's own home.

And so Tick sleeps in his bed across from me, and his painful moans and hollering in his sleep are slowly diminishing. He never remembers what he dreams.

Zee left some money for Tick and me, and in time I was able to jam a fistful of hundred dollar bills into Natalie's pocket and walk away feeling good about it. The funeral for Zee was a huge community affair at the Methodist church, with several fine speeches except for the preacher himself who gushed his praise that she "sacrificed so much and worked so hard to raise two *headstrong* boys whose mother left them in her care far too soon." I was tempted to saunter up to the podium to set the record straight but instead held my tongue and had words with the minister on the front steps after the service. I didn't know the man more than his name, but I felt he had to know the truth.

"Sir," I said to him, "Zee Morton was a good enough person, like you and I and many others. But I need to say, Tick and I raised ourselves as much as she did, and we did a fair job because we minded her and cared for her when she became infirm."

"Yes, son, I'm sure that's true."

"And as for sacrificing, it was money left to her by Uncle Carl, and most of the hard work fell to Tychander Williams, and before that, one maid or cook or another year after year. She was a good person, as I say –"

"Well, you *are* headstrong, aren't you?"

And with an annoying little snicker he tussled my hair, which infuriated me, but again I clamped down on my tongue.

"I s'pose I might be, yes sir."

Jupe's funeral was the next day at the First Baptist and most of the black population of Ogamesh showed up to bid him farewell. The casket had to stay closed because of his burned condition, and I wondered why Zane's Funeral Home, with Viola's consent, didn't complete the job by cremating him, but as life has taught me there's no accounting in this world for either taste or religion. The preacher hit upon a very good theme to draw lessons from Jupe's life. Jupe had a big heart and a ready smile, and he'd do most anything for anybody that needed it. But his death served a lesson to all of us – especially young black people in Ogamesh, around the South, and everywhere – that a big heart requires an even bigger head. Joy for living is a great gift from God, but exercising that joy with *responsibility* is a distinctly human obligation. I had to agree; Jupe had lost his direction and turned to criminal behavior to indulge his joy, with terrible consequences.

Nat and I gave good long hugs to Viola and Saturna. I told them both that Jupe had been a constant and good friend growing up together, and I was sorry it had ended like this.

Secretly, I always wondered about that stolen convertible overturned in the ravine, and if Jupe hadn't made a basic choice to sail off the road to his death rather than go to jail or be killed by police gunfire. I'll never know.

The last funeral wasn't really a funeral at all, but a graveside service officiated by our Presbyterian minister, Gregory Walden, who'd also been my third grade teacher and a man I liked. He had an especially deep sense of things that went far beyond the ideas of simple right and wrong, good and bad. It was my choice to hire him.

I worked my butt off writing a eulogy for Lyle McLean, then on the morning of the service crumpled it up and chucked it.

Zane's had delivered a nice brass urn to hold his ashes, and I cradled it to my stomach as Rev. Walden finished a short prayer and said,

"Woody Elmont has some thoughts to share. Woody?"

I moved to the center of the small crowd and stood over the neat square hole dug into the ground.

I could put him in there now, or wait till the end. I decided to hang onto him.

"I swear," I started, "Nobody knew him. Hardly even me."

I glanced around and saw Nat already blinking moisture from her eyes. Her mother had her arm around her, with the professor standing behind.

"We came together on the road for not even a full day. Like me, he was sixteen. Like me, he tended to keep his real thoughts to himself. And as you all know, he looks so much like me it caused quite a stir when word got out I'd been shot."

Well, I didn't intend any humor, but a few people chuckled, though I didn't look up to see who.

"Like me, Lyle traveled. Except, I did it for three weeks, and he did it his whole life. As soon as he could escape a mother who burned his back with cigarettes, he did. Foster families didn't work out too well. He kept moving, and when he did, he'd leave a piece of himself behind."

I caught a look at Dave and Trey Winkler. Dave's eyes were already bleary, probably from whiskey. Trey looked just as calm and thoughtful as Charles, who stood right next to him.

"Tick and I are blessed that Charles is staying with us. He's been a good guardian, and I hope it continues."

Somebody said, *amen*.

It was Tychander, who was holding Tick in front of her, her arms clasped around his chest. Normally Tick would squirm and wriggle free, but he actually had a hand wrapped around her wrist.

"Lyle didn't have that kind of advantage. He'd been bonked on the head a few times and it damaged his memory. He proclaimed that he told lies, but I swear for the short time I knew him I never heard a lie. He could be scary with his toughness, but his toughness saved him when a crazy man tried to kill him. His toughness kept him alive and moving, whether by hitchhiking or riding the rails like a hobo, the way I did, just like him."

That brought out a murmur because I hadn't shared that kind of detail yet with anyone.

"You should know what happened. Wanting our deposit money back, when the crooked motel clerk threatened us and insulted us, Lyle lunged at the man with his hands, not my hunting knife as you've been told. After they shot him and he died, the motel owners must have taken the knife out of the sheath and wrapped his hand around it."

I saw Charles taking notes in his head. Later, we'd agree not to pursue it with the Needles cops because they probably wouldn't believe us. What's done is done.

"I tended to Lyle's wound on his head when he was hit with a pipe. Those few moments were very important in my life, when I was attempting to heal him. I gave him my pills for his pain. I gave him clothing and my knife. I felt like I'd found a brother – another brother, someone close to my age."

I heard Natalie gulp, getting emotional from my story.

"In some ways, with Lyle, I felt like I'd found myself. Not the real me, but the kid I could've been if the dice had been thrown a little differently. I swear, for the short time I knew him, I've never had such a friend. I asked if he wanted to come to Ogamesh and live with us, and he said yes, he'd like to give it a try. He would end his life of roaming and try to settle down. And when they shot him and he went limp in my lap, I knew some of me died with him. I don't know which part yet, but it feels like a *big* part that may be better off dead. The last part of my trip to California was very tough. I was wounded, I got sick, I was hungry. If I hadn't met Lyle, I swear I don't think I would've made it. I wouldn't have been strong enough. But Lyle made me stronger.

"He told me, his name meant 'island.' That's how alone he was."

I knelt down with the urn, which was *heavy!*, and set it into the hole. I gave it a pat and said to it,

196

"I wish somebody had found you before it was too late."

I said good-bye to him, and now Rev. Walden stepped in to lead us in prayer. We followed with two verses of *Amazing Grace,* with me standing next to Charles, and that was the end of the service. Everyone was a little choked up, including me.

¤ ¤ ¤ ¤ ¤

It's funny, the more I saw Tick and Charles together, the more they looked and acted alike. And through the summer it seemed others in town were agreeing with me, and therefore suspecting the truth.

Why, he's applying for permanent guardianship! He's really taken to those two boys! Is it just because he likes them, or... could it be? Do you think? Wasn't it Milton Clayne?

You have to let people think what they want.

Charles and I had just one additional talk about his letter to our mother, and I put it very simply to him. "That was a personal and private letter, and it's good that just two people know about it."

In time, Tick might figure it out on his own, that the man who behaved like his dad really *was* his dad. But if you remember Tick's brain, that kind of curiosity generally escaped him and he might live his whole life not wishing to pursue it.

Gradually over the summer, Charles moved out of his old two bed-room bungalow south of town and into Zee's house, especially after he was granted permanent guardianship of us. He asked if he could use Zee's old bedroom downstairs, and we agreed it would be fine.

The problem was, as we'd learned from our first breakfast with him, he couldn't cook to save his life unless it was burgers on the grill or macaroni and cheese which came out of a box. So I slowly reinvaded the kitchen to try different things that were more nutritious, and Ty came back from time to time to help out, often with her favorite soul food like spicy shrimp, collards, cornbread and sometimes Bruns-wick Stew. Ty, in fact, was needed during the day again, once Tick was home from St. Anselm's, I was back at Winklers', and Charles was pulling his regular shifts at the sheriff's department. She believed, rightly or wrongly, that Tick still needed watching like a hawk –

particularly after all the "teaching" he'd gotten from Jupiter Strange on their adventure together.

As Charles settled more and more into his role as our father and guardian, his gentleness would sometimes give way to a firmness that I didn't always agree with. Getting my driver's license, for instance. There was still a part of me that saw it as bureaucratic and unnecessary, since I was well known around town, could drive perfectly well, and was also in the custody of a lawman. Well, that's just the *point*, he'd say –

"Every time you test drive a car you've fixed at Winklers, when you take it on a public way, you're breaking the law."

I gave in pretty fast when he added, "I don't want to have to arrest my own kid."

He also insisted I get back at eleven o'clock at the latest, if I'd been out with Natalie. A couple of times I missed the deadline by a half hour or so, and he sure would let me hear about it.

But neither of us ever got grounded. We knew Charles' limits, just as we'd known Zee's, and we stayed inside the lines as best we could.

Still, it was an adjustment for us – having a truly functioning adult in our house who cared about our neatness and hygiene, our grades in school, and our attitudes toward things. I had to give up some ground in my raising of Tick, and it wasn't as easy as I thought. I sometimes wondered if Charles was working overtime as a parent to make up for the thirteen years he'd lost with us, what with all his guidance, fishing trips, playing catch with the football and such. But then other times he'd let us wander off alone, even on a Saturday or Sunday when he was home, and I soon began to appreciate how respectful he was in apportioning his time with us. He was a much smarter man than he let on.

I also thought it was a kick having a sheriff's department cruiser in the driveway and a police band radio in the kitchen. We never had to lock our doors at night, the way most people do.

Jupe, Zee, and Lyle all had headstones not a hundred paces from each other, and from time to time I'd head over to the cemetery with flowers. Sometimes Tick and Charles joined me, sometimes Nat, but often as not I was alone, and I would spread the flowers evenly among the three gravesites and have a brief conversation at each stop.

I had my seventeenth birthday in late August, and Natalie and Charles conspired to buy me an enormous and expensive book, *Gray's Anatomy*, which is like the Bible for people who want to study medicine. I spent most of the morning going through it, fascinated by the detail of the drawings of muscles and tendons, arteries and veins and organs – everything that's inside all of us (or should be). Unlike cars, which have all kinds of mechanical variations in them, *Gray's Anatomy* was the blueprint for every human body on the planet. I spent day after day with the book, studying. I couldn't get enough of it.

In time, I knew this is what I would do. To me, the body was too fascinating to do anything else. This would be my life.

I could heal young people like Lyle, before they hurt so much they'd give up on themselves.

I could treat older people, like Zee, to help them avoid some of the problems of old age that would take their lives too soon.

I could work with little kids, and identify those whose smiling parents are secretly beating or burning them.

I could work with poor people, like Jorlane or Cletus or even Vic, and try to make a small difference in their lives so they wouldn't go out and hurt other people for no good reason.

I thought, with what I know, I could help almost anybody, whether it was a problem with disease or just loneliness.

As I write this, Natalie is sitting outside waiting for me to go to the river together for a picnic. It's a beautiful summer day, and though the river will be there forever, the day won't wait another minute, and, I'm afraid, neither will she.

ABOUT THE AUTHOR

Apart from his novels, Ned White has written widely for both public and commercial television – both documentary and drama – and for young adult theater and corporations. He is also an award-winning photographer and an occasional crossword constructor for *The New York Times*. He is the father of three grown children – a poet and illustrator, a theater director, and social worker – all living in the Northeast.

He lives in the Atlanta area with his wife, Carla, a public health specialist.

nedwhitebooks.com

Made in the USA
San Bernardino, CA
06 September 2013